Deborah Masson was born and bred in Aberdeen, Scotland. Always restless and fighting against being a responsible adult, she worked in several jobs including secretarial, marketing, reporting for the city's freebie newspaper and a stint as a postie – to name but a few.

Through it all, she always read crime fiction, and, when motherhood finally settled her into being an adult (maybe even a responsible one), she turned her hand to writing what she loved. Deborah started with short stories and flash fiction whilst her daughter napped, and, when she later welcomed her son into the world, she decided to challenge her writing further through online courses with Professional Writing Academy and Faber Academy, where she wrote her award-winning debut novel, *Hold Your Tongue*, the first in the DI Eve Hunter series. Her most recent book, *From the Ashes*, was longlisted for the 2022 McIlvanney Prize for Best Scottish Crime Novel of the Year.

www.penguin.co.uk

Also by Deborah Masson

Hold Your Tongue
Out for Blood
From the Ashes

I'll Be Watching You

DEBORAH MASSON

PENGUIN BOOKS

TRANSWORLD PUBLISHERS

UK | USA | Canada | Ireland | Australia
India | New Zealand | South Africa

Transworld is part of the Penguin Random House group of companies
whose addresses can be found at global.penguinrandomhouse.com.

Penguin Random House UK, One Embassy Gardens,
8 Viaduct Gardens, London SW11 7BW

penguin.co.uk

First published in Great Britain in 2026 by Penguin Books
an imprint of Transworld Publishers

001

Copyright © Deborah Masson 2026

The moral right of the author has been asserted

This book is a work of fiction and, except in the case of historical fact,
any resemblance to actual persons, living or dead, is purely coincidental.

Every effort has been made to obtain the necessary permissions with
reference to copyright material, both illustrative and quoted.
We apologize for any omissions in this respect and will be pleased to
make the appropriate acknowledgements in any future edition.

No part of this book may be used or reproduced in any
manner for the purpose of training artificial intelligence technologies or systems.
In accordance with Article 4(3) of the DSM Directive 2019/790, Penguin Random
House expressly reserves this work from the text and data mining exception.

Typeset in 11/14pt ITC Giovanni Std by Six Red Marbles UK, Thetford, Norfolk
Printed and bound in Great Britain by Clays Ltd, Elcograf S.p.A.

The authorized representative in the EEA is Penguin Random House Ireland,
Morrison Chambers, 32 Nassau Street, Dublin D02 YH68.

A CIP catalogue record for this book is available from the British Library

ISBN: 9780552178266

Penguin Random House is committed to a sustainable
future for our business, our readers and our planet. This book
is made from Forest Stewardship Council® certified paper.

To my childhood bestie, Nicola – a girl living her own story right now, and there's no one more deserving of a happy ending.

Six years ago

SHE PRESSES HER TOES against the accelerator, no more than a tap, before lifting her foot off again. The small red car sits back from the cliff edge, wet, saturated muddy ground sinking beneath it.

The North Sea swells below, opening out in front of her, the shredded white mist wrapped around the grey horizon. Waves crash and clap, loud as thunder, fighting through the silence of the metal box she sits in.

Her body is rendered rigid at the wheel. Face wet as the sea, breath as ragged as the wind outside.

Her foot hovers above the pedal. Does she have the courage to floor the accelerator, to cover the space between it and the cliff edge? To let herself fly?

One push . . . Mere seconds . . .

Her battered trainer brushes against the small pedal again. The blood rushing in her ears reminds her of the life still coursing through her veins. Of the lives lost because of her.

She groans and slumps back against the headrest,

tears spreading across her beige T-shirt, her throat gulping with the fear and sorrow that chokes her.

Her foot lifts clear of the pedal and flattens against the footwell.

She hits out at the steering wheel, grabbing at it with both hands, shaking it until it creaks against the force; howling at the windscreen, knuckles white.

Bang. Her forehead hits the wheel, and she sobs.

Forcing herself to breathe, her fingers feel for the keys dangling from the ignition. She turns the engine off, rips out the keys and lifts her head to stare out at the water.

She imagines what it will be to jump into its jaws, to allow herself to be swallowed whole by it – if drowning will feel as bad as living.

Coughing and spluttering, she puts the keys back in the ignition and lets them hang. She pulls down the sun visor and looks at the photo tucked there, tracing the faces staring back at her with her finger, before taking the picture out, into her hand.

She grips the photo and opens the door. The wind whips at her face and legs as she steps from the car, the sting of salty sea air assaulting her as she leaves the door ajar, taking nothing else with her as she steps forward, looking down at the feet still driving her to the nearby cliff edge, regardless.

She stops short of running out of land, so close to the edge that she can feel the freezing spray spitting on her face; her tongue licks at the salt on her top lip as her feet shift in the mud and her body sways in the wind.

Her head tilts forward, the jagged rocks beneath looking like teeth waiting to clamp themselves around her before they surrender her to the deep, dark gullet of the beast.

If only she could surrender herself to the force of the wind. Let it lift her up. Let it carry her to the sea.

She knows she can't go back. She knows what will be done to her if she returns. What's already been done to those closest and dearest to her.

She closes her eyes and thinks of the life she once had, of the prison her life became. With no one left to help her escape.

What will it be like when she joins them? Clutching the small photograph in her hand, she imagines being free of all this pain.

Her foot lifts, trembling as she balances on one leg, willing herself to step forward into nothing. The battle between heart and mind rages on, even as she imagines breaking free from her cage. Allowing herself to fly.

Chapter 1

Now

'Which one am I looking at?'

I stare up at the wall, the nine huge screens blinking down at me in the dark.

'Flailing arms. Roots that need doing. Seen more meat on a butcher's knife.'

I spot her on Camera Three. 'Jesus, there's no denying the genes.'

'Yup. I don't know about you, but I'm glad that's one gene pool my little fishies will never be swimming in.'

I glance sideways at Robbie. I'm not sure if his fishies have ever had the good fortune of swimming anywhere. He doesn't possess a neck, and his backside hangs off either side of his chair.

I curl my forefinger around the joystick on the desk and bring the girl and her windmilling limbs down to the curved monitor in front of me. A swift nudge of the stick zooms me in closer to her. The resemblance is uncanny. 'A year inside hasn't done her any favours.'

Robbie makes a noise, somewhere between a snort

and a tut, pink icing flying from his mouth and landing on the keyboard in front of him. 'The mother was in there too. Still is, I think.'

Shelley Barker. A woman at no risk of being nominated for Mother of the Year. You'd never mistake her daughters – doppelgängers she'd dragged with her into prostitution and drugs. The eldest, Sharon, now dead; the youngest, Sharlene, on the screen in front of him.

Sharlene's features are ravaged, old before her time. She's been in and out of the clink so many times, it's almost a holiday home to her.

Some folk never stood a chance, and the Barker girls are testament to that. Robbie has watched them since they were kids, the whole car crash unfolding in front of his eyes, and there wasn't a thing he could do about it.

And that's the problem. This job is just like driving through folk's lives. Us watching from behind a tinted windscreen; them out in front, oblivious.

Sharlene's not causing too much hassle yet, but it won't be long. The daytime drinkers on St Nicholas Street are becoming a regular problem, and a big one. There's daily radio contact between us and the community coppers. Coppers who listen to us; who go down there and take the abuse slung at them. The drinkers who scatter and, within ten minutes, are back at it again.

Robbie whistles. 'She's nae feart.'

Sharlene's getting up in some bloke's face, a guy twice her size, a bony, nicotine-stained finger jabbing at his face, her sore-covered mouth ranting at him. From the looks of folk's faces as they walk by, she's not holding back.

The guy stumbles backwards, one eye shut beneath shaggy, greasy hair. A once-white Kappa zip-up top hangs open, exposing a bare chest and protruding ribs.

Sharlene doesn't let up. Her palm bats at his cheekbone, making his head jerk. She raises a grubby Ugg boot and kicks at his shin.

The radio is in my hand a second before he retaliates.

'Altercation between a woman and a man on St Nicholas Street.'

He whacks her and Sharlene hits the pavement.

'Woman down.'

The radio spits before one of the community officers confirms they're in the vicinity.

The CCTV room goes quiet. Not a peep from me and Robbie, and definitely not a sound from the two other teams in here with us – Traffic and Housing, the operators about as dynamic as the job they do, the mice against us men. All three teams crammed into the one room. We're hidden away in the back arse of Marischal College, a building the tourist board likes to flout as an icon of the granite city. But to me, it's just another day in the office.

'So, what's for lunch?' Robbie asks, food the main source of excitement in his life.

'Half an hour 'til lunch. Greggs?'

'Your run, your choice. I wouldn't say no to a crescent.'

I've given up trying to get Robbie to say 'croissant', even though it's his usual chaser to two sausage rolls.

Robbie tuts and brushes at the pink crumbs sticking to the cracked yellow Batman logo on his top, the sickly-sweet smell of the bun still hanging around my nostrils as I look at the logo, knowing Robbie thinks this job makes him a superhero – and who am I to piss all over his fantasy?

And so today will go the same as every day. People-watching. Some of those people on our list of well-known names. A lengthy list, always by our side, of those known to the police. The troublemakers we deal with day-to-day.

We score through names as they drop off – sometimes because they've gone to prison, other times because death has taken them. Every three years or so, a spate of names is scrubbed through when a dodgy strain of drugs finds its way on to the streets. At one point, we were taking bets as we started our shift as to who might have died since the last watch. Some of the losses hit hard. You're as immersed in their life as you might be in someone's you follow on social media, forgetting that, in this case, you've never talked to them, and now never will. That, whilst they were still alive, they had no idea you existed.

And, of course, along with the regulars, there are always the average Joes. The greys amid the colour. Folk who rarely deviate from the norm, but who, every now and again, can surprise you.

But trouble or not, what I love about this job is that every face in the crowd says so much without uttering a single word; every nuance of body language revealing to me how they feel – and how they act when they think no one is watching. I get to see the 'hidden them'. The person beneath, who is rarely unmasked, even to those closest to them.

That's why I've never understood the guys who leave

this job, moaning it's mundane, complaining about dry eyes and stiff necks. What's mundane about the human condition? About that rare gift of delving into what makes folk tick? Being able to watch the masses go about their day, without a clue that I'm right there with them?

In a world where celebrity is the new royalty, where fame comes knocking for apparently doing nothing, where reality TV regularly draws in millions, what makes those wannabes any more interesting than the folk on the screen in front of me right now? All those inane online videos, clicked and 'liked' thousands of times. Subscribers in the millions signing up to the drivel of someone else's life. Or, at least, the life they *want* you to see and believe. Carefully filtered and edited.

But *this* – this *job* – is real life. Real people. Real time. Raw and unfiltered. Why wouldn't you jump at the chance to watch? To be *paid* to watch?

All-seeing. All-knowing. Travelling at speed without the need for feet or transport. Walking alongside – walking *through* – the crowds. Invisible.

With the mere flick of a joystick and the click of a radio, I'm able to change people's stories. Manipulating time, bending it. Averting crime, rescuing lives, saving people from themselves.

Robbie's staring at me. I'm always aware when his eyes are on me rather than the screens.

'I can't be arsed waiting another half hour. You on for Greggs?'

I guess even Batman has to eat.

Chapter 2

I BURST OUT THROUGH the revolving glass door of Marischal College and on to the pedestrianized strip, give a bus or two. October. A chill in the air that burns your lungs as you breathe in. Not long before the strip will be transformed into a makeshift Christmas village, there to entice you with fun and frolics – if you're willing to part with the cash in your pockets, that is.

My eyes take a moment to adjust as I walk down Broad Street, dwarfed by the towering retail and office buildings of Marischal Square to the right and my place of work to the left.

Robbie will be watching me, tracking the safe return of his crescent. I look up to the camera winking outside Costa, a small black orb that looks like it's wearing a baseball cap. Most folk don't know it's there. Not many people on the street to see it anyway – most of them inside the coffee shop and hugging their mugs for warmth. I stare up into the camera, crack a smile, and flip Robbie the bird.

As I pass the bus shelter outside the Illicit Still pub – now boarded up and for sale – I remember, not for the first time, waiting at that stop as a kid. Hogmanay, during one of the worst winters in years. A blizzard freezing our fingers and toes in their woollen gloves and fake leather boots as we attempted to get home from my auntie's. My parents had no idea the buses had stopped hours ago because of the ice. They'd wrapped themselves around each other, me taking the icy hit as they kept each other warm. Back when my mother still liked to make it clear where I ranked in her list of priorities. When my father was incapable of seeing anything beyond my mother.

She didn't die that night, but I often wonder if my mother might still be alive if CCTV had existed back then. If someone like me might've rescued her without ever leaving a seat in a darkened room, without ever taking their eyes off a screen.

But the only person who would've been shown on a camera was me. Left sitting out front whilst my father butchered my mother and hung her out to dry.

Literally.

Butchered and hung, through the back of the family butcher shop.

My Granda Joe had built the butcher's up from nothing and passed it down to my father, who then let me work alongside him, training me for when I was old enough. Mum probably shouldn't have let him. I was only eight. Far too young to see animals hung, drawn and quartered. The stench of blood never truly leaving you or your clothes.

I worked at the butcher's after school, throughout the holidays and every Saturday from then, right up to my early teens. Dad getting me as involved with the butchering of animals as I was with charming his customers at the counter.

But nothing could've compared to seeing my father rocking back and forth on his knees behind the counter, covered in blood and weeping. I say 'could've', because I don't remember any of it.

There would've been nothing unusual about finding Dad covered in blood, but I can't imagine him weeping, though I told the police that he had been. That's probably what led me to go searching through the back for the cause of it when my father wouldn't look at me or answer my questions. Again, so I was told afterwards.

They found Mum hanging by a hook. Naked. The gleam of a metal spike puncturing the skin beneath her chin and sticking up out of her mouth. Blood dripped and pooled on the floor beneath her. They found me covered in it too, reckoned I probably clung to her in my shock.

In the years after, I'd wake in the night. In my dreams I'd see her hanging there. As time passed, the images began coming to me when I was awake. I'd see flashes of her in front of my eyes, suspended on that hook, at the strangest of times, with no warning. When I was walking down the street or eating my tea.

The therapist they made me see said it would've been suppressed trauma causing it. PTSD – that's what they call it these days. But who knows? The therapist certainly didn't, because I remained silent, giving nothing away.

I always thought the job title said it all. Therapist – The-Rapist. He was someone trying to enter my mind without my permission, trying to take something from me against my will. No way. So, I listened and let him think he was helping.

He said a lot of things. Things I don't remember and don't care to remember. The only bit I could take away from it was this: whatever I saw, I had been too young to see it.

The death of my mother ripped a hole in my life. A gaping void I had to suffer and into which the rest of the country fell. My parents' faces were splashed all over the telly and the newspapers at the time, and for months after.

And mine.

The Butcher's Boy.

A whole new meaning to that moniker. The media scrutiny as intense as if I had done it. Before my father went to court, some reports even speculated whether I was involved. Reporters of all opinions hunted me down with a swarm of photographers, either looking for a shot of me in my orphaned despair or for the story that would confirm my guilt.

I worried that I didn't look the way I was supposed to – the way a child who had lost his mother, and in turn his father, would look. Emotion didn't come easily to me. This may have just been me, or it may have been the lack of feeling my mother had shown me when she was alive, or a mix of both. Did I look cold? Different from others? Like something was missing? It made me more insular with every passing day – withdrawing from others, from life; withdrawing even from myself, I think, looking back.

I lived those days afterwards hoping I could give those reporters and photographers the break that might catapult their careers from the locals to the nationals. Worrying that I may not be capable of giving it to them. Even more frightened that they would believe I had been involved with the murder of my mother. That the rumours would stick and grow, labelling me as something else altogether, the baying public seeing me hung, drawn and quartered myself, like a butchered animal. Like my mother on that hook.

The kids' home I was shipped off to did try to protect me, but it was a hard task. I was still living in the same city, still attending the same school. Minimum disruption was the argument – laughable, after the sledgehammer that had slammed through my life. I would never be able to step back into my life as I'd known it before. Eventually the photographers got their shot.

Seeing my face staring out from the newspaper stands made my life feel, more than ever, increasingly unreal, as if it was all happening to someone else.

But then my father admitted his part in the crime. He pleaded guilty and was sentenced to a life in prison. He cited sexual jealousy as the reason – my mother had been banging Colin, our next-door neighbour.

I hadn't seen my father since the day they took him away and I didn't attend court to see it happen. I wouldn't lay eyes on him again.

The rumours that had swirled around me were now just a whisper. I was left alone. The kids, none of them ever real friends, kept their distance, whispering behind hands, '*Do you think he did it?*'

Eventually, I shut down completely.

I yank open the door to Greggs, the smell hitting me at the same time as the hot blast from the overhead heater. The place is packed, and I wonder how I look to them all, what they see, my mask firmly fastened as I know I'm being watched. It's been years since anyone recognized me or talked about me from behind cupped fingers. For that, at least, I'm grateful.

What if we had done what Dad wanted and moved to the flat above the butcher's when Granda died? What if Colin hadn't moved in next door? What if we'd never found out what my mother had been doing? What if whatever had snapped inside . . . hadn't?

But no amount of what-ifs could change what had actually happened and, eventually, as the years passed, the torture lessened.

I reinvented myself. Straight out of the kids' home, I changed my name by deed poll. A fresh start: a new identity, feigned confidence, a new personality. Normal. I was determined I could and would play normal well. The years of adolescence filling me out both in build and height, gracing me with facial hair, the hair on my head darkened from the blond of childhood, taking me away from the photo of The Butcher's Boy that had stared out from the telly and the papers.

Reborn – and not to my parents, who I'd had such misfortune in being born to the first time – I even married; but, sadly, happiness was never meant to be mine, not even as someone else. Loss was in my blood and losing you – Beth, my wife, the life we had – was the most devastating of blows.

I was left living with the ghost of you every day, my old grief-stricken self threatening to return. Smiling and nodding my way through life as the war beneath twisted at my insides. Acting normal when it was the last thing that I was. The last thing that I am.

Only Robbie knows the truth of my childhood, and not because I told him. He recognized me – adult me, different me. He saw Wesley Harris in my eyes. The Butcher's Boy who I left behind on that hook with my mother.

I mean, what were the chances of Robbie knowing?

I guess when you're a man who harbours an unhealthy obsession with true crime, with a particular interest in local murders, there's every chance. Our Robbie's not averse to venturing into the realm of mystery and murder either. And supernatural stuff. He believes all that guff just as strongly as the proven stuff. He knows about the ghost of you too, Beth, believing it as keenly as what he sees for real in front of those cameras.

He accepts me as I am – who I am now. The person I present to him and the rest of the world. I think he even feels sorry for the boy I was. So I don't care what he does in his spare time – as long as he keeps the ghost of Past Me to himself.

Robbie once said that what happened in my childhood was probably why I came to the job. Perhaps my subconscious trying to somehow right the wrong. Amazing, really, that I'd come through it all so adjusted. That was the word he used: adjusted. If only he knew.

Unbeknown to me until then, Robbie fancied himself as a poor man's Sigmund Freud, spending hours of his life analysing murderers. So, it's not surprising that he came out with the bollocks about me being in the job now to save someone else when I couldn't save my mother – or you. Some – a shrink, for sure – might say there's a sliver of truth in that. The reason why I spend my days and nights watching.

Watching. Waiting.

Wanting and *needing* to spot the anomaly.

To find that glitch in the system.

Chapter 3

I FOUND THE GLITCH in the system the day I saw you. *You* – the wife I had lost. Beth. The only woman I'd ever loved.

I'd seen you before, so many times I'd lost count. Of course, I'd known at the time it wasn't real. It was tired eyes, long shifts, my mind playing tricks.

But that day, that last time, just three short months ago, when we were only an hour into our shift, my eyes and mind were alert. Robbie was already on his second iced bun, the sweet smell cloying in the office heat. July. The height of summer.

I was scanning Market Street, looking for a missing teen who hadn't been seen since the morning before. A sixteen-year-old boy who was untroubled as far as his friends and family knew, his disappearance totally out of character.

I was searching for that one face in a crowd of many. A face I hadn't seen before amongst thousands of other faces I hadn't seen before. One that needed to be found. Every bobbing head in that silent, surging, sunbaked crowd was made up of the same core features: two eyes, two ears, one nose, one mouth. It never failed to fascinate me how those same features ended up with such different results when you brought all of them together as one.

Face after face passed by my eyes until I felt it with a bang: that moment when those features all merged, sparking recognition – familiarity, experiences, memories, emotions . . . pain. And that's what happened that morning. All those features came together and there you were. *You.*

Everything in that moment aligned, simultaneously grinding to a halt.

My movement. Breath. Heart.

Disbelief as my breath and heart hitched and restarted, my fingers hovering at the joystick, scared to move in case I lost you.

It couldn't be.

I *knew* it couldn't be. You were dead.

The face I saw in my dreams, the image of those features that dwelled long after I screamed myself awake from my nightmares. Those watery blue eyes comforting me in my mind, in those quiet moments throughout my days. It was so long since I had last seen them for real. I wondered sometimes if any of it had ever been real.

And then, there you were. On that screen right in front of me, like a movie I'd played so many times over in my head. But you were real. It was as though I'd somehow imagined you into reality, like a mirage off in the distance of the desert that was my life.

Everything screamed that it wasn't you, but I couldn't risk losing your face in the crowd, my eyes struggling to see the whole of you, my vision via a lens blocked by other bodies, shoulders and heads.

'Casey?'

I was standing, ignoring Robbie, making my way around the desk in front of me, not letting you out of my sight as I walked towards the wall, my body pulled towards the big screen – drawn towards you. Seeing all of you for the briefest of moments. My heart stopping again.

'Casey? Casey! What are you doing, man?'

I glanced towards him, a split second of broken focus, and you were gone. I groaned, heart hitching again as I rubbed my eyes, willing you to reappear just as quickly as you'd disappeared. Feeling like an idiot standing there but not caring, left yearning in the haze of an illusion.

Still in the grips of your image, I reached out to the screen as if reaching out for that scarce sip of water. Thirsty for you, craving your touch. For those eyes to look at me as they once had.

I was aware of Robbie's hand on my shoulder. 'It's not her, mate. It's not Beth. You know it can't be her.' Pulling at me, dragging my gaze and my body away from the screen. 'Mate, it's not her ... *Casey?* Mate ... it's just a ghost. Nothing more than a ghost.'

But that day, it was the ghost of you – the fear that I was losing even the memory of you – that set me thinking; that set it all in motion. The longing. To find that glitch after all.

To find *them*.
To watch.
Needing to know where and who they were now.
What had happened after they took you from me – when they left you thinking there was no other way.

Chapter 4

Lewis Taylor is how I might've ended up, had I been a lesser man.

His childhood, like mine as I've found out, was no childhood at all. It was one marred by hardship and pain, profoundly affecting what kind of man he would become long before even a hint of stubble had sprouted above his top lip. Years before he chose the path that he did and took the catastrophic steps that he had.

In the hours and days that I've watched him, I've seen him move in plain sight. Striding the streets with forced swagger and feigned arrogance, desperate to be seen when he should want to hide; to hide from what has gone before him. But instead he was reaching, forever reaching, to reinvent himself, to rewrite his future. Hoping that someday, someone might want him.

But no one glances his way, unless in anger or ridicule. And Lewis Taylor has no idea it will always be that way.

I know it first hand. Not only because I've been watching him, but because I've walked in his footsteps, dragging myself along the edge of those same streets all those years ago, skulking in the shadows as I attempted to hide from a world that had labelled me The Butcher's Boy, yet still desperate for someone to see *me*. Trying to *live* day-to-day instead of only *existing* – but scared to truly live, scared that someone would recognize me. Scared of all those rumours and theories starting up again, the desire and fear of being seen threatening to swallow me whole.

The difference between Lewis and me? The reason why I've swum to the top and he's still drowning? I've been able to change, and I've been able to watch. At the bridge between childhood and adulthood, I jumped the divide. I reached the other side of the street a new person, the old me left staring across the road from behind.

I was then able to see, and study, what really sets people apart. Eager to explore the division between those who blend in to the grey of the world and become invisible to others, and those who splatter and splash colour across anything and everything they touch as they demand to be seen.

In order for me to leave the grey of Wesley Harris behind, to fully embrace the blank canvas of Casey Carter, palette in hand, I had to *see* before I tentatively applied those first brushstrokes. I spent endless hours carefully watching people interact and live out their lives. Listening to show after show on the radio, watching anything and everything on the telly.

I was an artist in search of his muse as I studied the nuances of facial expression and body language, the lilt and tilt of the voice – minutiae that anyone can access and that allow you to see what separates the mundane from the magical, the odd from the accepted.

And, oh, how I wanted to escape the skin I was in, to free that person trapped beneath. Doing everything I could to learn how to, forever mimicking and honing my acting skills in preparation for giving the performance of my life. For being able to move forward and live *any* kind of life.

This is something Lewis Taylor won't ever be able to do. His inability to see it evident to me in ways he doesn't even realize. He reveals it in the uncertain shift of his eyes, the nervous tic in his shoulder, the rub of his forefinger against his thumb. He radiates grey and carries himself like a man scratching to relieve himself of the skin he has found himself in. Fear, guilt – both of those things driving that scratch. Keeping him from moving forward, from breaking away from the things that've been done to him, and the things he's done to others.

What he did to *you*.

I recognize that itch. It was one that consumed me throughout the long days and nights after the incident with Mum and Dad, during those years in that kids' home. I could only burst free of that pox-ridden skin when I finally chose to erase Wesley Harris; when I changed the course of my future and chose instead to paint Casey Carter.

Another feat Lewis Taylor will never be able to achieve, because of the choices he's made.

Whilst he made his choices, I chose you, Beth. You and the life we lived were all that I needed. Even now, I'd still choose you. A thousand times over.

I watch Lewis and his mother come and go from that top-floor flat of theirs. I follow them, learning their routine – what little they have of one.

Him doing nothing when he ventures out. Barely living. Grey, grey, grey.

Her only leaving to check the weekly stock-change in Lidl's middle aisle. Her and her obsessive bargain-hunting for stuff she'll never use. It's not an invite that's ever extended to Lewis, or at least not one he accepts. He stays rotting in his pit when she goes.

Not for much longer, though.

I'm about to give him a reason to get out of bed. To jump out of it, in fact.

Lewis Taylor is finally going to feel seen; understood, even. I'm going to make him believe that he might just be able to stop his skin crawling at the thought of himself, at all the thoughts that he has.

I'm going to bathe him in so much colour that he'll be screaming out for a return to grey.

Chapter 5

It's barely gone 7.30 a.m. and she's arrived. I can't help but smile. Lewis Taylor's mother is a good twenty minutes earlier than last week. I must've really rattled her.

Her back is turned to me, but she knows I'm here. She looks over her right shoulder again, straight at me through the seagull-shit-covered car windscreen of my car, where I sit with the engine running, keeping the heat blowing. It's her fourth glance round at me in the last five minutes.

Her head spins back towards the storefront, her backside leaning against one of the metal bollards closest to the glass doors. The shopping trolley's scuffed wheels roll back and forth under the push and pull of her doughy, clenched fists, the trundling sound reaching me inside the car. It's as if she's revving up some invisible engine, ready to floor it as soon as the door opens – or as soon as I, the competition, dare to step outside of my car.

I look away from her rounded back and glance out of the passenger window. The traffic on the steep hill of Wellington Road is already building, the constant hum of cars and trucks bringing commuters to the many oil companies and car garages spread over the nearby industrial estates. But she sees and hears none of that, her focus on nothing but the blue-and-yellow overkill of Lidl in the heart of the city's East Tullos Industrial Estate, right in front of her.

A guy sporting a tired-looking blue polo shirt starts moving about inside the locked glass entranceway. He's doing a fine job of looking busy. He probably enjoys this little bit of power he has, making her wait. Her stare only breaks to check her wristwatch; she's checked it countless times. He fiddles with the keys at his waist with his hand, teasing as he lets them go, keys swinging as he turns and walks back into the shop, disappearing between the aisles, probably thinking how sad her little life must be.

I know how sad her existence is. How bad it is. The reason why she fixates on this place the way she does. There's not much else in her life to derive any pleasure from. Not when her son is Lewis.

I clutch the reuseable, oversized Lidl bag on my lap. The bigger the better so that she knows I mean business. It's important I get her attention from the off. But that's almost a given, after last week.

This is the third week I've watched her. The first week, I watched from a distance, and she had no idea I was there. Last week, I got up close as she urgently snapped up the latest middle-aisle deals.

She hadn't even been looking at the rainbow-coloured mug. Too busy unboxing and holding a thermal top to her chest before letting it fall back into the metal cage, making no attempt to reunite it with its box.

I stood just along from her, talking animatedly on my phone. No one was on the other end, but she didn't know that.

'Yeah, sweetheart, they've got them . . .' Unnaturally loud in my excitement to my imaginary whoever on the other end as I stared at the mug in my hand.

Her head perked up before I'd finished the sentence.

'There are only two left. Unbelievable bargain compared to those other ones we saw. Like Mike said, a deal like this won't come up again.'

She was already making her way towards me when I bent forward to pick up the second mug. She had no idea that I'd hidden a box of ten beneath the fleeces in the next metal cage. I straightened at the same moment the black rubber wheels of her trolley rolled over my left foot.

'Ow!' I jumped back for effect, dropping the two mugs back in the cage.

Her hand was already diving in and scooping up one of the mugs as I stared at her. I feigned disgust at her lack of apology.

Scowling, I mumbled into my phone, 'Honey, I have to go,' making a show of pocketing my phone, before turning to her. 'What the hell? You rolled your trolley over my foot.'

She didn't even look my way, staring instead at the rainbow-coloured mug as she turned it over again and again in her hands.

'Did you hear me?' I pointed towards the mug. 'And I

think you'll find that's mine. I had it before you rammed into me.'

This time she did look my way, her body turning slowly like the mug in her hands, as if she was doing me a favour by acknowledging my existence.

'Whatever. Nae like you'd paid for it.'

I let my mouth open and close before opening it again. 'No, but I was about to.'

I glanced into the cage at the remaining mug and back at her, the gauntlet thrown down in that split second. Both of us plunged into the cage for it at the same time, bumping heads as my hands grasped it first. To my surprise, she used the mug in her hand to hit the back of my hand in her attempt to make me release the other one.

'What's going on here?' The guy looked barely older than a teenager, the crack in his voice making the last word squeak as he tried to show some authority.

The woman's face was puce, cheeks filling and emptying as her wet lips flapped. 'He's trying to take these mugs from me.'

My eyes widened. 'Rubbish. She was two cages down when I had them both in my hands.' I set my hands on my hips, finding it hard to believe, in that moment, that I could stoop to this level of pantomime shit. But I needed to, for my end goal, and oddly I felt the adrenaline like it was a real feud. I could understand, in some small way, how people might end up like this.

She was rolling that trolley back and forth at speed now. 'I *wisnae*.'

And so it went on for a good five minutes, finally ending when the panicking teen called management, the guy just inside the entranceway in front of me right now, and it was declared that we could either do the decent thing and take one mug each to check out, or he would remove them, and us, altogether.

I smile at the memory and look down at the rainbow-coloured mug in the drinks holder of my car, wondering where hers is right now. Probably in that trolley of hers, ready to clock me with it if I cause her any trouble today.

She turns towards me in my car again and I lift the mug, sipping from it slowly, watching her fingers tighten on the trolley handle.

Her attention is ripped away by the keeper of keys who is back and making attempts to unlock the door as slowly as he possibly can. She's up and at the glass, so close her nose must be in danger of touching it. I switch off the engine and take my time opening the car door, making a show of getting out and pulling the giant bag out behind me. A bag big enough for any bargain.

She looks over her shoulder at me once more as she steps over the threshold, disappearing before I reach the shop door. Perfect.

By the time I get to the middle aisle, the smell of freshly baked bread is all around me and making my stomach growl. She's down at the first cage, rummaging through its contents like a dog digging for a bone, before moving to the next. She's systematic, not missing a thing, only occasionally raising her head to check my whereabouts.

I'm loitering at the other end of the aisle. She looks torn as to whether she should shadow me but is still far enough away from me that I can do what I need to.

Keeping an eye on her, I empty the contents of my shopping bag into the nearest cage before clutching it by my side again. She starts to stomp along the aisle towards me, playing into my hand.

I reach in and pick up one of the photo frames I've just tipped into the cage. Nothing but a standard decorative metal frame, chocolate-brown in colour. Asking only that you insert a favourite picture. Old school. Standard. Basic. But it may as well be one of those digital ones because she's going to want it regardless. Because I want it.

True to form, she leans over and scoops up the remaining two frames, smirking as she straightens and looks at me, and then to the frame in my hand.

'Do you want that one?'

I shake my head. 'I was after a set of two.'

She stares down into the cage. 'Seems you're out of luck. But I could do with a set of three.'

I look over the cage to the manager – the one from the front door, the same one from last week – who is hovering, expecting it all to kick off again. I sigh, loudly. 'Fine – have it. I'm not looking for any drama.'

She all but snatches the frame from my hand, all three of the frames swallowed by that trolley of hers before I've unclenched my fingers. *Bitch*.

I watch her flounce off back to the cage she came from, before I half-heartedly move on to the next. It doesn't matter what I choose to buy now. I'm only concerned about making it to the checkout at the same time as her.

Half an hour and several *almost*-rugby-tackles later, we reach the checkouts together. Me first. Behind me, she unloads her trolley making sure the frames are last on to the belt, as far away from me as they can be. Safe from any sudden moves I might make.

The light at Checkout Three glows above us, but the assistant isn't in their chair yet. I decide to take advantage of the situation. I turn towards her.

'Listen, let me get those frames for you.' I smile, feeling the extra effort required to drag my lips upwards and appear genuine. Her hands are already on top of the frames, holding them in place on the conveyer belt as she studies my face, and her eye twitches.

'Why on earth would you do that?'

'Call it a goodwill gesture. An apology for last week. And for the carry-on today.' I shrug as her hand lifts from the frames and hovers, contemplating. She'll say yes. She's a stickler for any deal at the best of times, but a completely *free* one?

She lifts them and passes them to me hesitantly, grudgingly, as if she's doing me the favour by letting me apologize, allowing me to pay for them.

I take them from her, the smell of stale body-sweat transferring with them, and place the frames at the front of my few random items, fussing with my oversized bag, laying it over my shopping, slipping those frames inside the bag at the same time as the assistant arrives and opens the till. I make conversation with them both, using the power of distraction until I'm through the checkout and over at the windowsill, already waiting with the frames outstretched to her as she ambles over to me, the till assistant too busy greeting the next customer, the two of us already forgotten.

She takes the frames and stuffs them in her trolley. A mumbled, guarded thank-you escapes from her loose mouth.

'No problem. I hope you make good use of them.' I smile and walk off ahead of her.

Mission accomplished. I just have to hope she uses at least one of them.

Chapter 6

Most guys go for a pint after work. Not Robbie and me. At least not *just* a pint.

Cosmo in Union Square shopping centre is packed. One of those all-you-can-eat buffet restaurants where every man, woman and child is sporting an elasticated waist and the tables are packed together so tightly that diners get stuck trying to move freely between them. The hum of chatter, clinking cutlery and the constant squeal of chairs being pulled back from tables is the soundtrack to our meal tonight.

Eating out following the afternoon shift was my idea, a silent congratulations to myself for getting those picture frames where they needed to be this morning. My time with Robbie is a distraction whilst I wait to see if Lewis's mother will play her part.

I've been sat for ten minutes and Robbie is already back up at the buffet, panting away on his second round of the hot plates. He's as aware as anyone else that he can go up as many times as he wants, but he likes to make the most of his first few rounds, layering his plate like some fucked-up trifle.

'Leave some for the kids, mate,' I snort as he sits down opposite me and lowers his plate to the table like the holy grail.

'Let their folks worry about that. Screaming little buggers.'

Our Robbie has never spoken about wanting a family; never so much as mentioned needing anyone. A man happy with the basics. Decent job, decent food. The one thing that slightly sets him apart, in his mind, is working with me – The Butcher's Boy. I think it makes him feel special in some sad way. I'm his rock star, he's my wingman. I'm the guy who's been on the other side of the camera lens and is now on the same side as him.

Despite his obvious fascination, Robbie has never asked me anything about the murder, or me in general. 'None of my bloody business,' he says.

Even if he asked, he wouldn't get to know me. Not the real me. No one does.

'Dumplings are top-notch tonight.' He stabs at one as he gulps down his pint of Guinness. Refusing to drink any other kind of pint.

'Always are.'

Probably why Robbie has stacked his dumplings like a profiterole tower. He rips into the one stuck at the end of his fork, a comfortable silence falling between us. Food is the priority for now. We exist happily alongside one another, knowing – without saying it out loud – that we've got bugger-all else.

Robbie finishes his second plate.

'Ding-ding. Third round.' He's up quicker than you'd expect his frame to be able to move.

'I'll catch you up.' I sip at my pint of beer – needing to let my first plate settle before I go up again – thinking how simple Robbie's existence is, and how simple mine has become since the loss of you. I imagine that Robbie was never the popular kid, never a best friend. Same as me. Robbie most likely because he failed to find that person who appreciated his hobbies. Me because no one was ever going to warm to the guy from the papers whose father killed his mother and who himself was a bit of a strange one.

But I'd built a life. A life with someone I could never have dreamt would even notice me: you. Until that life was taken. Whereas Robbie ... Well, Robbie was still locked in his hobby, poring over all those true-crime stories in his semi-detached home in the city's Bridge of Don suburb, when not in that CCTV room. A decent house, because what he earned went nowhere else except his obsessions: crime and food.

I think that's the whole Batman thing, and why Robbie went into the job. He dreams of being the superhero, the guy who spots the crime and saves the day. A day that will see his life start, the day he'll become someone. But he doesn't realize you can't rely on someone or something else to make it happen.

'You look like you're drowning your sorrows in that pint.'

I look up as Robbie returns to the table. 'Thought you'd never come back,' I reply, standing and making a beeline for the lamb bhuna.

The truth is, Robbie will probably never get his moment because he'll never try hard enough to make it happen. Folk like me make it happen. We turn everything on its head.

I killed a version of myself last time. I couldn't exist as I was, and I needed to make something happen.

This time, I'm going to make others wish they'd never existed.

Chapter 7

I'm in what's technically my spare room with a full belly and an even fuller mind. It's a square box room, too small to be used as an actual bedroom but perfect for what it's become, for what I've made it. I call it my control room.

I have no need for the hanging light on the ceiling above me, nor the window to the side of me, which is obscured by thick-lined curtains. What I do in here is best done in the dark, away from prying eyes. Not unlike the room Robbie and I work in. Except the camera feed on these monitors is for my eyes only.

Three large monitors stand abreast on the wide desk in front of me, all of them glowing and pulsing in the dark, heating the space around me. As alive as I am.

I had dared to hope she might use at least one of the frames but, even then, I knew I was leaving too much to chance. I'd really hoped that fate would land on my side, but I knew there was always a risk they'd be thrown in a drawer and forgotten about.

But instead, fate had come up trumps, delivering a hat-trick. In record time.

Three monitors. Three photo frames. Three rooms.

She didn't have a clue that what she'd actually taken home were three picture frames *and* the man who'd bought them for her. No idea that everywhere she went, he now went. That wherever she goes, I go too.

I'm right there beside her now, perched on top of the telly in her living room, watching her from my own home through the fug of smoke that hangs constantly in the rooms of her house, clouding the view from the tiny hidden camera in the top of the picture frame. Clouding it, but not obscuring it, and with absolutely no effect on the high-quality audio I'm able to pick up all the way over the other side of the city.

Thanks to my DIY expertise in doctoring the frames, the cameras are not visible – and there's no danger of them becoming so. Hacking into their Wi-Fi was easy – you'd think they'd have beefed up their security after what went down – as was downloading the app that worked with the cameras, allowing remote access from both my mobile phone and the computer screen in front of me now. Technology really is a wonder.

She's sitting on her own, chain-smoking as she watches a rerun of an old episode of *Coronation Street*. I can almost smell the smoke as she laughs and gasps, living a life through theirs, probably thinking of them as friends, as more like family than her own – a son who no one wants to befriend, a husband who did things that were so much worse than the things she sees most of those husbands and fathers doing on that screen. She accepts the people on that screen, no matter how many secrets they have, how many lies they tell, or what dirty deeds they do behind others' backs. Because Lewis's mother is in on all of them and she's lived through so much worse.

Meanwhile, Lewis is in his room. Alone. As he always is.

I'm sitting here watching them both, living their lives alongside them, and without them having any idea. As well as my spot in the living room, I'm perched on Lewis's windowsill, wanting to close my eyes to some of the things he's shown me. I'm also in their kitchen, looking out from where I've been hung on the wall, opposite the ageing gas cooker.

Lewis is sitting at a desk in his bedroom, a large computer monitor in front of him, a white PS5 lying to the side. Huge, padded headphones flashing neon on top of the console. I'd place a bet that the PS5 fell off the back of a lorry, the monitor too.

The screen is on but he's not looking at it; there's nothing but the screensaver moving – an image of a can of Monster energy drink. The can dances about the screen, in view either side of the back of his inclined head as he sits in the gaming chair, which I'm watching from the windowsill directly behind him.

Every now and then he spins on the seat, looking towards the window as if he's staring deep into my soul, before his gaze drops back to the mobile phone he's clutching in his hand. I wonder what picture he's put in the frame I sit in; which image sits below the place I watch from.

I watch his tongue probe his upper lip and I imagine it tastes of cigarettes. I have a good idea what he's watching. No matter, though. It won't be long before those eyes of his will be averted. Only seeing what I want and allow him to see.

Chapter 8

Lewis Taylor sat staring at the telly in the corner of the living room. Another day in paradise. His old lady was watching the same old bollocks – saddos running about, dressed up in blue and red fleece jackets, looking for shite that may or may not make a fifty-pence profit when it sold, if they were lucky. Not even watching it live. Nah, his ma thought it was exciting enough to watch on catch-up, some other programme pipping its excitement earlier in the day.

He sucked on his fag and glanced up at the picture frame on top of the telly. An ugly-looking thing with a stupid picture of his twat of a brother and his niece. Like he wanted to be staring at their mugs every day. He hadn't even wanted his own frame, but his ma had insisted on putting one in his room yesterday anyway.

'I play the bloody bills, so what I say goes.'

That's what she'd said. Not worth his breath arguing about it. At least he'd been allowed to pick the photo that went in the frame. A picture of a rapper that he'd printed off from the internet. He knew that photo pissed her off to no end. He'd made his own argument: 'It's my room, whether you pay the bills or not.' That had got him a clap on the lug, but she'd let it be. He smiled through the cigarette smoke as he exhaled.

Thick smoke drifted everywhere in front of him, his ma's last fag newly stubbed out, his own burnt almost to the filter between his fingers. His ma stood up from her armchair, groaning at her buggered knees.

She snatched up the tea-stained mug from her armrest and shuffled to the coffee table in front of him, knocking his forearm as he crushed his fag in the ashtray as she bent to pick up his mug too, the remains of its contents almost cold.

Lewis tutted. 'I wasn't finished.'

'You are now.'

He threw his head back against the sofa.

'You don't need any more caffeine.'

'Tea doesn't have fucking caffeine.'

The mugs clinked against each other in her one hand as she swatted at the side of his head with her other. He ducked, her slap swishing past his ear, the sweat ingrained on her making his nose curl.

'It's Candice's birthday on Friday.' Why tell him? He hadn't seen his brother in over a year and wouldn't know his sprog if he passed her in the street. 'She'll be five.'

'Good for her.'

She swiped at him again, this time with the two mugs. He lifted his hand and stopped them short of his cheek. 'What the—'

'I phoned Craig yesterday. Asked what Candice

wanted – some bloody American doll. I'm nae buying that. Expensive shite too good to give to kids. I got her stuff from Lidl last year. Moons-and-stars stickers or something. Just as good as anything else.'

He couldn't care less. It wasn't like he'd be putting any money towards it.

'Anyway, they're coming here on Friday after they've picked her up from school, so you'll need to skedaddle.'

'I live here.'

'Aye, rent-free. At twenty-three years old.'

'Nae my fault I canna get a job.'

'Your fault you lost the one you had. And what the fuck are you talking about anyway? You didn't pay bugger-all when you *were* working.'

Why would he? Fed, watered, washing done. Might as well milk his old lady's guilt.

'Anyway, you'll need to be out when they come. I don't want any shite between the two of you in front of Candice.'

Bloody Candice. Who the fuck calls their kid that?

'Your brother says I should throw you out, you ken. Place is a poky little fucking hole as it is.'

'Aye, well, I'm glad life's worked out just grand for him.'

Her lips pursed like a baby tasting a lemon for the first time. 'You're a queer fish. Get up off your arse and go get my prescription like you said you would. Make yourself useful. Maybe get the bus into town after, nip in by the job centre. Get out from under my feet.'

'Whatever, Ma.'

'Aye, whatever. Find yourself a job and then you can drink all the fucking tea you want on their time.'

Lewis slammed the door behind him, letterbox flapping, the crack of wood-on-wood echoing down the stairwell of the granite tenement on Tullos Place, his mother hollering something from inside about door hinges. He took the red, scuffed stone steps at speed, a smell of stale urine – where someone had taken to peeing in the stairwell – wafting up to his nose as the bunch of keys clipped to his waist jangled against his hip. The rucksack on his back bouncing about, a fag and lighter in his hands. Rust squealed as he yanked at the main door, the intercom pointless now after Kev downstairs got busted by the drugs squad two nights ago. The outside of the tenements down the length of Tullos Place might've been reharled, all sparkling-white in the sun, but the insides were still the same scabby shite. The lazy council fuckers still hadn't been round to fix the lock.

It was dry outside. Baltic but dry. He checked his watch as if he had some schedule to stick to; it was a while since he'd had to do that. Best thing that had happened to him, losing that job at the warehouse. Glad to be away from the bunch of pricks. All the wind-ups and shite they spoke.

Lewis marched along Tullos Circle, the school on his right casting shadows in front of him as he lit the fag and breathed in the hit of nicotine. Now he could do whatever he liked. His trainers faltered, thinking of who he had seen on this street just last week – the one excursion that had not involved jobs for his ma or drinks at the local pub, where at least folk tolerated him. He'd been scared to do anything since . . .

Lewis tutted and pushed away the thought, and the

reality of his life – the loneliness, the wish for anything, *anyone*, other than who he'd been left with. He thought again about last week and it spurred him on; he speeded up as he considered the chance it might happen again tonight, his shoes slipping on the fallen leaves sticking to the pavement, soggy and now rotting. His body jumped as the school bell rang, so deafening that he could feel it in his teeth.

He glanced at the kids as they fell out of the doors and gates, hearing them shouting, laughing, running, seeing the pupil support assistants already stationed in the playground – one of them looking his way before he fixed his gaze straight ahead and crossed over on to Oscar Place, focusing instead on the city buildings of Aberdeen jostling for space on the horizon. Torry Medical Practice, where he would collect his ma's bloody prescription, was just minutes away. But maybe a pint first wouldn't hurt.

Chapter 9

WHEN LEWIS BURST OUT the main door of his mother's flaking tenement, he did it like he was the man. But he's nothing but a walking joke from head to toe.

The oversized bunch of keys jangled against his faded-denim thigh, weighing the belt loop down, some ill-advised fashion throwback to the 1980s, when Pepe jeans were all the rage and all about the plastic-clip keyring. I wondered where he got all the keys and what they opened – someone who owns nothing and lives with his mum. He must think it makes him look important.

He was holding a fag between his thumb and forefinger as he strode down the path and out on to the street. Not because it's how anyone would hold it naturally, but because he thought it looked cool. He walked down the street and our journey was punctuated by clouds of smoke. Everything about him was wrong. Grey.

I crossed over the road and fell in behind him. Far enough back that he didn't hear me, didn't even look around. The shrill sound of a bell rang in the distance and he hesitated, then hastened his step. I matched it.

The kids spilled out of the doors like scurrying ants evacuating their hill. He glanced over. I knew exactly where he was headed, the details having been displayed on my mobile phone via the camera feed inside his home. It wasn't long before I was giving him time to get inside the White Cockade ahead of me.

He's already at the bar, pint ordered, by the time I pull open the door.

The barman looks up, past him, deciding I'm worthy of entry. The place stinks of stale beer and sweat – your standard working-man's bar with an extra layer of scum.

There are only two other punters here. There's the obligatory beetroot-faced, yellow-toothed guy perched on a stool at the end of the bar, and another guy, perpetually bent over at the neck by the ravages of time. He hunches by the window with today's *Sun* newspaper, a half-drunk pint and a half-eaten packet of cheese-and-onion crisps in front of him. I know they're half-eaten because the foil packet has been ripped down its side and splayed open, the contents readily available.

Lewis is too loud for the place. In fact, he's the *only* noise in the space. He's animated again, prattling shit to the barman as the bloke turns his back to him and replaces a box of crisp packets, perhaps preparing for a long stay by the hunchback at the window. Or it may just be a ploy to get rid of Lewis.

Lewis stands tall, looking at himself in the mirror behind the bar as he lifts his pint; thinking he belongs here. Too pathetic to realize that the barman is bored by him and visibly relieved when I approach the bar, or to notice the guy on the stool in the corner roll his eyes towards me in the mirror. A shared joke at Lewis's expense, my reflection smiling in response. The way I hold myself, after all my years of study, draws people to me.

Lewis makes his way over to a table, three away from the hunchback. He acknowledges the curved spine with a 'Hey, John,' but John barely looks up from his paper.

Lewis shuffles in behind the table, keys clanging against its chipped edge. He dumps his rucksack on the burst seating beside him, his back against the wall, looking out, able to see anyone approaching. He takes a sip of his pint and gives out an exaggerated sigh of contentment. He is indeed The Man. He looks my way for a split second and then his head is down, poring over that phone again, staring, his tongue wetting those lips.

He looks up periodically and scans the room; the dirt-streaked window out to the street too.

They say that your eyes are the window to your soul. That pains me as I look at Lewis. I think of all the things that those eyes of his look at. What those things would do to anyone's soul. I want to go over there and gouge those eyes out of his head.

I want to keep them. Lock them away where they won't look at things they shouldn't.

Chapter 10

Lewis shifted from foot to foot in the black night and blew smoke from his lips. He stood at the end of Grampian Place, just shy of Tullos Circle, clear of the pool of white hitting the pavement from the nearest street light.

He hitched the rucksack's canvas strap over his shoulder again and, for the umpteenth time, checked his jeans pocket to see that the glove was still there. His mother's glove – the smell of her still clinging to it. She'd find the other glove hanging out of the front zip of her handbag and think she'd dropped the other one somewhere without noticing.

The school looked ablaze across the road. Light was spilling out from every classroom window, landing like pools of fire on the darkened concrete playground and grassy field. The cleaners were in. *She* was in.

Another ten minutes and it would all be worth standing here freezing his arse off. At least he hoped it would.

He stared at the main double doors of the school, not risking looking away in case he missed her. Last week was the first time he'd seen her up close. In fact, he'd heard her before he'd seen her, as he'd headed towards home, up the hill from Oscar Place. The school day had been long over, and she'd been laughing as she made her way out of the grounds. She'd been mere metres from him when he'd finally looked up. He hadn't expected to see the details of her face under the street light, but he could clearly see her brown eyes when she looked at him and smiled. A genuine smile, something he couldn't ever remember seeing, at least not in his direction. He'd stepped down off the pavement, as if letting her by, though the pavement was more than wide enough for both of them. He'd wanted to look gentlemanly.

Her smile was a nervous one and her feet had picked up speed as she'd passed him, the sweet smell of her lingering in the breeze.

For a minute he'd stood there, watching her make her way round the curve of Tullos Circle, every now and then glancing back over her shoulder. Looking at *him*. Adrenaline had surged through his veins at the thought that she'd wanted to look at him, his blood pumping so loudly in his ears that he'd been sure she would hear it, his raw excitement mixing with the four pints of Tennent's he'd downed at the pub.

But the next second it had felt like those same four pints had been poured over him, extinguishing his excitement, as she'd got in a Mini Cooper, its engine idling kerbside before moving off, taking her away from him.

He'd walked home in a daze, seeing nothing but her smile. Daring to believe she might like him. Wondering who it had been in that Mini, the person lucky enough to go home with her.

He'd shoved past his mother when she came bursting into the hallway, trying her best to nag at him as usual, and slammed his bedroom door, shutting her up as he flung himself down on the unmade bed. He'd needed to see her again already.

He'd been back there every night since, but hadn't seen her once. All his hopes were riding on this chance that, exactly a week later, she might be there again at last.

The clatter of the reception doors opening brought him back to the here and now. His heart raced.

Please let it be her.

He heard her laugh first, the one that had rung in his ears on repeat since the last time he'd heard it. The sound was louder now as she separated from the others, pulling her coat around her as she said goodbye by the gate.

She'd taken ten steps or so as he took his first, hitching the rucksack up on to his shoulder as he crossed the road and fell in behind her. She didn't look back. He clenched the glove in his hand, raised his arm and threw the glove in her direction, watching as it fell silently to the ground.

'Hey.'

She stopped and turned. 'You've dropped your glove.'

He jogged and picked it up, holding it out to her.

She looked at it and then up at him. Her eyes . . . She was so fucking beautiful. 'It's not mine.'

'Oh, sorry. I figured cos you were ahead of me . . .'

She shook her head and turned to keep walking.

This was not how he'd imagined it going . . . 'Eh, I used to go to that school.'

She stopped and turned again. Slower this time. Wary. 'Yeah?'

'A while ago now.' Instantly kicking himself – as if it wasn't already obvious it had been a while ago.

She nodded and crossed her arms, hugging herself against the cold. He wanted to hold her himself.

He sensed she was trying not to be rude about it, but she glanced over her shoulder anyway, towards the Mini Cooper waiting for her.

He just wanted to *talk*. His fists clenched. He'd hoped she would want to talk too.

'Excuse me, mate, have you got a light?'

Lewis spun on his heel, coming face to face with some bloke putting a fag to his mouth.

Where did he come from? Anger prickled at his throat. 'No, mate. I don't.'

She was walking away, heading towards the car.

The man was talking again. 'You sure you haven't got a light?'

The rucksack slipped from Lewis's shoulder to his elbow. 'Look, fuck off, will ya?'

He should punch him in the face, but, right now, she was more important. He couldn't have her think he was that kind of guy.

Fuck.

His teeth squeaked as they ground together, fists clenching and unclenching.

He watched her moving further and further away as he hissed, *'Fuck!'*

Lewis spun round, raising his arm to punch the guy, his arm frozen in mid-air when he saw the smile on his face. 'What are you grinning at?'

'Never gonna make friends like that.'

Lewis stood, not sure what to make of the guy, expecting him to raise his own fist but staring at that smile instead. There was something in the way the man spoke. Open. Friendly. Something Lewis wasn't used to. 'Who the fuck are you?'

The guy shrugged. 'No one you know. Not long moved here. Just sussing out the place.'

Lewis unclenched his fists and dropped his arm to his side. 'You in the habit of just walking up to randoms whilst you suss stuff out?'

The guy nodded towards where the girl had disappeared. 'No more than you are, trying to flirt by using the excuse of a dropped glove. I was trying to save you.'

Lewis reddened. 'What the fu—'

The man lifted both arms in surrender, the scent of his aftershave or body spray hitting Lewis in the face. 'So, shoot me if I think you could maybe try a better chat-up line.'

Lewis smiled, despite himself. 'It wasn't ... I wasn't ...'

For a moment they stood there, each looking around. At the ground, a glance at one another, eyes back on the ground.

Lewis thought the guy looked in his thirties, a good bit older than he was. Bit weird he'd be out yapping to strange men. Unless ... Lewis looked up at him. *Nah.*

Lewis fumbled in his pocket. 'Do you have a smoke? I think I *have* got a light.'

The man grinned. 'I do.' He reached for his back pocket and held out a fag packet. Only one fag – the fag already in his hand, the one he'd wanted a light for – had been taken from it.

Lewis took a second from the pack and lit it, passing the lighter as he exhaled. 'So, you've moved near here?'

The man put his fag to his lips, holding it the same way that Lewis did, before pausing then lowering it again to answer. 'Over in Victoria Road. Shitty little flat. My ex screwed me over. Because of shite on my phone. Total violation of privacy followed by a huge overreaction. You?'

Lewis blew out smoke from his nose, peering through the cloud as he straightened his shoulders. 'Just over there. Same shit.'

The man cocked his head. 'A psycho ex?'

Lewis said nothing as the guy stared at him.

'Hah, don't tell me you still live with your ma?'

Lewis tutted and turned the fag to stare at its tip, striving for cool. 'Yeah, but plan is to move out as soon as I can afford to be rid of the cow.'

The man nodded. 'Sure.'

Lewis watched him wander over to the low brick wall next to them, then pull himself up until his backside was on it, feet just short of the pavement and swinging. 'So, what do folk do around here?'

'Fuck-all. Place is a boring shithole. White Cockade is about as far as I go. You going to light that fag or what?'

'Yeah ... Was hoping you'd forget and I could steal your lighter.' He grinned and lit the fag, pulling it away from his face just as quickly as he exhaled. 'Think I might've seen you in there the other day. Only been the once. Been in the flat a few days.' He motioned to the empty spot by his side. 'You can sit. I'm not going to fight you or snog you.'

Lewis grimaced. 'You're not into that shit, are you?'

The guy let out a belly laugh. 'Eh, no, mate. Ex was most definitely a bird and let's just say I did a lot better at getting her than throwing a glove.'

'Fuck off.' Lewis pulled himself up on to the wall, leaving a gap between them, trying not to be the saddo that he was being, getting a little kick out of the guy calling him 'mate'.

'You like that bird?'

Lewis looked at him quizzically.

'Ah, come on, man. You're not the only one looking for a lady. Couldn't see much of her in the dark but I bet she's a looker. Maybe a bit young for me but not far off.'

Lewis bristled. 'She's not that young. And I'm a fair bit younger than you.'

'Cheeky bastard. Maybe that's why you'd struggle to get a mature woman.'

Lewis flicked ash to the pavement. 'I'm nineteen. I'm not after someone your age.'

They sat in silence, Lewis's heart beating at someone sticking around to talk to him, at the banter being thrown his way. Almost scared to say anything that might make the guy leave.

The guy turned to him. 'So, what's the name?'

A first name couldn't hurt. 'Lewis. You?'

'Mitchell.' He held out a clenched fist. Lewis took a moment to realize Mitchell was waiting for him to bump it, instead of his face being on the receiving end of it. He met Mitchell's knuckles, hiding his smile as he looked down at their feet swinging.

Mitchell threw his fag to the kerb.

Lewis's gaze followed it. 'That's half-smoked, mate.'

Mitchell laughed. 'Money to burn now I'm shot of the bitch. And, actually, now I am rid of her, the way I see it, you and I could be of use to each other.'

Lewis raised an eyebrow.

Mitchell laughed. 'Nae in that way, you twat. I think we've sussed I'm a woman-only kind of guy. But I reckon you're sound. Plus, I could teach you a thing or two about how to get a girl.'

Lewis raised his eyes this time, not interested in the promise, just that Mitchell might want to hang out again. 'Pretty sure of yourself, aren't you?'

Mitchell shrugged. 'Someone's got to be. I'll teach you how to chat up a bird, you join me for a pint downtown. Be nice to have a drinking buddy. Get us both out of this shithole.'

Lewis's heart quickened. Mitchell didn't have any other mates either. And he wanted to go catch a pint with *him*. Lewis jumped down from the wall. 'What, you want to go now?'

Mitchell laughed. 'Nah. I'm going to head home for some scran, and I'll see you back here tomorrow.' Mitchell stood too, spitting on the pavement and wiping his chin. He looked up the street. 'In fact, which flat's yours?'

Lewis managed to stop himself from skipping along the pavement. 'I'm walking back that way. I'll show you.'

'Come on, then.'

It was mere minutes before they were standing at the end of the path into Lewis's block of flats.

Lewis nodded up at the building. 'Top floor, right. Ma's a bit touchy so just throw a stone up so she doesn't go nuts at you buzzing. Nae too hard, though – you'll hear her if you smash the window.'

Lewis kept looking upwards, hoping he didn't sound like a nutter, not wanting his ma to know about Mitchell or for Mitchell to meet his ma.

Mitchell peered at the window. 'Shouldn't be a problem.'

Lewis had to fight the smile on his lips. 'You fancy a pint tomorrow, for real?

'More real than any chance you had with that bird.'

Lewis pushed at Mitchell's shoulder. 'Knock it off.'

Mitchell grinned and turned to look down the road where he was headed. 'Right, I'm off.'

Lewis rubbed at his thumb, trying to think of something to say, something that would make tomorrow a definite, but not wanting to look desperate.

Mitchell was already walking.

Lewis shouted after him. 'So, tomorrow?'

Mitchell raised his hand without looking back. 'Tomorrow.'

Lewis watched until he was no more than a spot in the distance, hoping more than anything that he'd see him again.

Chapter 11

I BLOW INTO MY cupped hands, having been trying to get up a heat since getting home, the smell of smoke still on my breath after brushing my teeth three times. I didn't inhale, just pulled on the butt and pushed it out of my lips as quickly as I could get away with, but I can still taste the stink. A means to an end, well practised so I didn't collapse in a fit of coughing.

The light from the three monitors in front of me has turned the skin on my hands to a blueish hue, looking as cold as they feel. Lewis is on one of those screens, lying on his bed. Flat on his back, nothing but a pair of boxer shorts on, his face illuminated by the cracked bedside lamp, by the promise made between us.

His hands are locked behind his head, wide blue eyes staring at the ceiling. Not seeing whatever's on that ceiling – probably nothing more than cracks and cobwebs – his mind in overdrive, thinking of what and where tomorrow might lead. No trace in his body language of the rage on the street earlier. That girl he was trying to get, already forgotten.

I'd promised him friendship, human connection, starting tomorrow.

My room is silent but for the constant tick-tock of the clock on the wall, the place in darkness except for the flickering colours of my screens and Lewis's home. A sickly glare. Most likely akin to the contents of his mind – the tick-tock of the clock making me think of the mechanics of that mind, and I'm forever grateful that I can't see what makes him tick, that I don't have to bear witness to the images behind those staring eyes of his.

Forty-five minutes I sit alongside him, both of us barely moving, that silence stretching out both sides of the camera. Nothing wrong with the audio feed. Both of us wrapped up in thoughts of tomorrow. His fuelled by excitement, mine driven by purpose. I could've made it all so much quicker – avoided the build-up to what's to come, but I want him to believe that he has something to look forward to. I want him to feel, for a single, brief moment, what he's longed to feel.

Fattening the goose if you like, and then taking it away. That crushing loss hitting him. Never as brutally as it hit me, but enough to ensure he knows and thinks hard about what he's done. Ultimately understanding what he took. Why he must pay.

Lewis sits up and swings his scrawny pale legs over the side of the bed – his lungs need that last nicotine hit of the day. He sits still, every rib visible on his bare back, enjoying each inhale and exhale before he stubs the cigarette out in the overflowing ashtray on the bedside table and reaches to turn off the lamp. There is no shout of goodnight to his mother, only the rustle of the thin duvet as he moves beneath it.

I imagine he's smiling. He won't be for much longer.

Chapter 12

Lewis dreamt in waves, flickering images and heightened sounds pulsing and beating throughout his mind and body, causing him to twitch, moan and cry out. A hard kick to his shin from a kid's scuffed boot in the playground; the brown eyes of the girl in the street smiling as he reached out to stroke her cheek; the bright lights and cameras being shoved in his face as he opened the door to the flat; the sting of leather against his skin as his father hissed in his ear, the stench of whisky pushing at his nostrils.

He was moaning, being dragged into consciousness.

Lewis's eyes shot open to darkness, the blackout blind drawn, his ears already alert, trying to figure out what had woken him. Why nightmares always woke him. Mere seconds before, his mind's eye had seen his father's face, the face he always saw. Those piercing eyes glaring at him, the memories ripping him from sleep. Almost as if his subconscious knew that those memories, that face – all of it – were things his body and brain wouldn't be able to deal with; had never been able to process. It was all safer kept locked away. Out of sight, out of mind. The only way to protect himself: to keep going.

Lewis's eyes strained against the darkness, looking for anything, the smallest chink of light, to drown out that face, to dissolve the memories. He pushed the images from his mind, forcing himself to remember last night, recalling Mitchell and his promises, daring to believe there would be or could be only good dreams ahead. Wanting to hear the tap of a stone on his window. Hoping that today would be the day when the nightmares would stop.

Chapter 13

'You want one?' I hold out the packet of Polo mints to Robbie. He yawns, and stares at them as if he should be checking them for pocket fluff.

'Jesus, Casey, breakfast fit for a king or what?' Robbie helps himself to one and stares at it. 'I prefer a wine gum.'

'Buy your own, then.' I wait as he helps himself to two more.

He chucks them in his mouth, the smell of mint between us. 'They'll do until Greggs opens.'

I tut and turn to the screens up on the wall, the street lights ablaze on Union Street, the place all but deserted. That lull before the city awakens and the day begins.

'At least we'll be finished by lunchtime.' My eyes don't leave the screens, mind deciding which camera to pull down to my monitor.

Robbie stretches, looking like he rolled out of bed five minutes ago. 'Aye, nae much handover from night shift. Mind you, that Alan doesn't do more than the bare minimum these days.'

I click on another screen, looking for something, anything, to focus on, all the screens empty of any drama. '*These* days? Never bloody has.'

That raises a smile from Robbie, before we fall into the usual comfortable, compatible silence. Nothing but the buzz of the overhead lights, the squeak of a joystick, the sound of our own thoughts. This morning, my thoughts are deafening. Exhausting.

It takes it out of a man, being up close to someone like Lewis. Feigning friendship with such a pathetic, loathsome bloke. A man with a lesser motive than mine might've been taken in by pity for him. I can sort of understand that; of course I can. Someone else could feel that way. But not me.

Not when I know about *you*.

Robbie pulls himself up from the chair and shuffles towards the door. 'I'm going for a piss.'

I nod. 'That's the coffee going through you already.'

I wait until I hear the door shut behind him and look to my mobile phone on the desk in front of me. Face down. Same place as always. Rarely anything incoming, rarely any need for me to lift it for anything outgoing. As I've said before, Robbie and I have each other.

Except that now that little black rectangle gives me as much power as I have sitting at this desk. With the click of a button, I can travel across town. See life in real time. Up close. Closer than the cameras I watch here, which are always restricted, only able to follow people whilst they're within range. But now I can travel through the walls that wouldn't let me in before, windows only giving a glimpse of the life within if the camera angle is just right.

My cameras are now positioned perfectly, smashing through those windows, taking me deep within those walls. I lift the phone and turn it over, the screensaver springing to life, my thumbs jabbing at the screen. My eyes looking within Lewis's walls within seconds.

He's lying on top of that bed again. Already awake. Smiling. Maybe seeing me, thinking of the adventures we could go on. Lads' holidays, strip clubs . . . No clue I'm there right beside him already, or that I'll be there in person by his side this afternoon.

I rub a thumb over the screen, scoring right through him. Again and again, moving back and forth across his body. Then turning the phone at speed and putting it back down on the desk as I hear the door, as Robbie plods back in moaning about something to do with no bog roll.

I'm smiling in the dark, matching Lewis's lips, thinking about scoring through him for real, rubbing him out. Erasing him from his life within those walls, and from the little life he lives outside them. Gone.

Chapter 14

Lewis paced the small rectangle of his room like a caged animal. He'd lost count of how many times he'd looked out of the window. *He should have asked what time. What if he somehow missed him? Would he come back?*

He had woken up at 10 a.m. Unheard of. Over three hours he'd been awake now. He was starving, but he didn't dare attempt to leave his room, to go through to the kitchen for something to eat. Sod's Law that Mitchell would turn up the very moment that he did, and he'd never know. Lewis had already peed in the mug his ma had failed to collect from his room last night. He'd need to get rid of that little surprise later, before it began to stink even more than it already did. Not worth the earache.

He could hear her grumbling in the living room, arguing with something they were saying on *Loose Women*. She hadn't come near him yet – not needing anything done, obviously, enjoying the peace; little point in trying to get him to move, unless she wanted the fight.

Where was Mi—

Lewis's head turned towards the tap against his window. It took him all his time not to dive towards it. Mitchell had hit the windowpane just enough, four floors up. Impressive.

Lewis made himself move slowly, sleepily, seemingly stumbling to the window at the same time that another small stone hit the window at eye level, making him flinch. He wiped at the condensation on the glass and squinted. Mitchell stood there, on the small patch of grass in front of the tenement.

Lewis took his time releasing the latch on the window, feigning a yawn as he leaned out of it. 'What's the time?'

'One thirty. Half the day gone. Had stuff to do.' Mitchell shrugged.

'No worries. That's still night to me, mate.'

Mitchell grinned. 'Get dressed. Meet me at the end of the road in twenty.'

Lewis moved away from the open window, jumping into his clothes in his eagerness to get downstairs, grabbing his fags and all he needed from the bedside table.

He came back. He was going out. Going to do something different. With a mate.

Lewis checked himself in the mirror, stood up straight. Things were going to get better. This was just the beginning. He could feel it.

Lewis's ma snarled. 'Where the fuck are you going?'

'Out.'

'Out where?'

Lewis ignored her as he grabbed his jacket from the

back of the kitchen chair, desperate to get out before Mitchell disappeared.

His ma's hands were glued to her hips. 'You better not be involved in any funny business.'

He'd heard that statement a million times since . . . well, since his life had imploded. But now – now he was about to rebuild it. In time, she'd see.

'Ma, it's no funny business. I'm off to see a man about a dog.' His answer to anything he did in life. Telling her nothing just to piss her off.

'You're a waste of fucking space.' Another thing that played on repeat in the soundtrack to his life.

'Whatever, Ma.'

He slammed the door and made his way down the communal stairs, bursting out into the afternoon. Lewis marched down the road, the school in the distance; Mitchell too, as promised – his mate leaning against the street's low wall sign, one knee bent, foot pressed against the brickwork behind.

Mitchell turned his head and raised a hand at Lewis. 'Thought you'd fallen asleep again.'

'Ha. So, where do you fancy?'

'Let's start at the Market Arms.' Mitchell winked as if that was only the beginning.

Lewis smiled. 'Sure. As good a place as any.'

Together, they set off down the street, Lewis swaggering alongside Mitchell. Hoping everyone could see.

Chapter 15

'Been years since I've been in the Market Arms.' Lewis looked around the pub.

Mitchell patted Lewis's back. 'Same old.'

He wasn't wrong – the same smell of stale beer, the same old sticky God-only-knew-what on the floor. Lewis felt like one of the boys as Mitchell placed his hand on his shoulder blade. He looked ahead to the bar, willing to bet it was still the same lass serving as the last time he was here, same guy sitting at the end of it. He wasn't wrong about the barmaid. One thing was different, though. This time Lewis wasn't alone.

Mitchell smiled at the barmaid. 'Two pints of Tennent's, please.'

The barmaid didn't crack a smile back as she slowly lifted two glasses from beneath the bar and poured from the pump, banging the glasses down before barking how much they owed.

Mitchell fished in his pocket and lay a note on the counter. 'Keep the change.'

That did raise a smile.

Lewis looked at Mitchell, expecting to be asked to pay his half, but Mitchell just motioned to the glasses as he picked one of them up.

'Come on, then, mate. Pick it up. It's not going to drink itself.'

Lewis couldn't move fast enough. 'Cheers.' He almost followed with 'mate', but didn't want Mitchell thinking he was assuming anything.

He followed Mitchell over to a small round table in the corner by the door and sat, before looking around. No one looking his way, no one staring; they were oblivious to him, as if he fitted in the same as everyone else. He never wanted today to end. 'So, what's the plan?'

'I say, let's be on the lash for the day. No pub left standing by the time we're done. You and me, mate.' Mitchell raised his pint between them.

Lewis's chest swelled as he clinked his glass against Mitchell's. 'Cheers to that.' He gulped at his pint, half of it gone when he put the glass back down on the table, and belched.

Mitchell's tongue wiped the foam from his top lip. 'I reckon we head for the Snug after this.'

Lewis nodded. 'Maybe Wilson's after that.'

'Whatever you say, my man.' Mitchell drained his pint.

Lewis grinned, excitement at his throat as he raised his glass and matched Mitchell. The quickest he'd ever drunk a pint, but he didn't want to look like a wuss. He banged the pint glass down and pointed at it. 'See how many of those babies we can down today.'

Mitchell leaned forward. 'My kind of man. I knew you and me would make good mates.'

Lewis wiped at his mouth trying to control the grin. 'I aim to please.'

Mitchell grinned this time, doing nothing to hide it. 'You sure do. The Snug first and maybe Wilson's after that. What d'ya reckon?'

Lewis nodded. 'For sure.' He looked out the window behind Mitchell's head, closing his eyes at the slight blur in his vision, rubbing at them. Not surprising, given he'd been up earlier today than he'd been in a long time. Lewis looked at Mitchell again as his new mate spoke.

'I'm thinking a nightclub later. Somewhere with banging tunes.'

Lewis doubted he'd still be standing by that time if he kept drinking at the same speed as their first pint, but he didn't want to look like he couldn't hold his drink. 'Fancy a second one in here?'

'Not going to say no.'

Lewis stood and paused, surprised to feel his head taking its time to catch up with his legs. It can't have been anything but the excitement of what was to come, though. He'd only had one pint.

He gave his head a shake and walked to the bar, hoping he was walking in a straight line.

One pint?

He took hold of the edge of the bar, working hard to focus on the barmaid's moving lips. As he started to talk, his own mouth stopped as he felt a hand on his shoulder.

'Actually, scratch that, mate. Let's just head to the Snug

now. New rule for the day – no more than one drink per pub.'

Lewis nodded and turned towards Mitchell, the room spinning as he did.

'You all right, mate?' Mitchell smiled.

Lewis raised a hand and pinched at his forehead, feeling something weird. Definitely not excitement. Didn't feel like the familiar buzz of a first drink either. 'I don't feel so good.'

Mitchell's hand was at Lewis's elbow. 'You're just revved up for hitting the town. Come on, let's go.'

'Maybe.' Lewis let himself be turned by the arm and led over to the bar door, aware of Mitchell shouting to the barmaid over his shoulder, something about his mate being a lightweight. Lewis licked at dry lips, his stomach rolling as his legs shook. The day blinding him as he stepped out on to the street, eyes squinting against the pain in his head.

Mitchell raised the arm not propping Lewis up and pointed down the street. 'The Snug is just across there. Bit of fresh air will do you good. Although, I don't know, mate. I mean, what the hell? Might be a taxi you're needing.'

'Tax-ay . . .' Lewis could hear the slur, panic rising.

Mitchell shook his head and laughed. 'Jesus, mate. Just lean on me and I'll get you to the rank.'

Lewis leaned into Mitchell, fear prickling at his chest as to what was happening – seeing the cobbled street beneath him as they crossed from the pub, sure that the taxi rank was the other way, as Mitchell dragged him along.

Lewis groaned, feeling worse in the fresh air, not better. 'Need to go humm . . .' Unable to say or finish the word, his heart banging.

No answer from Mitchell as the grip on Lewis's arm tightened and the pace sped up. Or was he imagining that?

Lewis's eyes drooped, his feet stumbling on the street as the cobblestones rose and fell in front of him. 'Mit . . . chell?'

Maybe Mitchell was talking, but he couldn't hear him. Everything was so far off in front, so deathly quiet around him.

Darkness ahead, that grip on his arm ever tighter, travelling upwards. The grip now . . . *Jesus* . . . The grip now wrapping around his throat.

Coughing. Trying to breathe. Struggling to see.

Mitchell's face swimming in front of him. Smiling.

Smiling.

A woman's name ringing in Lewis's ears as everything went black.

Chapter 16

I come back to work hoping to feel cleansed in some way. Easier said than done when the waft of Robbie's armpits keeps hitting my nostrils. Batman needs a good wash.

Another morning shift. Yesterday's early stint, and what followed after, feeling like another lifetime. I watch the screens, as always. Concentrating on the cameras covering the main heart of the city – Union Street, its arteries branching off and through the city, oxygen-rich life travelling through its side streets. Everyone going about their business.

Knowing that my business, the task of ridding the world of Lewis, of avenging you, is done.

Back to normal. A return to the job. Nothing much happening today. No visible crimes to pre-empt, stop or report. The heartbeat regular for now; healthy. Everything fine on the surface. As if Lewis's removal has balanced the scales of life, all being right with the world again. Except I know the truth. That beneath is diseased, the plaque silently building, one wall at a time within those arteries, until it attacks. That it will strike again.

Robbie stretches back in his seat, arms above his head as far as he can lift them, dragging me from my thoughts, making my nose curl with the pungent stink of BO. He yawns. 'Not much going on so far, mate. Got some photos through of two fourteen-year-old girls to look out for. Came off yesterday night's train. You seen the pics?'

'Yeah.'

'Suspected trafficking. Other than that, no new Missing Person reports, the drunks at St Nicholas are still in their scratchers, the thieves too – and anyone else with half a brain. Won't last.'

'Never does.' I swear sometimes that Robbie can read my mind, and then I remember he definitely can't. He wouldn't be here beside me if he could be in my mind. And maybe vice versa. The truth of anything – of anyone – has to stay hidden beneath. That's where you find the guts of the story.

Robbie is staring at me.

'Casey?'

'Yeah, mate.'

'You OK?'

I turn to him. 'Sure. Why?'

He shrugs. 'You seem a little distracted these last few weeks.'

'Nah, just not been sleeping the greatest.'

He doesn't need to know that last night I slept like a baby.

Robbie turns back to his screen, seemingly placated. No reason not to be, not with the number of times I've fought his corner. Putting the boss in their place about cutting the guy some slack about his workwear, covering for him whenever he's late, as he often is; that time he ballsed up royally on a missing person and I swooped in, dug him out of it and saved the day.

Loyal Casey. Reliable Casey. Saviour Casey. Robbie thinking he does the same right back. That we know each other inside out. That he can see right into my soul and knows my secrets because he knows about my childhood. Not a clue.

I'm no different from every face that will appear in front of me today. Each one of them a cover. Each with secrets to keep in the pages beneath.

My own face is a cover. The name associated with it not even mine.

In Aberdeen there are secrets. There are people, and there is a city. Union Street itself hides a whole other world, a place out of view. Hidden from the camera lens. Unseen. A place we walk above every day without a second's thought – the forgotten vaults beneath.

Union Street. The Granite Mile. A city centre essentially built on stilts. Stretching from the Mercat Cross at the Castlegate, all the way up to Holburn Junction – a feat of engineering at the beginning of the nineteenth century. The roots of the old town still beneath the shiny new one above that welcomes visitors to the city.

The whole city is an ocean to explore, though the CCTV cameras only cover the surface. But I'm everywhere. I'm watching them all. As much as I can. As far as I can. Going down under.

Blind spots which only I have access to. Those that I intend to make full use of.

Because there is more to do. Much more. Our Lewis was only the beginning.

Chapter 17

THE RINGING WAS FAINT and seemed far off.

Jennifer Scott looked out of the open, white-framed kitchen window of her home, expecting to see someone rummaging in their jacket pocket or bag for their mobile phone, but seeing no one.

She glanced down at her own phone lying on the worktop, always nearby, knowing before she'd even looked at it that it wasn't her phone that was ringing. Jen frowned and put the knife down beside the half-cut onion on the chopping board. She turned, staring at the slightly ajar kitchen door that led out into the corridor and to the front door.

Maybe someone was at the door. The postie, or a delivery driver. Taking a call, maybe; it had to be that. She was in the house alone, Daisy at school, Tom at work. Jen being sure she hadn't left the telly on in the living room.

She lifted the bottom of her apron and wiped at her eyes as she walked across the kitchen. Lola, their golden labrador, following at her heels as she stepped out into the hallway. Jen paused in the narrow corridor, the ringing louder now, Daisy and Tom staring out at her from the framed pictures on the walls either side of her. Jen stared at the frosted glass panel of the front door straight in front of her, baffled not to see any silhouette through it. The ringing was insistent. Not a ringtone she recognized.

She looked at the countless coats weighing down the coat-hooks on the wall to the left of the door. Wondering for the briefest of moments if the phone might be in one of the pockets, mild panic rising that Tom might be the kind of man who hid a secret phone, doing whatever men do who have secrets to hide.

Her gaze fell to the wellies, shoes and trainers piled high beneath the coats, to the carpet runner beside them, to the rubber mat behind the door. Jen's forehead wrinkled as her eyes fixed on the doormat – on the small, yellow padded envelope lying there. The *ringing and buzzing* yellow envelope.

What the hell?

She crept towards the mat, her eyes never leaving the yellow envelope as she walked past the side dresser and the wall mirror above it. Stepping gingerly, as if the bag might jump up at her or explode; Lola circling her feet, both of them coming to a standstill by the doormat, looking down at the envelope.

Still ringing.

Jen crouched and touched the package, her hand springing back at the vibration. She stretched her hand out again, noticing the tremor there as she lifted the envelope. Jen turned the buzzing blank parcel over in her hand. She straightened and stared at it, finally taking a deep breath before ripping along the seal at the back. She hesitated as her fingers found the opening, then slowly dipped them in, feeling around inside.

Jen's fingers brushed against cold, vibrating plastic. Her hand grabbed at it, pulling the small, black, ringing handset out into the daylight.

Into her home.

She peered down at her hand. Holding a phone she'd never seen before. Hearing a ringtone she'd never heard.

Old school. One of those flip phones she hadn't seen in years.

Posted through her door.

Jen scowled and grabbed at the door handle with her free hand, pulling open the door with force and sticking out her head, looking this way and that, ready to ask what the hell was going on. But finding no one to ask. She stepped back inside, closed the door and squinted down at the phone.

What the hell? she asked herself again.

Jen turned the phone in her hand, the flashing screen coming into view.

Number withheld.

She stared at the black letters, the phone pulsing like a living, breathing thing against her palm. Black. Ominous. Refusing to be ignored.

Jen swallowed, her finger trembling as she hit the answer button. The ringing was silenced but her mind was already dreading what she might hear next.

Jen put the phone to her ear.

Chapter 18

'Hello?' The line was silent, but Jen sensed someone there, waiting. 'Hello?'

'Hello, Jennifer.'

Jen's heart lurched at the voice. Male. Deep. Someone who knew her name.

'Who is this?' Jen bit at her lip.

'That's not important right now.'

The voice was almost jovial, friendly and familiar, though Jen didn't think it was someone she knew.

'What?' Her brow creased. 'Who is this?'

'Jennifer, stop talking.'

She fell silent, bristling at the jaunty tone that scolded her, but somehow knowing it was a voice she didn't want to upset.

This wasn't some nuisance call. Whoever this son of a bitch was, he had been at her door. Moments ago. Since she'd got back from driving Daisy to school. Jen closed her eyes, thinking about that drive. How she'd tried to calm herself once home, by cooking. This man, whoever he was, had been at her door. Mere metres from her, posting the phone through the door whilst she stood preparing to make soup.

She heard him sigh, as if she were some child whose behaviour he needed to rein in. 'Thank you, Jennifer. Who I am doesn't matter right now. What you think you need to know is of no importance either. What is imperative is what *I* know.'

Jennifer's grip tightened on the phone at her ear. 'What are you talking about?'

'Jennifer, I asked you to stop talking.' Condescending. Infuriating. Something else beneath.

Her hand shook.

'You know what I'm talking about.'

Jen's heart thumped, the dryness in her mouth making her tongue click as she tried to speak but failed to find the words.

'You know exactly what I mean, don't you?'

Her heart thumped still harder, as she thought about the other night with Tom, about this morning. 'Who are—'

'Shhh . . . you need to listen to what I'm saying.'

Still talking to her in that bouncy voice, like some long-lost friend.

Her stomach flipped, adrenaline surging through her veins. Wanting, needing, to take the upper hand – unsure whether she was right to play it the way she was about to, hissing down the phone through clenched teeth. 'I don't need to listen to shit.' She hung up and stared at the phone before taking shaky steps towards the dresser and stopping dead as the phone vibrated in her hand again, the ringtone loud and intrusive, making her ears and her head ache.

It rang. And rang. And rang.

Jen looked above the dresser, seeing her haunted face in the wall mirror. Who was it? How did they know? What did they want? What would they do if she didn't pick up?

She glanced at the coat-hooks again. At Tom's Barbour jacket, her gaze dropping down to Daisy's wellington boots.

She couldn't risk finding out what might happen if she didn't answer.

She stabbed at the green-lit button.

He was speaking before she had a chance to. 'Jennifer, didn't your parents teach you that it's rude to hang up?'

'Just tell me what this is about.' Her voice caught.

'Now, now. What would Daisy think of Mummy's manners?'

Jen froze. He knew her daughter's name too. It sounded sour, dirty, coming from his mouth. He had no right to utter her daughter's name. 'Who the hell is this?'

'I'll say it once more.' The tone was no longer jovial, ice travelling the waves between them. 'You do not need to know who I am. What you need to do is listen and do exactly as I tell you.' Firm now. Anger at its edges.

Her voice trembled. 'I don't need to do anything you say.'

'You might believe that, for now . . .'

A beat, the threat left hanging for her to consider.

'. . . but after this call, when I'm finished giving you your chance, it's what I *then* go on to do. What I *say* – to Tom, to Daisy – to anyone and everyone you know.'

The voice fell silent, Jen sure she could now hear her heart instead.

And then, 'Jennifer, I think you'll wish you had listened.'

She snapped her eyes shut, trying to calm her breathing. She wanted to reach down the phone line and scratch at his eyes. 'Keep my family out of whatever this is.'

His laugh was dry, rough against her ear. 'What, to protect them? Do you think you've done that, Jen? After everything you've done? After all that's happened?'

She was stunned into silence. Anger and fear replaced by gnawing guilt.

'Were you protecting your daughter this morning?'

Jen rubbed at her forehead, the fingers of her other hand turning white with the force she was holding the phone with. Trying to ignore the burning shame, the sickening feeling that what he was saying was true. *How did he know?*

She couldn't show fear. 'I'll call the police. Get them to trace this phone.'

The laugh was cruel. 'Really? You think I haven't covered all of that?'

Jen felt a spike of fear.

'After all, Jen, that would come down to my word against yours. Let's just say I have a little insurance – *assurance*, if you like. Something that would most definitely cast doubt in their minds as to whether anything you were saying was true.'

Jen slumped to the floor, her legs buckling and crossing beneath the weight. *What could he possibly have?*

The phone pinged, making her pull it away from her ear but not far enough that she couldn't still hear him.

'Look at the phone, Jennifer. Play it.'

Her finger shook as she pressed it against the screen, opening the attachment. Bile rising in her throat as an image sprang up and she saw the freeze-frame of a video. Of her. *Inside* her car. Telling her everything she needed to know already before she even clicked play.

The video rolled in slow motion, Jen's gaze glued to it no matter how much she wanted to turn away.

She closed her eyes as the phone pinged again, then looked back down. Another video. Her finger hovered before she stabbed at the screen. A different shot this time. *Outside* the car. From a distance. She played the video, reliving every minute of that morning, before the screen went blank.

Jen swallowed, her tongue feeling fat and thick as she looked up towards the coat-hooks. Her home, a place of warmth and comfort just minutes before, now feeling cold and dangerous.

Tears sprang at the corner of her eyes as the phone pinged yet again, making her jump where she sat on the hallway floor, even though she should've been expecting it. Jen stared at the phone, desperate to look away – for all of this to stop. A photograph this time. The image sent a chill down her spine.

Jesus. He'd been in her garden.

Behind the sprawling old oak tree in the corner of their lawn, by the looks of the angle. The tree where she and Daisy would sit in the summer and have a picnic. Where she would lean against its trunk during Daisy's time at nursery, and read a book. The same tree where she and Tom had kissed, that first time they viewed the house.

How long had he been watching her? Jen swallowed as the voice came back on the line.

'Now you know.'

Jen was trying to stand, her legs quivering with the effort.

'I'm sure you appreciate, Jen, how easy it would be. One text. Those attachments, from the many others that I have, sent to multiple numbers. Numbers I already have: Tom, school, extended family, Facebook friends, the authorities . . . I could take out the bottom of your world as you know it.'

Jen slumped again. 'What is it you want from me?'

'I want you to do exactly what I tell you. And I want you to tell no one.'

She had to think. What if she agreed but found a way to alert someone – to tell them she needed help without them knowing what she was trying to hide? Jen glanced at the notepad and pen on the side dresser. A note. She could leave a note. But then she saw those images again in her head. How close he had been to her and her home. Possibly *inside* her home. She looked around, sure her eyes would come to rest on a camera or something. Seeing nothing but knowing there was no way to be sure. She couldn't take the chance. Jen jumped as he spoke again, as if reading her mind.

'Leave nothing and take nothing except the phone in your hand.'

Panic squeezed at her throat. 'But Tom will worry if he

can't get me on the phone . . . And Daisy . . . What about Daisy coming out of school?'

'None of that is important.'

A flame almost sparked in her belly and her teeth clenched as she spat the words: 'What do you mean, none of that is important? This is my life!'

'No, Jennifer, that is your life as you know it right now.'

His calmness only intensified her unease.

'Where am I going?' She looked to the door, half expecting to see his silhouette through the glass.

'You'll find out. Not far.'

'Will I be safe?' She looked at the little wellington boots once more. 'Will I see my daughter again?'

'If you do as I say. Instructions will follow by text. Be ready to follow them.'

'But . . .'

'There are no buts. Remember, take only the phone. And, Jennifer . . .?

Jen scowled through her tears. 'What?'

'I'll be watching you.'

Chapter 19

AND I AM WATCHING.

Life360 tracking is downloaded on that phone she holds, the app hidden from view whilst she remains in plain sight. In my sights. All the way until she gets to where I want her.

But first, let's up the ante. I want her to pay. To be made to think. To feel fear. She'll think it's for what she's been doing recently, but I know it's for what she did. That all of this is for you.

I want Jennifer to fear every text. To think that every instruction I bark at her from afar is the tick . . . tick . . . tick . . . of that timebomb. Making the threat of that colossal explosion real – the thought that her life as she knows it might be destroyed. That thought as real to her as I now am.

A countdown – ensuring, as I did with Lewis, that she comes to me. That she does as she's told. Except, this time, not with promises of what I can give – but rather, the promise of what I'll take. Letting her believe that I can influence in any way the *when* of her arrival, not just the *where*.

What she doesn't know won't hurt her.

But what I know might.

Chapter 20

JEN FROZE AT THE ping of the phone in her hand, which hung down by her side. She stood in the hallway of her home, on the same spot she'd been since the voice went dead on the other end. Lola whined as Jen stared at the wall, seeing nothing. Trying to make sense of the voice that had come crashing into her life. An intruder. Switching her home, her life, from safety to danger.

She lifted her hand, heart pumping. She didn't want to look at the message. She squeezed her eyes shut again, hoping it might all somehow disappear – the phone, the text, the man at the end of it all. Whoever the hell he was. She opened her eyes slowly, dread spreading in her chest as she focused and read:

Get the No.11 bus. Take nothing but cash for your fare.
No bank cards. No ID. No phone but this one. Nothing.

A second later . . .

Talk to no one.

The screen flickered. The text disappeared and was replaced by a clock. Jen stared at it. Large grey digits against a black background. Not a clock: a timer. The seconds already counting down. Making Jen think of New Year and new beginnings, but thinking that this clock may instead signal the end.

She looked from the timer up to the wall clock, assuming the digits were counting her down to the bus's arrival time. Less than twenty minutes to get to the stop. Her chest flipped. What would happen if she didn't make it? If those digits ran to zero?

She swallowed and slammed the mobile phone down on top of the dresser, wishing it was the unknown caller's face she was in danger of smashing. She glanced at the ever-changing numbers taunting her as she grabbed at the collar of her Barbour jacket on its hook and shrugged herself into it, swearing as her arm pushed at the silk sleeve-lining that had turned itself inside out.

Money. She didn't carry cash. She rubbed at her forehead. *Think.*

Daisy's piggy bank.

Jen snatched the phone and ran to the foot of the stairs, sweeping up them two at a time, Lola bounding up by her side as they both burst on to the upper landing and through the first door off to the left. Her daughter's bedroom. The porcelain teddy money box sitting centre of the chest of drawers under the window. The light brown bear standing out like a beacon in a sea of pink.

Jen put the phone down on the white-stained wood and lifted the teddy, relief flooding her as she heard the jangle of coins inside. She pinched the grey rubber stopper beneath the bear and pulled, turning to the low single bed, letting the coins fall to her daughter's pink heart-strewn duvet.

She shook the last of them from the teddy. Daisy's teddy. She was taking this nightmare into her daughter's room. The place where her daughter felt safe. Where she slept through innocent, childhood dreams. She'd brought this man into their lives, the bogeyman suddenly as real as Jen stealing from her daughter.

Lying. Again.

Jen shook her head free of the thoughts as her hands dived for the coins, scooping them up, stuffing both pockets with coppers and silver, hoping it would be enough. She couldn't remember the last time she'd stepped on a bus.

She ran into the bathroom and opened the mirrored cabinet, her fingers grasping what she was looking for. *Take nothing.* But she couldn't not take this. She stuffed it in her pocket and bounded back down the stairs.

All she knew was that the No.11 came through Hazlehead – down from the academy, and over the Hazlehead roundabout, by Daisy's primary school. And she only knew that because of the school commute every morning and passing the bus too many times to remember. Jen pictured the road, sure that there was a bus stop just down and across from the Hazeldene Road junction that she regularly turned into and drove up, to their home. Sure, but not certain.

She looked back at the phone: fifteen minutes. She'd have to run.

Chapter 21

JEN CLUTCHED AT HER stomach, bent over by the kerbside on Queens Road, panting and wheezing. She wiped at her dry, cracked lips, her mouth feeling like a sandpit. She looked left, towards the Hazlehead roundabout, and gasped: the bus was just crawling into view, its bulk spread across both lanes as it navigated the grassy mound.

She flipped open the mobile phone clutched in her hand: two minutes. Her head whipped right, left, and right again, her heart sinking at the steady stream of traffic, the smell of petrol fumes making her queasy. She stepped from side to side, needing to be in motion. Her feet squelching – realizing for the first time that she was still wearing her slippers. Grey furry boots with a rubber sole that had done nothing to keep out the puddles she'd splashed through on the run here. She looked down at her zipped Barbour jacket, knowing that her kitchen apron was still beneath it too.

The bus was indicating to pull into the bus stop

opposite. She looked left and right again, and stepped out into the traffic. Brakes squealing, horns blaring, heads shaking as she raised a hand and parted the cars.

The bus was already indicating to leave the kerbside. She waved frantically, failing to attract the driver's attention before running right in front of the bus as its horn deafened her, then around to the door before the driver had time to argue. She pounded on the glass and glowered at the scowling driver.

'Open the door!'

She glanced at the phone screen: thirty seconds. What would happen if he didn't let her on? *How would he know?*

Jen looked along the bus windows and saw a face staring out at her as the door thundered open. She immediately bolted on board.

'You trying to get yourself killed?' The scrawny bus driver sat behind his Perspex screen, safe in his see-through box, safer than she felt on the other side of it. Out here. He drummed bony fingers against the steering wheel and stared at her as she fumbled with the loose change in her pockets. She had no idea of the amount to pay or how to pay it.

Tell no one.

That's what the text said.

What if she said something to the driver? Something that meant he might somehow be able to help her? Jen looked around as the driver sighed and pointed to the cash machine. She pulled coins from both pockets and dropped them all from cupped hands into the machine without saying a word. A few coins hit the edge of the machine, missed, spilled and rolled on to the floor, then towards the rear of the bus. She didn't move.

The driver tutted. 'Single or all day?'

She looked at the machine, past him, and out the window towards her home. Would she be coming back? Would she ever see her family or house again?

'Single,' she mumbled.

'You've paid too much.'

She shrugged and looked up at his creased face, keeping her own features blank. Desperate to say *something*.

'Oh well, it's your money.'

She grabbed at the slip of paper escaping the machine. Not exactly the portly, smiling, ruddy-cheeked bus driver from the kids' books. Perhaps not someone who would be willing to help her even if she did ask.

She stuffed the ticket in her pocket, stumbling as she was almost propelled down the aisle by the speed with which he pulled away from the stop. Her hand grabbed hold of the pole by the nearest seat, using it to save herself from falling forward, spinning around before she slumped down to sit.

A tap to her shoulder made her jump. An elderly gentleman with a flat cap and kind smile stood over her. 'You dropped these, dear.' He handed her the coins with his shaky, frail hand, the crepe skin almost translucent, revealing a road map of blue veins.

She took the coins and dipped her chin in thanks before he walked back to his seat. Her head turned to watch him, her gaze darting to scan the other three passengers on the bus. Were any of them *him*?

There was a surly-looking teen on the back row, his

head down and face hidden by greasy curls, thumbs flying over his phone; a doughy-faced woman, the fat of her neck pushed up and over the high collar of her beige quilted coat, any hair she might have had hidden beneath a white woollen hat; and a bald man with thick, black-framed glasses who looked away from the window, towards her, pausing briefly before settling his attention back outside the window again.

Could the man with the glasses be him? She wondered if any of the people on the bus had been planted to watch her. If any of them knew why she was here. Where she was going.

She shuffled forward and perched on the edge of her aisle seat, blocking access to the window seat beside her. She wouldn't be letting anyone past her to take it. The last thing she wanted was small talk, and she needed to stay as close to the exit doors as possible. No way was she moving over if someone asked her to – she couldn't risk being blocked in, missing the stop. Assuming she got a text telling her where to get off, that was.

The phone pinged as if it had heard her thoughts:

Good girl.

Her head whipped around, the only person with a phone in their hand being the teenager. *How the hell could he know she'd made it?*

She tried to find a way to reply but the phone locked out just as fast as the text arrived. It appeared to be set up for the basics, for whatever sick game this was. No internet access and no way to make a call or reply to a text. And no countdown this time.

The phone bounced in the hand resting on her jittering leg, as uneasy as her mind. Her other hand still held the pole in front. She could only surmise that the bus would head into the city centre. But what did she actually know? She knew nothing. Not who was doing this. Not if she was in danger. Not if she, Daisy and Tom would be safe.

All she did know was that, if she had any chance of returning to her life as she knew it, she needed to do exactly as she was told.

Chapter 22

I'M WHERE I NEED to be. Where she'll be before long.

I'm huddled in a doorway, in full view of the people who pass by, if they cared to look. But they don't care, their heads down, oblivious to me, to the world around them. Wrapped up in their own lives, their own stories, as they travel through the streets – my esteemed colleagues watching them. All eyes on them in the places where they become visible, following them until they disappear out of range again.

But here, there's no camera focusing on me. I made sure of that, obviously. I'm invisible. There's nothing to see here.

I look at my phone, anticipation building as I watch that little green dot crawling towards me on the mapped streets of Aberdeen. Making its way down Union Street, being dragged along the arteries, straight towards that diseased city heart.

Straight to me. To my heart, which was only ever yours. Every beat of it now marching towards justice.

She's almost here.
Her own heart probably beating as fast as mine, her mind thinking of that ticking bomb.
Not knowing what's about to happen.
She can't do anything now.

Chapter 23

THE LIGHT FROM THE telly flickers on the wall. Moving images from a real-life movie silenced long ago.

It's how I've spent my nights since the loss of you. Alone, in my home. Sometimes watching people live. But mostly watching you, over and over. Living in the past.

I wonder if Lewis's mother might now do the same, if Jen's husband and daughter will find comfort in living in the before.

I get scared that I'm forgetting how you sounded. The way you would say my name. Your laugh. Your sigh. Your cry.

I wonder if you cried out. If you called my name. If you screamed.

Did you think I'd let you down? Were you scared? Did you hate me in that moment?

Or did it happen too quickly? No time to think. Not a spare breath to shout.

I hope for that, at least – not that there's any hope in

what happened – and that, other than it being quick, you still held nothing but love for me. Those things are what I cling to most. Where I try to find at least some shred of hope.

It never lasts, though.

Easier to torture myself. Feeding my guilt. Fodder for my failure. Fuelling my anger.

I pause the film. Your face fills the screen, that dimple in your cheek close enough to touch. A memory of pinching it gently; your smile before I kissed it.

I clutch at my stomach. Physical pain. Wishing I could reach into that TV screen and pull you out into my arms.

Comforted by the fact that I have, at least, found those who took you from me. That instead of watching only you on repeat every day, I have watched them too. Two of them now fully aware they were seen. By me. By you. Knowing that we saw right through them.

Only one remains. His time is coming.

Maybe then, there will be peace. Justice.

I stare at your frozen image. Wishing I was up close to you, now more than ever. Needing to feel that warm flesh again. To smell that hot, sugary smell of yours.

A heat gone cold a long time ago.

A smell that never lingered.

Chapter 24

BILL WEBSTER'S HOME SMELLS musty, with an undertone of furniture polish, because he never opens the windows. He does, however, pride himself on keeping a tidy and clean house. The way *she* used to; the way he knows *she'd* want it.

Bill keeps a spare set of keys in the grey metal mailbox bolted to the side of his heavy, expensive-looking front door. Expensive but not practical; how can it be when it doesn't have a letterbox? A simple metal catch allows access to the mailbox. Bill probably figures no one will ever think him stupid enough to store anything of any importance in there.

His son, Simon, comes to visit and stays for tea every Thursday evening. Bringing his mousey wife, Kelly, and their small boisterous child, Brandon, who already exploits his mother's timidity – scarily so, at this young age.

Bill's son does the same thing every week: pretending to check the mail, but really fetching the key without even trying his father's door first. He knows it'll be locked because it always is. Bill must make sure she can't get out.

His son most likely has his own keys somewhere, but it's habit just to help himself to the one in the mailbox; so ingrained that he's long ago stopped checking to see if anyone is watching.

He doesn't see me watching.

I let myself in on a Thursday morning. Right after Bill's car backs out of the driveway, and he and his wife head off up the hill towards Aldi for their weekly food-shop. Getting in supplies for the family visit in the evening. The same time every Thursday; it's the only time they go out during the entire week.

Bill's laptop is surprisingly new. An Apple MacBook Air. It's a high-end piece of technology for someone of his age. I'll admit, I didn't have him down for a laptop. I'd have expected an old, yellowing, boxy monitor – maybe a freestanding clunky disk drive at its side – if he even had any technology at all. The laptop sits centre of a small, polished mahogany desk. A patterned, upholstered hardback chair is tucked in beneath the desk.

I doubt he needs something so fancy. Probably wandered into the Apple Store, no clue what he was looking for, until some pimple-faced, overconfident nerd with a tablet in his hand convinced him to buy something he never knew he needed.

I tap the trackpad and the screen springs to life. No password request, just straight to the home screen. Our Bill is clearly a trusting kind of guy, or rather someone who figures there's no one here who'd pry. No one but his wife, and it seems she wouldn't know where to start.

The bookshelves that sit behind his mahogany desk and laptop are against the wall by the living-room window. Weighed down by books about dementia – caring for someone with it, to be precise.

I open Safari on the laptop. There are no mentions of dementia in the recent search history on Bill's shiny new MacBook Air. Maybe he finds the reference books easier than a screen when there's a need to read in detail. Perhaps he doesn't want the MacBook to be about that; something just for him.

I don't know what type of man Bill is, not yet, so there's a small chance that he doesn't have a password because he's the sort who actively wants people to see his searched-for answers on the condition, for them to know that he's doing his best. Either because he enjoys martyring himself or because he has a genuine need for others to see how much he cares.

I continue to scroll through his search history, thinking that poor Bill has most likely paid over a grand to play solitaire and look up information on Google, because that's mainly what he does. He checks up on animal facts (with a particular interest in birds), plays music by The Beatles – no other artists – and educates himself on the gardening seasons.

I close Safari down, my eyes scanning the few files saved to the Mac's desktop – shortcuts to websites of interest, sitting on his home screen for easy access.

My finger hovers over the trackpad, then pushes the cursor towards each of the shortcuts on the home screen. Clicking on them one by one – the one labelled 'Winter gardening tips' making my finger freeze in surprise when it springs to life, the website accessed definitely nothing about any garden.

Senior Singles.

Clearly our Bill is searching for something else. Something outside his usual interests.

A smile spreads across my face, but how can I be sure? Perhaps I'm jumping and missing the landing. Maybe the website indicates nothing more than morbid curiosity, something to while away the lonely hours.

I play with these thoughts as I move to the bathroom and then the bedroom, searching for something, just like Bill. I'm relieved to find it, taking it with me as I head back down to the living room.

I look around the room, checking I've left no sign I was ever here. I glance over at the framed wedding picture of Bill and his wife, Trish, on the dresser. Thinking for sure how senior Bill looks all these years later. But single? Nowhere near it.

I stare into Bill's eyes in that black-and-white image. Young Bill. Married Bill. Vows newly made. *In sickness and in health.*

I look at those books again, and at the shortcut on his laptop.

Thinking about those vows. Wondering if Bill remembers them. If he still honours them.

Chapter 25

BILL DIDN'T WANT TO get out of the car. The little black Kia might as well be a coffin – him trapped inside it, buried alive, feeling the same claustrophobia, panic and hopelessness as he did right now, sitting here next to Patricia.

Thursday morning and folk were coming and going through the doors of Aldi at Cornhill Shopping Centre. Fraught-looking mums with overexcited kids, skinny teenagers spitting their phlegm on to the pavement, the odd lone, dishevelled shopper probably just glad he was able to feed himself.

All of them people he and Trish used to pity. Folk they felt sorry for but, if the truth be told, they also felt superior to. Middle class to their working class, or, worse still, to their impoverished, benefits existence. Their semi-detached granite home on Cairncry Road, with its sprawling garden out back, had always seemed at odds with the skyscrapers and shabby tenements across the way.

Now it was them, he and Patricia, who were looked

down upon. Folk's stares, whispers and barely concealed laughs as they made their way around the shop every week as he tried to move Patricia as fast as he could through the checkout without her shouting out; trying to avoid her demanding to see the manager or, worse still, asking the cashier who the man was that she was there with. Why he wouldn't let her leave.

Their son, Simon, had offered to get their weekly shop. When Bill refused the help, Simon tried to get him to consider online shopping. What Simon didn't understand, even though Bill couldn't ask for a better son, was that their world, *Bill's* world, was becoming ever smaller. Unable to get out on his own, for fear that Trish might kick off or hurt herself – or, even worse, wander out the door.

It was why he'd . . .

Bill rubbed at his forehead, thinking about what he'd done, what he was doing – forcing those thoughts out of his head, burning guilt gnawing at his insides, sitting here next to Trish. The bottom line was that he didn't want to be seen asking for help. So much of what used to make him feel like a man had already been stripped away from him. He had to at least try to keep these little routines going. The ones they'd always had as a couple; so set in their ways that folk used to laugh at them. Mince and tatties on a Monday, chicken pie on a Tuesday, whatever they fancied at bingo on a Wednesday, and so on – rarely breaking that routine.

But now he'd broken that routine, done something so out of routine, so out of character . . .

Bill forced himself to focus on that old routine. The

one that always worked for them. The doctor said it was a good thing that a firm schedule was already in place, that the familiarity could only be helpful for Trish. Bill had secretly hoped that, over time, it might stir something within her. But that glimmer of hope had vanished a long time ago. As had the few friends he'd had outside their marriage. The guys that had long ago stopped calling, without him really noticing it happen.

He looked at Trish. She hadn't moved since they'd parked up. She was sat staring into the distance. At the rows of cars; the numerous posters plastering the glass doors of the Cairncry Community Centre; the skyscrapers behind it. There was no way of knowing what was going on in that head of hers.

He looked past her, out the window. His old local, Murdo's Bar, was up the slope behind the bare bushes and low wooden fence. He could see the smokers gathered outside. Jim, one of the regulars – so regular that no one dared to touch his stool in the corner of the bar – was standing there, puffing away.

The guy was staunch Scottish. Broad Aberdonian accent. He'd wrap himself in the blue-and-white flag if the pub would still let him in, but regardless, he'd welcomed Bill into the fray four years ago when he and Trish had first moved up from Whitley Bay. Even though he was 'bloody English' – the rivalry jabs becoming part of their banter; all part of that old routine . . .

He itched for that banter. Just plain, straightforward human contact. The urge had been coursing through Bill for some time now – a quick, simple conversation between him and another, where they would engage and reply with sense to whatever he said. The urge so strong, for something others took for granted.

Bill glanced at the doorway of Aldi. They probably had enough stuff in the house to keep them going until Monday ... If he parked in Murdo's car park, at the side of the building, far enough in the corner that folk wouldn't notice Trish sitting there, but close enough for him to keep an eye on her ...

He shook his head. *What was he thinking? He couldn't do that.*

If Simon and Kelly knew he was even thinking of leaving Trish alone – in a car outside a pub, for God's sake ... If they thought he might drive her home after drinking ...

But being in the house day after day, stuck – it was akin to being slowly suffocated. Dying alongside a woman he would once have happily barricaded himself in with, now a woman he no longer knew.

Trish was now a shell of someone he had shared a whole life with. All those memories were still clear in his mind, but, over time, hers had slowly, ever so slowly – and then, eventually, completely – been washed out of her with the tide. Buried so deep in the sand that no amount of digging could bring them back to her. And he'd tried. God, how he'd tried. It was as if Trish was already dead. Dead, yet here she was still, sitting and breathing next to him.

No. He wasn't going to do it. And he didn't need to. He could find company, human contact, at home, without putting Trish at risk. Without leaving her in a pub car park on her own.

He knew what he was doing was wrong. He felt awful about it. But what more could he really do?

Bill shook his head, trying to get rid of the thoughts circling, gathering so much speed they were in danger of making him dizzy.

He spoke without looking round at Trish. 'Let's go get the shopping, then, love.'

Trish continued to stare straight ahead.

Chapter 26

BILL SAT AT HIS desk, the glow from the laptop screen in front of him the only light in the room.

He'd told himself he shouldn't do it again, that he should delete the thing altogether. Yet here he was, that little black arrow pointing at the logo on the screen, his forefinger poised.

Just this one, last time. He needed the distraction. Trish's tears had been flowing when he'd put her to bed earlier. It had taken an age to calm her. He hadn't meant to shout at her at the table. He'd made her favourite tea: two fried eggs on buttered toast with fried mushrooms on the side. The care was still there, the duty, but he wasn't sure it was something he could call love any more.

They'd sat opposite one another at the dining table; no chat, just some music playing from the radio on the sideboard. He'd been too tired to try to talk to her. The toilet trips the night before, for her and then in turn for him, had left him unable to get back to sleep, just staring at the ceiling. Then there was his inability to switch off from what was going on inside his head. Unable to ignore what he was doing behind her back.

Trish had eaten the meal in that robotic way that she did things now, her face a mask devoid of any emotion, her movements stiff. Doing nothing about the egg yolk dribbling down her chin, even when it fell to her chest, landing on the paper napkin that he'd tucked into her jumper.

He'd cleared the plates, not putting up an argument when she'd silently refused to let go of her fork and knife when he tried to prise them from her fingers. Her physical strength never failed to surprise him.

By the time he'd washed up what he could and come back to her, she'd licked the cutlery clean and was sitting with her forearms on the table mat, the fork and knife still clutched in her hands and facing upwards, as if ready to go again. Nothing he said could convince her that they'd already eaten. Not even the fullness she would've once felt in her stomach, telling her otherwise, as she'd argued. She'd point-blank refused to get up from the table. Even when he'd tried to cajole her with the promise of a chocolate treat before bed.

She'd started to shout then – swearing, using words that, before the illness, he'd never heard her utter in their lifetime together. He'd taken the barrage, clinging desperately to the patience he tried to exercise every day.

Then the knife had hit his eye.

It had landed near his eyebrow on the handle end, but nonetheless, it had snapped the last strand of patience still hanging.

He'd lunged for her, taking hold of her upper arm more roughly than he'd meant to, towering above her where she sat, his face up against hers, his spit flying on to her pale skin. And then he'd realized what he was doing and let go. Instantly. Retreating in shame and mumbling his apologies repeatedly as she cowered, eyes wide with fear and brimming, matching his.

If their son had seen that . . . Simon was a good son, and he had always looked up to Bill, but if he knew what his father was capable of – of how he had treated his mother . . . Bill couldn't bear to think of what his son's reaction would be. What he'd have thought about him considering leaving her alone in the car. The way he was treating her every time he visited this website.

What kind of man was he?

Bill didn't want to answer that.

Especially when he was going to click that link again, regardless.

Chapter 27

He looks conflicted, I'll give him that. I'm watching Bill from my control room, through the top of the laptop screen in front of him. So close that I can almost count the pores on his ruddy skin.

I'm looking out at him, but I'm still able to see what's happening on his laptop screen. Still able to know what he's doing, as and when he does it. Camera planted, remote access granted. It's easy when you know how.

Her name is Norma. She likes knitting, cats and long walks along the beach. At least, her profile says she does.

Bill likes Norma, the heart he placed against her bio one week ago confirming so. The same night after I'd been in his home, Bill accessing the Senior Singles dating site at five past ten, most likely when his wife, Trish, had been asleep for at least an hour.

Norma sent an electronic heart back to Bill that very same night.

I know because it was me who sent it.

Bill sat on that heart for some time. Two further days

before he attempted to make conversation; perhaps it was after a particularly fraught day with Trish. Not that he told Norma that. He didn't mention Patricia. He gave no hint that he had a wife.

It took Norma exactly eight minutes to reply.

Eight minutes where Bill probably wrung his hands, berating himself for acting, wondering if she'd reply, asking himself what he'd do if she did.

Norma made it easy. Chit-chat. Mundane. Safe. Boring text after boring text – telly, food, pastimes. Nothing serious, absolutely nothing deep.

Two hours they chatted, with a polite sign-off from Norma thanking Bill for his time and telling him how much she had enjoyed talking with him.

The following night, Bill ignored Norma's attempt at contact. But not the night after that. And not any – not one – of the days or nights since. Chatting back and forth, almost non-stop. Scrolls and scrolls of typed messages, at all times of day. Messages I've had to keep up with at home; sitting next to Robbie at work; everywhere.

Endless drivel. Except for the last message: the five-word one from Norma to Bill. The one I'm now willing him to respond to.

Hoping he'll say yes.

Chapter 28

BILL CUPPED HIS HAND around one of the tired flowers on the rhododendron bush before letting it go and making his way towards the raised vegetable beds. He stopped and bent over the wet soil that was now sprouting more weeds than anything remotely edible. His fingers brushed the dirt, pushing and pulling at nothing. Pottering in that sliver of a window between dusk and darkness, thinking about the message he'd left unanswered.

He straightened, bones cracking as he wiped his calloused hand against his jeans, ambling on past the empty greenhouse to the bottom of the garden, coming to a standstill beneath the branches of the towering oak tree. Enough leaves still clinging to its branches for him to be out of view from the upper windows of houses that overlooked their property.

Alan and Betty next door had been there for years, long before he and Trish had moved in. They'd been nothing but welcoming, but they kept themselves to themselves most of the time. He loved the privacy of the garden, proud of what he'd turned the space into over the last few years.

He looked back at the house, towards Trish and his home, knowing she couldn't see him. Wondering when the last time was that she really had *seen* him.

He scratched at his neck; his khaki-green cable-knit cardigan was zipped to his chin and itching the skin there. The zip sounded loud in the silence as he pulled it down a little, feeling hot even out here in the night air. Uncomfortable. Guilt, perhaps.

Another fraught day. The morning, at least, had passed without incident; Trish had seemed OK. In the afternoon, he'd brought her a cuppa by the telly, a plate of chocolate digestives too. At the same time as always, whilst she watched *Doctors*. He had no idea how much she took in of the soap these days, but she'd always loved it, and the routine seemed to bring her comfort. He'd told her he was popping upstairs with the washing and that he'd be back in a jiffy.

Putting the folded and ironed clothes away in their drawers as quickly as he could, he was back in the living room within fifteen minutes. He could see that Trish had taken a bite of a digestive, and now she was staring straight ahead at the telly. She didn't turn to acknowledge him.

It had been a shock when the front door burst open. It did so with such force that it banged off the wall that separated the living room from the hallway, leaving a dent in the thick, flowery wallpaper.

'Dad? Dad!'

Bill collided with his son in the hallway. It was the fastest Bill had moved in a long time, adrenaline surging at the prospect of challenging intruders in their home, before he heard his son's voice. The tight features on a face, though familiar, drained of any colour – Simon's face – was not what he'd been expecting.

'What is it, son? What's wrong?' Bill put his hands on Simon's forearms, bracing himself for the worst.

'Where's Mum?'

Bill frowned with confusion as he turned his head to the living-room door. 'In there. Watching *Doctors*. What is this?'

'She rang me, terrified, saying there was a stranger walking round the house!'

It was only then that Simon's wife, Kelly, appeared in the doorway and Bill felt Simon's frame physically soften under his hands, realization dawning on them both at the same time: that the stranger had been her own husband.

Five minutes later, Bill sat at the kitchen table with Simon whilst Kelly stayed with Patricia, who had gone back to her cuppa and the telly. Thank God Brandon had been in school.

Simon had driven at high speed from their house after answering the phone to his mother, Kelly jumping in the car, by his side, asking what was wrong.

Patricia had been in tears on the call, panicked, telling their son that there was an intruder in the house, someone she didn't know. Simon had asked her where his father was, demanding to speak to him, but Trish had been unable to give him any kind of straight answer.

He had dropped the phone and run – to find his father there at the house as usual, realizing his mother had believed her husband to be a stranger. Simon and Kelly were shocked at how much worse her illness was than they'd been led to believe.

Bill had assured them that everything was OK, and they'd left.

But afterwards, he'd slumped into his chair and cried.

It was supposed to be their fresh start. His and Trish's chance to have the retirement they'd always dreamt of, cultivating together the gorgeous garden he was standing in. Moving up to Aberdeen from Whitley Bay, for no other reason than to be near their son, his wife and their grandson, Brandon. It had seemed a no-brainer to switch from one coastal home to another, but with another ocean of love and memories to be made.

At first, he hadn't wanted to believe what was happening. The forgotten words, the odd wrong date, the snatches of confusion. He thought it had been the stress of the move. The eventual diagnosis had been devastating, crushing – but doable. He'd reassured Trish that, as always, together they could do anything.

Except that now they weren't even together. How could they be, when Trish was having more days than not of questioning who he even was? Her mind and memory ravaged, and unable to remember him. Nothing about the illness made any sense but there was no mistaking its cruelty.

He'd let the tears fall, eventually gathering himself enough to put Trish to bed.

She'd gone down peacefully, thank God. Then, back in the living room, relieved to finally have some time to himself, he'd heard the ping of the laptop.

When he'd signed up for Senior Singles, he'd had no real idea what he was doing; he just let himself be carried along by the pop-up messages telling him to like other profiles, to let people know he was there and ready to chat. And chat was all he wanted. All he'd ever intended. Until he'd started talking to Norma.

Bill shook his head and looked up at the branches of the old oak tree above him – his mind thinking about the message. About the question.

Norma's request to meet was probably as innocent as his initial click on that link. A cup of coffee, a chat in person, nothing more.

Friendship.

Except Bill hadn't told Norma about Trish. But why hadn't he?

Bill shifted his gaze from the branches above, towards the bedroom window, to the glow of the lamp behind the curtains, where Trish slept, reaching out to him like a beacon. A room once filled with laughter and so much love.

He wanted nothing more than to climb the stairs to that bedroom and for her to recognize him. For them to lie together and talk, to laugh long into the dark.

But he knew that wasn't to be.

It left the smallest part of him yearning for something – anything. For someone to see him. For something more than this life he'd ended up with – living with a stranger in his own home.

But if he did it ... If he answered Norma's message ... If he *did* say yes to Norma's question ... What then?

Because then he'd have to ask himself: was it Trish who was the stranger in the bed? Or him?

Chapter 29

Norma asked to meet Bill in the car park at Duthie Park. Not the busy, overpacked one on Riverside Drive, but the one around the back. The small one. The quieter one. Down from the old Deeside railway line, nestled behind the park's cafe, where she promised him the fruit scones were to die for.

Bill had seemed nervous about meeting in such a public place, but Norma had to insist. For safety, she'd said. Softening her insistence with an offer to meet him at her car. Telling him they could maybe go for a walk around the park first.

Bill had agreed to that and asked for details of Norma's car – the make, the colour.

It's the same car I drove over here. The one I'm hiding behind now, awaiting Bill's arrival.

My hand tightens around the wet material in my hand as I raise my head up above the boot, peering through the rear window, out of the front windscreen. Ducking down just as fast when I see Bill locking his own car door, as he turns to stare over at mine. Perhaps wondering why he can't see Norma sitting in the driver's seat, nor standing by her car.

I'm banking on him walking over, on him coming close enough for me to pounce, too late for him to cry out or move away when I clamp my hand over his mouth.

Poor, trusting Bill. Unaware, as he walks towards me, that he need not have worried about the meeting place being so public. About who might see him or who he might see. Not when he'll only ever be seeing the car, right before he sees nothing at all as I bundle him into it. Never seeing Norma. Not knowing that Norma's safety was never at stake.

But definitely knowing, before long, that it was never the park cafe's fruit scones that he was going to be dying for.

Chapter 30

My fingers fly over the keyboard and then the joystick, instantly bringing the camera feed from outside Primark on Union Street down on to the monitor in front of me. It's a notorious hotspot.

Robbie wipes at the strawberry jam on his chin. 'You seem a bit more yourself, mate.'

'Yeah. Better sleep, I guess.' And as I give another quick flick of the joystick, varying the angle and the zoom, I guess I may be coming across like that.

I look at the screen and I'm there in that hotspot. Right next to one of my regulars: George, an old guy with a set of false teeth in his head better fitted to a horse. He favours standing in the wide, deep doorway of the clothes store, where he's sheltered from the wind and able to stay dry. He also favours cigarette butts that have been flicked to the pavement, their smokers too busy to aim for the ashtray on top off the bin right outside the shop. I watch him crouch to the ground and pick up a butt, still glowing orange at the tip after narrowly missing a puddle, and not yet trodden on. A rare find – as his overcrowded grin goes to show.

The wiry-haired security guard is standing just inside the glass doors, his hands behind his back. He stares out at George but does nothing to move him on. Months since he even tried. That guy has a heart.

On my days off-shift, I sometimes think of my regulars, missing them like old friends, knowing they'll be there when I get back to work, giving me meaning and purpose.

'Casey? Casey!'

I drag myself back into the room. 'Sorry. I was miles away.'

Robbie shakes his head. 'Jesus, and here was me just finished saying you seemed back on it. Fat lot of use you are if you're not watching.'

He doesn't realize how much he's summed up my life in that one sentence.

He tuts. 'I *said*, she's got a brass neck for sure.'

I lean back and look over at Robbie's screen. He's targeted a female youth running from the Bon Accord shopping centre, a shitload of clothes clutched to her chest, all of them still on hangers and swiped from one of the shops inside – New Look, most likely. A smash-and-grab. Robbie's tracking her, mumbling into the radio, keeping the police up to date with where she's headed. I lean back further, Robbie's curved monitor otherwise out of view from my desk.

The security guard who gave chase has given up. He's stopped short of the pedestrian crossing on Schoolhill, panting and bent over, with his sausage-fingered hands clasped over his knees through trousers that have given up on keeping his backside hidden. The girl sprints, a checked shirt and its hanger falling to the ground behind her as she runs to the rainbow-coloured steps, then up and over the roof of St Nicholas Shopping Centre.

The radio crackles before a breathless voice confirms what they were hoping. A security guard in Marks has grabbed her out front, lying in wait as she ran down the stairs over the other side.

I look back at my own screen. Back at George. Good old George, who has found another used tab. Wet this time, but he pockets it anyway. A hidden treasure for later. His secret stash.

I pick up my phone and turn it over, Robbie still by my side basking in the aftermath and not looking my way. What I see, via the camera feed to that little mobile phone screen, makes my heart soar. A place . . . things . . . that I've been planning for all along. A place I'll be going. Things I'll be doing before long. Somewhere I'll finally feel close to you again. Doing things that will finally put you to rest. Not caring what comes after because nothing past it matters any more.

I glance back at the screens. At good old George. Feeling like I've taken a leaf out of both his and Bill's books, my own secrets stashed for later.

Chapter 31

LEWIS STIRRED, PAIN FLARING in his shoulder blade as he moved, the jutting bone scraping against a solid coldness beneath him.

Am I naked? he wondered.

He opened his eyes. To black. Panic rising... So dark he saw nothing, no matter how wide he stretched his eyelids. He squinted against the pain in his head which pulsed at the centre of his forehead, feeling like he'd eaten a litre of ice cream at speed. Skin cracked at the outer edges of his eyes where a crust had formed. His eyeballs aching as they moved, but they could find no chink of light to focus on.

It was so fucking freezing that his teeth chattered. Loud enough that he could hear them.

What the hell happened?

His stomach lurched, reminding him how he'd felt in the pub, forcing him to remember what had happened. The only thing that must've happened. *Mitchell.* Hating the feeling of sadness, quickly replaced by embarrassment and then anger. *That fucker had put something in his drink.*

Mitchell. If that was even his name.

Lewis was flat on his back. He flexed his fingers either side of him, half expecting his hands to be tied to something, feeling a tightness at his wrists. But his hands were free. He patted at his stomach.

What . . . ?

The material was smooth to touch, plastic maybe. His hand slid against whatever it was that he wore. He lifted his arms away from his stomach, using one arm to slide down the other. Long sleeves. The tension at his wrists caused by elasticated cuffs.

Jesus.

He rubbed his legs against one another. Feeling the skin, the bristle of the thick fair hair on his legs.

But he'd been wearing jeans . . .

His heart thudded as the smell of the plastic garment – coverall, apron, or whatever the fuck it was – wafted up at him.

This guy said he wanted a drinking buddy. To chat up birds together. What was this?

Maybe he *was* into him after all.

Lewis groaned. There was a gnawing feeling in the pit of his stomach. This was no bad dream. Instead his nightmares had been dragged into the real world.

His heart thumped to the beat of the pain in his head as he moved it from side to side against the hard floor, the back of his head lumpy, each ear flattening in turn against what he assumed was stone. Some kind of concrete floor.

The darkness was so close it pressed hard against his nose. Wrapped itself around his throat. Suffocating him. He straightened his arms out either side of him. Nothing.

Slowly he lifted them. An inch at a time, eventually bringing his palms together above him, relieved at least that he wasn't in some box. That he hadn't been buried alive.

He pulled his body up, stopping with his elbows at right angles, the plastic sleeves squeaking and crinkling as he put pressure on his forearms against the ground to keep him there, needing a moment before pulling himself up any further. His head was swimming in the black. He felt lost at sea, no flare to let off, no rescue party searching for him. Imagining he might look like the guy in that scene – that actor with eyes as big as saucers, piercing, making him look as mad as they needed him to when he supposedly woke up to a world where he seemed to be the only one left in it . . . The name of the movie was on the tip of his dry tongue . . . *28 Days Later*. That was it. That opening scene, of him stumbling on to the streets in a hospital gown.

Lewis patted at the plastic again. He himself was wearing a gown now. Except his appeared to be fucking wipeable. He didn't want to dwell on that.

Lewis shifted focus to his body. To how he was feeling. Not thinking he was injured, just bloody stiff from lying on concrete for God-knows-how-long, from whatever he'd been given to get him here in the first place. Wherever 'here' was.

That guy undressed him. Took his clothes. Put him in some freaky suit.

Lewis took a deep breath and pulled himself up to sitting, his mind taking its time to catch up with his body. He lifted his heels from the floor, keeping his legs straight. Bare legs. No pain. He dared to bend his knees and stumbled up to standing, feeling a thickness between his thighs. A softness. No pain. Not ready to investigate there yet. Needing to find other stuff out first. Like, was it safe to move, to take a step forward?

Lewis rubbed a fist against his nose. Numb with cold, aware for the first time of the smell. The odour in the air above the plastic. Musty, reminding him a little of the warehouse where he used to work, when the roller door had creaked up and open after the place had been shut down for a fortnight over Christmas.

Cold. Dank. Oily.

He stepped tentatively forward, arms out in front of him, palms outright, flat, and ready to press against whatever was there. Maybe *whoever* was there. He tried not to think of all the horror films he'd watched as the coverall squeaked and slid against his skin, pulling taut at his armpits.

Lewis felt sick as he blew out through trembling lips, the sound echoing around the space. He psyched himself up, flexing his outstretched fingers, and took eight steps before his body jerked in shock at his skin making contact.

A wall. *It was just a wall.*

Rough. Skimming his hands and arms outwards

and away from one another against it. Bricks. Lines of grooves rising and falling between them.

He took a step left, keeping his hands on the wall as he moved. Another step. And another. Five steps before his shoulder hit a wall. The same brick surface. He stepped right and made his way back, taking steps sideways as before, his right shoulder hitting another wall after twelve sidesteps.

His breath was ragged in the black. He turned, backside pressed against the wall, and stepped forward, his left shoulder trailing along the adjacent wall as he moved, hands out in front again, going back the way he came when he first started moving.

He took seven steps and stopped dead as searing light flooded the space, blinding him. He clapped his eyes shut, the sound of buzzing overhead like the crackling of an electric fly-killer.

He struggled to breathe. Body tense, waiting for whatever was to come. Nothing arriving. Slowly, he prised his eyelids open, the constant deafening yell in his head screaming against the sudden light.

There was a metal door in front of him. An upright grey rectangle in a granite brick wall. No handle – nothing but a flat panel reflecting light back at him. The granite walls, the floor, the ceiling, all black and white mixing to grey.

He looked down at the bright blue of the coverall he wore, at odds with his drab surroundings.

To the left of the door panel was what looked like some sort of metal office stationery cupboard; pipes covered in flaking white paint ran up from it and off into the brick.

He turned slowly.

His heart lurched as his mouth cried out. An animalistic sound ricocheted off the stone walls and back at him.

Lost on the two bodies lying on the floor.

Chapter 32

JESUS. WERE THEY *DEAD*? Lewis covered his mouth, unsure what he was trying to keep out, thinking of all the telly programmes he'd seen of folk stumbling across the deceased. Imagining he could smell the stench of death now, wondering if some kind of chemical gas was lurking in the air, about to swirl its way into his nose, force itself downwards and wrap itself around his throat before taking him too.

He edged towards the closer of the two bodies. A woman. Lying flat on her back, eyes closed, mouth open, arms and legs splayed. Slim. He stared at her chest, willing it to rise, to show some sign of breathing, that she was alive. Nothing. Realizing that her chest was beneath a coverall identical to his.

Who the hell was she? How the hell had she ended up here? How had he ended up here? And who the fuck was Mitchell?

The woman's face and legs were as pale and as still as Lewis imagined those of a dead person would be. She looked in her thirties, forties maybe. Kind of pretty for an old bird. He lifted a scuffed trainer and jabbed his toes into her side, feeling the skid of plastic but also the flesh and ribs beneath, pulling his foot back just as quickly, repulsed by the contact, sickened by the fear of getting no movement in return from her.

Lewis pictured her upper body shooting up straight, like some nightmare where the dead rose again – her bloodshot eyes springing open, her head spinning as blood dripped from her mouth.

Stop it.

But his cry, his foot . . . *Surely* she had to be dead?

He looked past her to the other body lying still beside hers. A guy. Older. Elderly. Looking as dead as she did, although he'd probably looked like he'd had one foot in the grave when he was alive. He was rocking the same attire as them.

He shuffled back from the bodies, not wanting to take his eyes off them but not wanting to be any closer to them than he had to be. Should he feel for a pulse? Put an ear against a mouth to listen for breathing? What else was he meant to do?

Anything but that . . .

He dragged his gaze away from them and scanned the space around him. Four black, flimsy-looking folding chairs rested flat and upright against the wall. Bizarre. Nothing else in the room but the chairs, him, and the small issue of the two bodies by his feet.

His eyes kept scanning . . .

Nothing . . . Stopping—Not nothing. A blinking red light up where the walls curved inwards to an arched roof, no break in the brickwork between the walls and the ceiling. Lewis squinted. *A camera?*

Flashbacks. The lights and cameras up close in his face on his doorstep. His ma shouting and crying.

He peered closer. It *was* a bloody camera. What the hell was this? Who was the guy that had brought him here? Was it anything to do with what had happened? Had this all been a test? He swallowed, tasting acid in his throat before glancing at the bodies. But what about them?

Shit. Was he being set up to take the fall for murder?

Lewis stared back at the flashing red orb, seemingly beating in time to his thudding heart – and saw the speaker on the wall next to it. Feeling the fear that if they'd already exposed him *above* ground back then, with all eyes on him, if they'd already almost ruined his life, how far would they be willing to go *below* ground, with no one watching?

A cold sweat crawled up his neck and spread over his scalp as he stared at the blinking light and bellowed, 'What is this? What the fuck is it that you want?' Lewis's arms were spread wide, his voice echoing back at him from the stone walls. He waited, hearing nothing . . . dropping his arms to his sides, the red light forgotten, as he heard a guttural grunt.

He spun towards the two dead bodies, one of them no longer lying on the floor but slowly rising, blue tied bows spaced out over bare flesh along the length of the spine, holding the coverall shut. The body sitting up now, dragging Lewis's nightmare of only moments ago into reality, making his scream echo in his ears.

Chapter 33

'Please . . . Stop.'

Lewis's mouth clamped shut at the old man's words, watching as the man – who he had thought dead only seconds ago – sat upright, covered his ears, and scowled. Alive. Talking. Polite, even. A far cry from the horror he'd imagined.

'What the fuck?' Lewis backed away as the man opened his eyes and squinted against the light.

The old guy stared at Lewis from beneath grey bushy eyebrows, confusion flitting across his lined features, his large hands still over his ears, as if cradling his white-haired head against pain. His gaze darted from Lewis to the walls around them, to the woman's body by his side, his gasp loud, even against the squeak of plastic, as he lowered his hands and used them to reverse-shuffle on his backside across the stone floor, away from the woman, only stopping when his back hit the wall.

His eyes were wide. 'What the hell's going on?'

'Mate, I've been asking the same question.'

The man stared at the body. 'Is she . . . is she dead?'

Lewis shrugged. 'Thought so but, then again, I thought you were a goner too, so that means nothing.'

The man looked up at him. 'You haven't checked?'

Lewis tutted. 'Sorry for not getting around to the whole doctor bit but, like yourself, I've been trying to figure out what the fuck is going on. What the hell I'm doing here.'

The man rubbed at his forehead. 'Where is here? Why are we all wearing these . . . these . . .' He stared down at himself. 'What even *are* they?'

Lewis looked around. 'No windows. I'd say wherever here is, we're below ground. The suits? Not a clue but not my style choice.'

The man's eyes widened. 'How long have I been here?'

'No idea.' Lewis thought about how he himself had come round on the floor, the same as this guy just had. 'But I reckon about half an hour ago I looked as dead as you did.' He tipped his head towards the woman. 'And her over there.'

The man stared at him before looking at the woman. 'How do I know I can trust you, that it wasn't you who did this?'

Lewis shrugged. 'I couldn't give a fuck whether you trust me or not. But I'll tell you something for free, I have no interest in you or her. I've never seen either of you before.'

Lewis looked towards the red pulsing light. 'Whatever psycho did this, he did it to all of us. I reckon that same person is behind that light over there, in the corner.'

The man turned, grimacing at the discomfort from the movement. 'What is that?'

'A camera.' Lewis's mind was already turning over the last things he remembered, and who 'Mitchell' might really be. How he could be linked to an old codger and a woman in early middle age.

Lewis was pulled from his thoughts as the man spoke.

'We're not going to achieve anything, me just sitting here and you standing there.'

Lewis swallowed, walking over to the door. 'Ain't no window to shout out of and I'm betting this door isn't just going to fall open.' He stared at the metal panel, no handle, before patting at its edges, his hands skimming down them, pushing at its centre as if it might just open like some secret entrance. Nothing.

Lewis turned back to the man, keeping his eyes away from the woman on the floor. His mouth wanting to say the obvious. That surely the old guy had some memory of how he got here too. That he must somehow know Mitchell as well. That he brought him here. Brought all three of them here.

Unless ... Unless there were more folk involved in all this than just Mitchell. Cloying sweat spread over Lewis's skin. Should he ask this pensioner his backstory? Should he tell him how he thinks he got here himself? Lewis looked at the guy, the woman. She was still lying unmoving on the hard ground.

No, not yet.

And not the whole truth, even when he did give something away. People reacted badly to the truth of who he was. Besides, like the guy had already said, how would he know that he could even trust Lewis – that he wasn't somehow involved in all this?

Lewis watched the old man motion towards the woman with a point of his pale finger, forgetting all about the thoughts that had just tumbled around in his head as the man's voice broke through them.

'We can start by checking she's alive. Try to wake her. Then we can figure out what we're all doing here.'

Chapter 34

Jen groaned, and batted away the hand shaking at her shoulder. Shaking her shoulder hard, her limp attempt to get rid of that hand no competition for the grip she was being shaken by.

Her teeth clamped together, body rigid, heat travelling up her body, rage building and getting ready to burst free. 'Knock it off, Tom.' Mumbled, her own voice unrecognizable to her ears. Ears that were ringing.

She turned her head away from the shoulder that was starting to hurt with the force it was taking to try to wake her. There was a crinkling sound every time her shoulder was shoved. A squeak, even. Her head pounded, getting worse with every jerk to her body. 'Stop it!'

Not her voice.

Her heart lurched at the same time that her stomach sank. Did something happen? Was Tom angry at her? Where was Daisy?

Her eyes snapped open – to grey; granite brick walls all around her – the floor and roof above doing nothing to break up the gloom. She bolted upright, now sitting, her legs out straight in front of her. Bare. Some kind of blue skirt at her thigh . . . No – covering her whole upper body too.

The hand stopped pushing and pulling at her shoulder, but her legs still shook against the ground. The hard, concrete ground.

Not her bed.

'Tom?'

Her voice again. Not her voice.

'I'm not Tom, lady. I'm just the guy who got the short straw to try and wake you.'

Jen turned her head to the right, towards the voice. A voice she didn't recognize – deep and rough. Seeing the young guy straightening from his crouched position, now standing above her, looking as friendly as he sounded. Wearing the same blue as her.

'Who are you?' Her racing heart making her feel even more sick. Sweating but, wherever she was, freezing. She lifted her arms, looked at her hands. Long plastic sleeves gathered at her wrists by elastic. 'What the hell am I wearing?'

'Seems to be a common question around here. Call me your new roommate. Him too.' Lewis nodded towards his fellow captive. 'Can't give you anything about the suits.' He looked over his shoulder, his legs partially blocking whoever was behind him from Jen's view.

She leaned forward, her head feeling as if it would carry on tipping over as she peered at the old guy sitting about a metre away. Another blue suit.

Jen swallowed the bile burning at her throat. 'What's going on? What are you talking about?'

She tried to bend her legs, groaning at the stiffness in them, the numbness in her backside. Her hand instinctively going to push down the plastic material between her thighs, to protect her modesty. Her mind questioning what exactly was covering her modesty, as it didn't feel like her pants.

The rough man spoke again. 'We haven't got a clue what's going on, but it seems we got a fucking room for three in whatever shithole this is. And going by our outfits, the host is into the whole doctors-and-nurses vibe.'

Beneath the bravado, he sounded as confused and scared as she felt. Jen needed answers. Now. 'Where are we? Was it you who brought me here?' Slurring. The thing that was wrong with her voice.

'Fuck knows where we are, and no, I didn't bring you here. Didn't bring myself here either.'

Jen wiped at her mouth, lips dry and cracked. 'What? How did we get here, then?' Her hand trembled with more than the cold. She instinctively reached for her back, making sure that whatever she was wearing was still fastened. Water. She needed water. Her throat felt like sandpaper and her tongue stuck to the roof of her mouth every time she spoke.

The guy gave a dry laugh. 'Well, it wasn't a date, although I guess this is becoming a bit of a love-in. Cosy little threesome.'

'Enough.' The old man's voice was firm but soft.

Jen stared at him. He had a kind face. Not threatening, not like the young guy, or as brash.

Then she remembered. *The phone*.

The old man was rubbing at his forehead, eyes bleary, apparently not as awake as the younger man. Maybe, like her, he'd not long come round. She thought again about the phone, the voice. Not either of the voices in here with her.

She watched the white-haired man lick at his lips, trying again when he found no moisture there, then speaking anyway.

'We need to find out what's going on. Why we're here.' He groaned as he pulled his legs towards him.

Jen was still trying to work out what she should be asking. The obvious, probably. 'Do I . . . do I know either of you?'

The young guy towered above her, making her feel uneasy as he kicked at the stone floor with a scuffed trainer. He spat an answer at her. 'I already told you. I don't know either of you. You're a bit posh for the company I keep.'

If only he knew.

She looked up at him. 'Do you have a name?'

He tutted. 'I might not be posh, but, like most folk, I do have a name. Lewis. Yours?'

She didn't want to tell him, but figured she had nothing to lose. 'Jen.' She glanced over to the elderly man, now hugging his legs to his chest. Flexible for his age. 'And you?'

'Bill.'

Jen didn't miss Lewis's glance, the way he looked around on hearing that information, as if they hadn't got that far with each other yet. She wondered again if the old guy was just waking up, if maybe they hadn't had the time.

'How long have I been here?'

Lewis smirked. 'Gee, Jen, you like a question.'

'How long?' She was aware that, even through the slurring, her voice sounded as blunt as her senses.

Lewis clucked his tongue. 'Not exactly a wall clock to go by.'

Jen closed her eyes against the pain in her head, but also at the thought of Tom and Daisy. *Did Tom know she'd gone? Daisy – where was Daisy? She had to think.* She opened her eyes, squinted – the head pain worse, the harder she tried to think. Remembering the rush to get here. Then the nothing.

Her gaze darted around the stone walls, settling on a flashing red light. 'What's that?'

Lewis, above her, answered. 'Camera.'

Her breath caught, hearing the word, thinking of the camera that had been in her car. The video sent to her phone. More than one – the videos. The photo. She looked to the floor either side of her, her eyes ignoring Lewis and Bill as she looked back at that scarlet light, seeing the speaker on the wall beside it.

She looked at the doorway beneath it. 'Has anyone tried the door?'

Something stirred in her mind, tickling at her subconscious, just out of reach.

Bill unclasped his hands, manoeuvring himself to a seated position, the movement laboured and not without its moans. 'I woke only moments before you.' He looked up at Lewis. 'But he tried the door just after I woke up.'

Lewis stared back at Bill. 'I wasn't long before you, except I woke up in the dark. Took me a while to try and suss out where the hell I was. Felt like some kind of fucking cave. Then the lights went on, only seconds before I saw you guys on the floor.' Lewis glanced between them. 'I thought you were both dead. Bloody looked like you were, all trussed up for the morgue in these get-ups. Then our Bill here sat up like Dracula awakening for the night shift.'

Jen stared at the door. The 'something' that might explain everything was still scratching at her mind, the flashing light constantly blinking, like a fingernail picking at her brain. She looked down at her shaking hands, knowing what the tremor was as she worked her tongue against the roof of her mouth, her stomach rumbling loud enough for Lewis and Bill to look towards it.

'Someone's starving,' said Lewis, pausing to rub at his own stomach as if realizing he was too.

That fingernail inside Jen's head was scratching harder, but not yet breaking the surface.

She rubbed at her legs, trying to stop the shake in her hands. Telling herself it was the after-effects of whatever they'd been given to knock them out – the same drugs causing the tremor that was coursing throughout her whole body – but knowing that was bullshit. Knowing that it was the *want*. The *need*. She didn't just need water, for her dry mouth; she needed something else, even more than she needed food.

Jen tried to refocus, looking between the faces of the two men, nothing but strangers to her, but still people who surely somehow had to be connected to whatever this was. To *her*.

She needed to think, to concentrate on anything but the thirst she was fighting. She tried to swallow the rising fear of not satisfying that craving – she'd always been able to remedy it. But this time she couldn't, and now there was so much more to be afraid of.

Jen swallowed hard. 'I have a kid. A husband. I want to know what the fuck I'm doing here.' Hating herself as she said it, knowing what she'd left unsaid.

Lewis paced. 'Well . . . Jen . . . I have neither – no bird, no rug rat. Just a crabby old bitch of a mother who's probably smoking all my fags right now, thinking I'm up to no good.' His footsteps were loud in the space, his voice just as loud – booming as he moved closer, then ebbing away again. 'I'm bloody itching for a smoke.'

Jen doubted that itch would be as strong as hers. Relentless, like the fingernail scratching in her head. She listened to him spout on.

'Doesn't matter what we've got at home, but the old man's right: we need to figure out what the fuck's going on.' He stopped pacing and turned to face them both.

'Maybe we should start with how we all ended up in this shithole. Maybe that'll—'

Lewis visibly shrank as a voice boomed into the space – an electronically enhanced voice that seemed to be blasting from the speaker up by the camera but which was bouncing around and back off the stone walls at them, as if connected to surround sound. A voice demanding to be heard as all three of them scrambled to crouch together on the floor.

'Let me help you. You are all here for different reasons. It's up to you to uncover why. To do that, you must work together. Find the answers. When, or *if*, you do, you all move one step closer to being freed.'

Chapter 35

THE SPEAKER CRACKLED AND hummed before falling silent, all three of them sitting equally quietly, still huddled together in the centre of the room.

Jen brought her legs towards her, crossing them in front of her like Daisy did on the floor in front of the telly. The ground was too hard for kneeling, and she didn't trust her shaking limbs enough to stand, not after what they'd just heard.

Lewis shuffled over to the wall, clearly wanting to forget how quickly he'd moved towards Jen and Bill. He sat with his back against the stone, forearm resting over bent knees.

Bill didn't move from his spot, instead rolling on to one buttock and bringing his legs to the side of him. Looking far from comfortable. Looking like all of them felt.

Lewis rubbed at his forefinger with a grubby thumb, over and over, in the quiet, the silence stretching, before finally talking again. 'What the fuck is this? He's not all that, you know. Can't even speak to us with his own voice. Acting the big man. Doesn't even have the balls to come in here and say it himself. See how friendly I'd be if I met him now!'

Jen looked over at him. 'You've seen him?'

Lewis stared at her. 'Yeah. Haven't you?'

She shook her head and turned to Bill. 'Have you?'

'No.'

Lewis frowned. 'I assumed we all would've met him.' He kept rubbing at that thumb. 'Seems I was a special case, then.' He closed his eyes, looking as if he was battling something, like he should've known better.

Jen sat up a little straighter. 'Lewis, with you, did it start with a phone? Did he send you a phone?'

Lewis's brow furrowed. 'No phone. Met him in the street.'

Jen's nose twitched and curled as a smell hit her nostrils without warning. Not something she was smelling now, but a memory. The street. An arm around her throat from behind, her Adam's apple crushed against the crook of someone's elbow, struggling to breathe as their other arm came around, that hand holding something that smelled bad. Chemical. Then nothing.

She closed her eyes, willing the smell and the memory to go back to where they'd come from, desperate for a hit of something else as she spoke, her voice trembling as much as her body. 'I was in a street. Attacked from behind. Didn't even see him. Must've come out of a doorway or something. A wet rag over my mouth. A smell, such a horrible smell . . .'

Bill squirmed beside her – his discomfort on the floor, though by the look on his face it was more than that. 'I remember that smell now. Same way.' Bill's eyes were wide, remembering.

Jen shivered, a cold sweat coming over her. *Do Lewis and Bill know why they're here?* Jen thought, knowing full well why she herself was. No doubt about it, after those videos. But why would that matter to whoever had put her in here?

She looked at Lewis. 'You've seen him. What does he look like?'

Lewis tutted. 'Regular Joe. Nowt outstanding. Thirties, brown hair. Could take him out with one punch. Knows it too, I bet. That's why he's hiding behind that speaker.'

Jen doubted Lewis's knock-out conviction, and his description of their captor could be describing a large number of the city's population.

Lewis hadn't finished. 'You said you didn't see him, but you mentioned a phone.'

Jen sighed. 'He posted a phone through my door.'

Lewis's eyes widened. 'That's fucked-up.'

Bill's face echoed the words. 'He phoned you on it?'

Jen nodded. 'Yeah.'

Jen said nothing else. She wasn't going to be the first to say why she thought she was here. For all she knew, the others were perfectly aware why they were here too. Neither one of them telling her.

She thought back to the call, to the videos. All that time spent watching her to capture the footage and photographs that he had. Even if they were able to figure out why they were all here, what really were the chances that he was going to just open the door and let them go?

She stared at Lewis, not wanting to think about the

answer to that, needing to keep her focus on the belief she'd escape, that she'd soon be back with her husband and daughter. But to have any chance of doing that, she had to work out why Lewis and Bill were here.

Yet both he and Lewis were saying next to nothing. Like her.

Were they having the same thoughts? Not wanting to go first?

She looked at both of them, pausing on each of them in turn, staring at their heads as if she could somehow burrow beneath their skulls – see what they were thinking. Were they going to tell her why they were here? Would sharing their secrets, getting them out in the open and putting them together, give any clue as to what was going on? Would it reveal who was keeping them here? Was that what this was? What he wanted them to do?

Jen couldn't be sure. For all she knew, it could be Lewis or Bill themselves who had put her in here in the first place. *Oh God*, she thought. Maybe that was it, maybe one of them was pretending to be in as much of a mess, acting as clueless as the other two were.

Lewis. Lewis had been awake first . . . He was the only one who had tried the door.

Jen brought her knees up and circled them with her arms, making herself as small as possible. Protection. Or as much as she could have in here. Noticing that strange feeling again, as she bunched herself up, the strangeness where her pants should be. She looked at Bill and Lewis, making sure they were looking elsewhere before leaning her head over and lifting the coverall quickly, daring to peek beneath.

Suddenly not caring any more if Bill and Lewis were looking, as she slammed her legs back down against the ground and sprang to her feet. 'I'm wearing a bloody nappy.'

Lewis's hand was under his coverall before she'd even finished shouting. Not caring whether any of them saw. His contorting face as he felt down there, telling her all she needed to know. Bill's too, as he mirrored Lewis's search.

Jen raked her hand through her hair, head pounding. 'Jesus. What *is* this?'

Is the nappy soiled? she wondered.

She looked at the light, wanting to tear the thing from the ceiling, needing to calm herself to think; to try to remember more than she could. Dizzy . . .

'I need to sit down.'

Lewis and Bill watched her in a daze. Despite her own shock and disgust, she figured the men's discovery and realization that they were each wearing a nappy would be sure to strip them of their masculinity. It would strip—

Jen's thoughts froze at the word.

Think . . .

That chemical stench again . . . So strong that she looked around, half expecting to see a green mist seeping into the space but knowing it was her memory coming at her – the arm, the rag. The nothing . . .

That same scratch again as she looked at that red light and stared at the sheet-metal door. All of it pushing her to remember; to recall something important. That scratch drawing blood as she realized that the nothing didn't stay that way . . . That there were other memories, blurred images, mumbled words, swirling in her mind. She was in danger of being pulled under again as she tried to swim to the surface with them.

Something was fighting to burst free. She was almost sure of it. She straightened, Bill and Lewis staring at her.

No, she was certain.

She shook her head, as if the thoughts were about to shuffle and fall into place – gasping when they did. That scratching finally scraping free. Coming up into the light now.

With startling clarity, Jen knew this wasn't the first time she'd woken up here.

Chapter 36

Jen's head whipped from the door to Lewis, to Bill, to the door again. 'He's been in here.'

Confusion contorted Bill's features. 'The voice? When?'

Lewis looked to the ceiling, shaking his head. 'When do you think? We didn't somehow fly in here on our own.'

Jen ignored the sarcasm. 'No, I mean he's been in here. *With all of us.* So many times. Whilst we were passed out.'

Bill was getting up now, grumbling against whatever numbness or pins and needles he had before he spoke. 'How do you know that?'

Jen rose alongside him as she spat the words, needing to get it out. 'Don't you know it too? Can't you feel it? Don't you remember?'

Lewis looked up at them, not fired up enough by this new information to move. 'I can't remember shit apart from waking up earlier. Finding you two looking as dead as dodos on the ground.'

Jen lunged down towards him in her need for him to remember. 'Think. *Really think*. Like a dream, a nightmare even. Like it didn't really happen.'

Lewis was looking at her as if she'd lost it. 'Like what didn't happen?'

She felt breathless, needing him and Bill to listen. For them to remember what she could. To *confirm* her memories. 'Shadows. Voices.'

It was Jen pacing now. 'Physical contact. Stripping us of our clothes.' She hesitated. 'Changing the nappies.' She closed her eyes, repulsed. 'All of it. I remember. Like broken pieces in my brain but they're all there.'

Jen turned towards the door and stared, seeing something that wasn't there. 'Waking up, panicking because it was dark, feeling cold. So, so sick. *Being sick*. Choking. Lifting my head from the stone when I heard a noise. Seeing light. A circle. A blurry circle that wobbled and moved.

'Someone coming towards me from the door. Kneeling. Him cursing as he wiped the sick from my chest, from this coverall. Me trying to get up, screaming again and again – stopping as I felt the slap to my cheek . . . Hearing a deep groan beside me, away from the light, from the torchlight above me . . .' Jen's breathing was ragged, her chest heaving. 'And then my head being pushed back down against the stone, the hand at my mouth. That smell . . . Then the nothing.'

Lewis's forefinger and thumb were back working overtime. 'I think I heard those screams.' He looked up at her, a haunted look on his usually smug face. 'I thought I was dreaming. But that smell – a strong stink, like it was burning my nostrils.'

Jen looked to Bill. 'Do you remember, Bill?'

Bill's mouth opened, closed, and opened again. 'Nothing, until I woke up and saw Lewis.'

Jen's mind was racing. 'I bet you were last in.'

Bill stared at her. 'Last in?'

'Yeah.' She looked at Lewis. 'Maybe you were first in – maybe it was you grumbling, the noise I heard beside me when I was sick.'

Lewis's gaze darted from Jen to Bill, and back to Jen. 'What makes you think it was staggered?'

Jen shrugged. 'It had to be. He's targeted us all. He had to get us in here. No way he could've overcome us all at once. He must've brought us here one at a time.'

Bill nodded, warming to her theme. 'But how long between us? Are you saying you think he's been knocking us out every time we were in danger of coming around?'

Jen nodded. 'Maybe he wanted to wait until we were all in here – couldn't deal with any one of us being awake until that happened – whilst he was away luring the ones of us who were left. Maybe he didn't want us fighting back as he brought someone else in.'

Lewis's lip curled. 'You're saying he put us in these fucking oversized plastic kiddie smocks and these . . . these . . .' He clearly couldn't bring himself to say it.

Jen finished for him. 'Yes, to make it as easy as possible to keep us under for a while. Either he knew the drugs would cause us to be sick or that we'd maybe need to "go" – if you know what I mean. And whatever was on that rag did make me sick. This . . .' Jen pulled at the plastic. 'This made it easier for him to deal with that.'

Bill didn't look convinced. 'Why bother? Why not leave us in our own waste?'

Jen didn't have an answer to that, other than: 'Maybe he thinks he's above that. Maybe he's a neat-freak.'

Lewis grunted. 'Maybe he's a lover of plastic. Kinky, like. One of those guys who also has a thing for adult babies.'

Jen groaned, but she didn't believe it; more inclined, for some reason, to believe it was for practicality, ease – hygiene, even. Everything about the way he'd been with her on the phone seemingly self-righteous. As if he was better than her.

Her thoughts were interrupted by Bill. 'You realize what this all means, don't you?'

Jen and Lewis stared at him, waiting.

'All of this.' Bill looked around the room, at the door. 'All of what you just said . . . It means we could've been down here for days.'

He looked at them both in turn, worry etched on his face, the fear they were both feeling reflecting back at them in his eyes. 'And we have absolutely no way of knowing.'

Chapter 37

Jen jumped up from the floor, her head regretting the move but her resolve to figure this out not caring. 'OK, so he said we're all here for different reasons; that we need to figure out what those reasons are.' Jen looked between Bill and Lewis. 'Surely there has to be a link, similar reasons that brought us here, if not exactly the same one.'

Bill stared at her. 'How do we even begin?'

Jen paced. 'I don't know. Maybe we just start somewhere ... Anywhere. What you said, Bill, about having no way of knowing, no idea of how long we've been here. What if we each look at the day we think we ended up here. Maybe something we were doing that day ties into all of this.'

Lewis tutted. 'Maybe we were doing bugger-all.'

Jen's pitch rose, an unexpected excitement that they were taking action, at least. 'Nothing to lose by trying. Think of the day we were knocked out. What day it was. I bet we were all different days.'

Bill spoke first. 'I can't remember any of the things that you can.' His hand fluttered at his belly. 'I'm not hungry, so I don't think I've been here long at all. In fact, I'm willing to believe that I was maybe brought here only a matter of hours ago and, if that's the case, then it's Tuesday.'

Jen nodded vigorously. 'Which means I was brought here yesterday. Daisy was back at school after the weekend and Tom was at work.

Lewis shrugged. 'Saturday.'

Jen's feet increased speed as she continued to pace. 'OK, good – it ties in with what I said earlier. Going by those days, it was Lewis first, then me, then you, Bill. Making me think it's all been over the same week. It might be different if any of us had been taken on the same day of the week – then we would've been left questioning if it had been the same date, or if we had been taken a week apart. But maybe even then, we could work out what the weather was that day, remember what was on the news, if it somehow might be longer than one week. But I don't think it was.'

Jen had no idea how she knew this, but she just *felt* she hadn't been here that long, without noticing that, if she had been, by now her body would probably be fighting a lot more, struggling to survive. She realized in that moment that her coat was gone. What she'd stuffed in her pocket, before she ran from her home, gone with it. She swallowed down the panic, hearing the pop of Bill's tongue as he spoke, his voice brittle with dryness.

'But how can we be sure?'

Jen sat, momentarily losing momentum with Bill's

doubt. 'Wait a minute . . .' She was up again. 'Bill, you said you remembered the smell, but from when he first attacked you. You don't remember anything else, do you? You said you can't remember voices, him being in here, me screaming, etc.?'

'No, I can't remember any of that.'

Lewis laughed, a cruel sound. 'He's geriatric – maybe just shit memory.'

Jen glowered at him. 'I don't think Bill has been in here long, as he said. Maybe just since earlier today, perhaps yesterday at most.'

Bill spoke. 'For the reasons I explained earlier, but also because I'm on medication. I think, I mean, I don't know for sure, but I think I'd know by now if it had been any longer.'

Jen stared at Bill and said nothing, the rumble of Lewis's belly making her turn. 'You're as hungry as I am. I bet we haven't eaten on any of the days we've been here. He's probably given us water, at most. Maybe that's what my memories of choking are – not just being sick, but struggling against water being forced down my throat.'

Lewis patted his stomach. 'I'm starving.' He looked around at the walls. 'All this . . . He must be here now. Here all along.'

Jen nodded. 'If not, then he must stay somewhere close by when he leaves, that camera meaning he can see us from wherever it is he goes – able to get back here when he sees us coming around.'

Bill rubbed at his mouth. 'Lewis, if you've been down here the longest – say, it's for three days – then people must be looking for you. Maybe even looking for all of us. My son; Jen, your husband.' He turned to Lewis. 'Your mother.'

Lewis grunted. 'My ma'll be glad of getting the place to herself. There won't be her or any other search party on the lookout for me.' He paused. 'So, you better hope that your son, and that husband of yours, are jumping up and down making a racket around about now.'

Jen spoke, her voice quiet, hesitant. 'I didn't tell anyone about the phone. It'll look like I just disappeared off the face of the earth. Nobody will have a clue where I've gone.'

She waited, hoping Bill or Lewis might say something different, that they'd somehow told someone, left a clue; that one of them had thought to, before they were knocked out. But she heard nothing except silence, before thinking about the phone again. About what she was thinking not long ago. How he'd made that call to her, threatening her, promising what he'd expose. The things she had done in her life; the things she was doing . . . wrong. Had he done the same to Lewis? To Bill? Telling them how they'd be made to pay for their . . . mistakes?

Jen glanced at Bill and Lewis. She could well believe Lewis would be involved in something unsavoury but Bill . . . *well, they always said never to judge a book by its cover.* Jen was picking at her thumb, her mind whirring. Was that what this was? Were they all here because of something they had done, something they were doing?

She looked at the door. All she knew was that she had to get out of here, that they had to figure it out, even if it meant grasping at any reason at all, hoping something might hit the mark. That it might give this nutter the answers he wanted.

Jen jumped up, ignoring Lewis and Bill, seeing only Tom and Daisy's faces in her mind's eye as she ran towards the camera, stopping just short of it. Tilting her head up towards it, like a child looking up to an adult for approval as she stared into the lens, the words tumbling out of her: 'We're here because we've made mistakes. Bad choices. Things you somehow know about. Stuff you disagree with. You've brought us here because of them. You want us to answer for them.'

Jen stared at the blinking camera, waiting. Jumping as the speaker hissed.

'Good, Jennifer. One point awarded for your thinking. But it's *your* thinking. Yours alone. This isn't a one-person game, Jennifer. Teamwork is required. Several puzzles must be solved if you are to win the prize. If you are to buy your freedom.'

The speaker suddenly went dead.

Jen scowled at the camera, heart racing. What the hell did that even mean? Her stomach rolled. Daisy. She had to see Daisy. Jen's temple pulsed as she shouted out, right up at the camera, 'I need to see my daughter! I need to know she's OK!'

Nothing.

Jen rushed at the door, slamming her palm against the smooth metal panel, feeling at its edges, pulling at them trying to prise it open with her fingertips. Kicking at the door, the crash of the impact echoing around her. Crying in her frustration as she screamed at the door, 'You need to let me out! I need to see her! Let me out, you son of a bitch!'

Jen felt a hand on her shoulder and spun round. Bill.

'It's OK, Jen. It's OK. We're going to figure this out. I promise.'

Jen fell into his arms, sobbing.

Both of them breaking apart and turning to stare up at the speaker as it started to crackle again.

'Find the answers.'

Chapter 38

JEN AND BILL CONTINUE to stand looking up at the camera. Looking for answers they're not going to get from me – the two of them, and the man behind them, holding all the answers they need.

I look at the three of them in the vault next door via the monitor in front of me. None of them have any idea what's to come.

I've done a good job of the camera, considering. Everything requiring any power down here now working because I was able to tap into the electrical supply. Infra-red sensor, able to watch around the clock – lights on or off; audio tracking, to hear everything being said – to *record* everything being said. Because, until now, I couldn't be listening and watching twenty-four/seven.

I had to bring them here one at a time. They've done a good job working that out. One question answered, at least. But I also had my day-to-day job to do. Keeping up the act. Seeming normal. Giving Robbie no reason to question anything whilst I continued to protect the city and its people. As always.

The camera feed down here delivers to both my mobile phone and my laptop at home. Even the overhead lights are set up to work remotely.

I've been able to dip in whenever and wherever I need to. At work, sat in the CCTV operating room right next to Robbie. In the control room I've set up at home. And now, in my underground control. The room where I've brought down a makeshift, foldable desk, my laptop, and a chair – once a decent chair, leather and all, but that same leather now cracked and stain-ridden. At least the chair still spins – not bad after being pulled out of a nearby skip. So you can forgive its burst back and broken innards. A little like me, after all life has dealt me with. That same life experience meaning I'm comfortable enough in my seat as I preside over proceedings.

Robbie would pee his pants if he knew a crime was happening right beneath his nose. In real time. You could say that happens in his job every day, and that's the whole reason he does it. But this – *this* – isn't like any of those petty crimes we see on those screens above ground. This is a hero's dream. The thing Robbie has been waiting all his life for. I'm almost sad that he won't get to realize that dream; no idea what's going on beneath the streets of Aberdeen.

Beneath the main strip. Union Street. The city centre. If you build a mile-long street on stilts, you create a world underground. Vaulted caverns shouldering the weight of the world above. A dark, damp, cavernous land beneath.

They're not all as dark as they sound. Some are just

underground car parks, others commercial storage. And there's the odd restaurant or nightclub, whilst some are basements to shops. So many of the doors to the staircases, leading to the interlocking tunnels and vaults beneath, are hiding in plain sight. Right there, if you know where to look. I've always known.

It's been a fraught four days. Jen reported missing, her face staring out from television reports, from Missing Person reports at work, demanding us to be on the lookout. Jen's husband all over the media, begging for any information, for someone to bring his wife home, for his daughter to be reunited with her mother.

Lewis's mother decidedly quiet, even though he was first to go. Perhaps not caring, maybe knowing there's no sympathy for Lewis's disappearance. Many being nothing but glad he was gone.

Bill hasn't made it to the news yet. Too soon. I wonder if his son, Simon, has even realized he's gone. That his mother is all alone.

All of their disappearances are ones that Robbie, if he hasn't already, will come to know about. People he'll be asked to look out for on the screens. With no idea they're all connected, that I'm at the forefront of it all. Thinking I'm off for the next week, having nothing to say to that except 'lucky bugger'.

No one wondering why I'm missing from the desk. No one asking if they can see me during my break. No one thinking to check in.

Still, I can't take any chances. Even here, I can't risk being seen, being found. The only entrance is via a door set into the belly of a building that was, until recently, hidden by the sprawling beast that was Aberdeen's indoor market, but is now laid bare next to hills of rubble, the fallen building exposing the forgotten backs of shops that have their fronts facing on to the main strip of Union Street. Those façades once all fresh and glowing. Colourful. Now grey and broken.

A camera is set above the outside of that narrow door now. Linked to a dedicated screen for that entrance. The door's alarmed too.

I've waited a long time for this. Gone to great lengths. Finding them, watching them. Targeting them through their weaknesses. Getting them here.

Jesus, I've even cleaned up their spew, changed their waste. All for this. The moment to see it through.

To watch them uncover the answers.

All the while, thinking of you, Beth.

Of how this all started. How it's going to end.

Chapter 39

Then

I FIRST SAW YOU on a rainy Monday night in October. You were alone, trying to move at speed across Union Street, diagonally, at the crossing from Marks and Spencer. Right towards me.

At least that's how I remember it now, looking back. What you were really running towards was a place out of the downpour and a hot coffee.

You were weighed down by an oversized, overfilled black canvas bag hanging from your shoulder – your arms clutching a stack of books at your chest, attempting but failing to shelter them in your half-open blue duffel coat.

Your coat reminded me of Paddington Bear, and, in that moment, I imagined that, given the chance, I might find a brown luggage tag hanging from one of the wooden toggles. Asking for someone to take care of you. At least, I hoped I might.

I watched you run beneath the awning outside the glass doors where I worked. Caffe Nero. Me, the curly-haired barista extraordinaire inside, the only person I'd demonstrated my coffee-making skills to in the last hour being a stout elderly guy who'd barely grunted his appreciation, and who was now snoozing in the corner, his cappuccino long gone cold.

Seven o'clock and I was single-handedly manning one of the only cafes still pumping out coffee at that time of night. Always with a smile, of course, even if the reality was that I was heating the place for the lonely. Those looking for anything but the quiet of their own four walls.

I knew that because I was one of them.

I propped the mop I'd been washing the floor with against the nearest pillar as you pushed against the heavy glass door with your back, the books in your arms almost toppling to the floor as you turned and dripped your way into warmth. I was, of course, already valiantly coming to your rescue, albeit in a green, coffee-stained apron, which I appreciate wasn't quite as romantic as shining armour.

I smiled. 'Here, let me take those for you.'

You grinned and thanked me, your long, straight, blonde hair clamped to your head, the rain caught in your fringe dripping into your eyes and down your freckled nose. A dimple creasing your cheek.

Cute. Definitely cute.

I looked at the book that was on the top of the pile in my hands. 'You're a student?'

'Yeah, or at least I'm trying to be.'

'Hey, we're all trying to be something.'

You smiled, blue eyes twinkling. I tried not to follow the bead of rain sliding down your chest, disappearing into your top. I was trying to be a gentleman, but you must've noticed as you looked down, catching the drop with your thumb before our eyes met and our cheeks turned pink.

You glanced away first and looked over to the counter. 'My flatmate is a little noisy and the library shuts early so I reckoned I'd chance coming here. Eight o'clock you close, isn't it?'

I nodded and led you to a table for two, beside the window, looking out on to Union Street, far enough away to leave the elderly guy slumbering in peace. That, and because I was already thinking I didn't want us being interrupted.

I couldn't explain it then and I still can't now. Call it something about you, an instant connection. A crazy feeling that I had before you even made it through the door. As strong as all that bullshit women read about in books and get peddled to them in films. With you, in that moment, I was willing to believe it all.

I served you a latte. Skinny, extra hot, and on the house. The least I could do by way of thanks for promising to be the one customer to stay awake and keep me company whilst you drank it. You laughed at that, and it made me feel good. You thought I was funny. I hovered by your table, mop forgotten.

'So, Casey, are you studying too?'

It took me several seconds to respond, surprised that you knew my name and still getting used to the sound of it myself. Remembering I was supposed to answer to it. Realizing that it was emblazoned on the name badge pinned over my left nipple. You thought I was a student, like you. There to make ends meet. I wondered if you'd still want to talk to me once you realized that this was it for me. Me in all my dead-end-job glory.

'No, I work here full time.' I looked around the place as if I'd made it, ignoring the sleeping guy in the corner who clearly didn't recognize my success. 'I'm obsessed with coffee in all its caffeinated and decaffeinated glory. I see it as my mission to bring it to the masses.' I stood to attention and saluted. 'Captain Barista.'

You laughed again. 'Commendable.'

I shrugged. 'What're you studying?'

'Nursing. I'm in my final year.'

You were kind and you were intelligent. 'Impressive. The two of us will bring care and caffeine to the people of Aberdeen.'

You slanted your head to the side, perhaps intrigued by me, maybe thinking how it was even possible that I could be such a loser, but you smiled. 'What a team we could be.'

Maybe, just maybe, you found me cute too.

I stuck my hands into the deep pocket at the front of my apron, digging for something to say, not wanting the chat to end. 'You don't sound like you're from around here.'

You shook your head. 'Inverness. Came here to study. I love it; can see myself staying here after I graduate. If I can get a job.'

'I'm sure Aberdeen Royal Infirmary would be glad to have you.' I knew that I would be. 'Won't your parents be devastated when you don't come back home?'

You shifted in your chair. 'My dad died when I was

young. My mum's remarried, had a couple more kids. I don't speak to her much.'

You said it in a way that required no more discussion about whether you'd be missed or not. You wiped the lip of your latte glass cup with your forefinger, wiping away memories.

We had both experienced the loss of a parent, and my dad had remarried too; was now committed to the inside of a prison cell. Of course, I didn't tell you that.

It was refreshing that you weren't local, that you were less likely to have heard about my own sad story. My name changed by deed poll. Wesley Harris and Harris Butchers long since dead; Casey Carter born. Fresh out of the care system at eighteen, heir to the proceeds from the sale of my parents' house, their butcher's business, and their life insurance policies. Comfortable for life. No actual need to be working here. But you didn't need to know any of that either, and I didn't want you to.

I did tell you about the care bit, that both of my parents were dead. Not that I wanted you to pity me. I wanted you to think of me as strong. To believe that I could survive and succeed in the face of adversity. That there was more to me than coffee and frothed milk.

'So, you never knew either of your parents?'

I shook my head slowly, bit the inside of my cheek.

'That's sad.'

I stood there like a lost and unloved bear. Just a softie waiting to be cared for. It *was* sad, and not a complete lie.

I thought I knew my mother, but I never thought her capable of banging the next-door neighbour. I thought I knew my father, but I never thought him of capable of murder. I hadn't spoken to him since the day I found my mother hanging from that hook, and I obviously hadn't spoken to mother. Casey Carter *was* an orphan.

You were too, really. All alone here in Aberdeen. I wanted to adopt you. I wanted you to be mine.

Maybe you sensed that I could be good for you because you felt it enough to motion towards the empty seat beside you. 'Are you allowed to sit down on the job?' Your eyes moved from sadness to playful.

It was my turn to laugh, giddy. 'No one here to tell me I can't. Although, I should know who I'm sitting with before I do. Never talk to strangers, and all that.'

You smiled and pointed to your chest where your badge would be if you had one. 'Beth.'

You suited your name. I sat and I brushed my forefinger down the spines of the piled books on the table between us. 'I don't want to interrupt your studying, Beth.' Your name felt good in my mouth, right.

You sipped at your coffee and smiled that smile again, your dimple folding. 'Can't be all work and no play.'

You were flirting. I was there for it.

'You're pretty intense.'

My eyes widened. 'Who, me?' You had no idea how intense I could be.

'I feel like you're looking into my soul with those dark brown eyes of yours.'

You were staring just as hard.

'I like looking at you.'

That dimple again. 'I know.'

My gaze never left yours.

We chatted for hours. Long past closing time, hours

after the only other coffee drinker had awoken and been shuffled towards the doors and out of them, the doors locked behind him, one light left on, both of us beneath it, huddled over steaming mugs. Me wondering what we looked like to passers-by on foot, or on a near-empty bus as it thundered past. Not wanting to put out the light above us any time soon, grateful for once that I was trusted and left to lock up on weeknights.

Listening, learning. Starting something unspoken between us that went far beyond sharing a hot beverage. You were the first person I had felt alive with. Not just the first girl. The first anyone.

You could see me for me. Not the boy that everyone knew from the paper. You didn't glance away or avoid eye contact like so many others had when I was a kid. Before I reinvented myself. You didn't seek distraction or escape.

It was a moment that I replayed again and again and again in my head afterwards. A pause in time that I still revisit, even now.

I never wanted that night to end, but I knew it had to. You did too, when you reached over, nudged the books to the side, and placed your hand on mine. Both of us joined across the table.

Your hand gave off a warmth that spread throughout me.

'It's been great chatting, Casey. I'm beat. Long lecture tomorrow, so I'd better get going.'

I looked out the window at the black night. 'It's late. Can I get you a taxi?'

'No, it's fine. My place isn't far. I'll walk.'

You took your hand from mine, and we stood. I helped you gather your books, moving as slowly as I could. I wanted so much to ask for your number, but I wondered if what I felt had just happened between us was normal. I was too inexperienced to know. It was probably nothing more than a chat in your world; us being forced together, as you might have seen it, just because there was no one else to talk to.

As we walked to the door, I wanted to believe that wasn't true. I was waiting, waiting, for you to ask for my number. This couldn't be it. I didn't even know your second name.

We reached for the door handle at the same time, our hands coming together again. You stared up at me, your blonde fringe now dry and curling in on itself. Your voice cracking when you spoke.

'So, are you going to ask for my number or not?'

My heart soared and I grinned. 'I thought you'd never ask.'

We stood there, both of us grinning, my hand clasped over yours on that handle.

A hand that I inexplicably knew I never wanted to let go of.

Chapter 40

JEN'S TEETH CHATTERED. 'It's freezing. Maybe we should get those chairs. Get up off the stone.'

Lewis tutted. 'It's not that cold.'

Jen wondered if it was something else causing the shivers. She wasn't going to go there. 'Well, I'm freezing, and I want a seat.'

Lewis sighed. 'The old codger could probably do with a proper seat anyway.'

'Bill. His name's Bill.' Jen walked over to the chairs, wondering why it had taken them this long to get them. Probably because acknowledging them would be accepting they were settling in for a long stay.

Bill cleared his throat as Jen walked past him. 'You don't have to talk for me, Jen. I'm long enough in the tooth to speak for myself.' He sounded weary, his voice small as it travelled upwards from the ground where he sat.

Metal scraped against stone as Jen unfolded the chairs. Leaving one against the wall.

Lewis made his way over to the closest chair, shaking

it as though he didn't trust it. 'I guess we blame you, Jen, if they collapse.'

Jen ignored him as she looked towards Bill. 'Do you want a hand up?'

'I'll manage. Thank you, though,' said Bill as he pulled himself up from the floor.

Jen sat, Bill filling the seat opposite her and Lewis. She squirmed against the chair, clasping her hands in her lap. 'So now what?' Jen looked towards the door, to the camera above. Imagining that they looked like some circle of truth. Junkies or drunks ready to stand and take their turn. Desperate.

Not her. She swallowed. 'So. He wants answers.'

Lewis scoffed. 'Don't we all.'

Jen ignored him. 'Maybe we should start with what we know. How this all started. With me it was the phone. Lewis, you said the street. Bill?'

'Duthie Park. In the car park. Didn't even see him coming.'

Jen could feel Lewis by her side, staring at her. She turned to him.

'What?'

'I'm just thinking . . . What Bill said: didn't even see him coming. But you, you had a phone put through your door. You say you didn't see him, but you obviously spoke to him. What I'm thinking is, what exactly did he say to you to make you leave your house?'

Jen froze. Not ready. Not ready to say.

Think. Why had she said anything about the bloody phone?

She had just woken up in a bloody basement with

two strangers and she hadn't been thinking straight. She needed to think now, though.

She shifted in her chair, relief flooding through her as something came to her. 'What I said . . . earlier . . . to the camera. About mistakes. About us all being here because of them. Neither you nor Bill have said anything since. And neither of you said anything at the time. Which makes me think what I said was of no surprise. That it all made sense.'

Lewis fidgeted, his chair squeaking as Jen carried on.

'Granted, with Bill not seeing or hearing this guy, he may have been wondering why the hell he was here.' She looked at Bill. 'Sorry, Bill, I don't mean to hone in on you, I'm just saying what's in my head. I imagine you know what you may have done to end up here?'

Bill dipped his head and stared at the floor.

Jen turned back to Lewis. 'And I bet you have a pretty good inkling as to why you're here too. You know the things you've done, don't you?'

Lewis's face flushed as he glowered at her.

Jen's heart started to slow. 'So if you're not willing to spill your guts about what that is right now, neither am I.'

Lewis sat silent.

Jen looked to the ceiling. She sighed, moving the conversation on. Protecting her secret. 'We're in some kind of basement, aren't we? Somewhere he was able to bring us to without being seen. Able to keep us here without us being seen or heard.'

Lewis spoke. 'Place reminds me of the Tunnels nightclub. The place just off the green.'

He sounded oddly animated, maybe glad he might

know something they didn't. He looked at Bill. 'I guess you're not the kinda bloke that goes to the Tunnels. But you must know of the other tunnels around there. Like the hill down past the Frigate Bar. Under Marks.'

Bill shook his head. 'Not really. Although, I'm not from Aberdeen. I only moved up a few years ago.'

Jen looked at Bill but said nothing as Lewis went on. 'The nightclub takes up, like, two tunnels. This place looks a bit like it. If it was stripped back and burnt to the ground.' A dry laugh. 'A shell, I mean. A lot smaller. Like an individual vault. A basement, like Jen said.'

Jen could hear Lewis's Aberdonian twang. Born and bred. Bill not local. Jen neither, from Edinburgh herself. *Probably not important.* Not ready to share anything about herself yet. Keeping things general as she spoke. 'OK, so we have an idea where we might be. We don't seem to know one another but we were all brought here by the same person. Are we sure there's not some way we might know one another, but we just don't recognize each other in person?'

Bill coughed and shifted in his seat. 'I'm sixty-five. Don't get out much. I tend to stay in Northfield.'

'I'm forty-five.' Jen still found her age hard to believe. 'I live in Hazlehead.'

Lewis sighed. 'Nineteen. Born-and-bred Torry loon.'

Bill shrugged. 'It's a bit of a wildcard, but do either of you ever drink in Murdo's Bar? Or shop in the Aldi beside there? That's about as far as I travel.'

Lewis shook his head. 'Nah, mate. White Cockade. Torry.'

Jen's face burned. 'I don't drink in bars.'

Lewis smirked. 'Told you she was a posh bird. Don't think Murdo's or the White Cockade would be her kinda place, Bill.'

Jen didn't want to acknowledge that with a response. Silence fell. Jen squeezed at her fingers, thinking, seconds turning to minutes as no one spoke.

Breaking it, Jen said, 'Maybe we do need to say how and why he got to us. Either of you ready to talk?'

It was the logical place to start – the one thing they all had in common. Which would mean her talking about the phone. Telling them what he had said to her. What he had threatened her with. To make her act. Which meant saying things out loud. Things she hadn't even admitted to herself yet. Not fully.

Jen looked up in surprise as Lewis started talking. He was jumping first.

'He came up to me in the street. Close to where I live. Told me he'd just moved to the area. Asking what there was to do around the place . . . type of thing. Friendly.' Lewis straightened. 'Not that I'm in the habit of just yapping to randoms. I guess he played the part well.'

Jen wasn't sure what to make of that. Doubtful that she would've been taken in by some friendly chat in the middle of the street. Unless she was desperate for company – any kind of company. Or . . . unless Lewis was lying. She stared at him. 'So, you trusted him? Even though he just approached you in the street?'

Lewis picked at his thumb. 'I guess. One of those "had to be there" things.'

Jen nodded slowly. 'And he didn't give any hint to anything else? Anything about what's brought us here?

Lewis shook his head.

'Your turn,' he said.

Jen wrung her hands, not wanting to push Lewis because it would mean her having to give more away too. Not even wanting to talk at all. Knowing she had to, if there was any hope of getting back to Daisy. 'The phone was posted through my door. Started ringing in a jiffy bag on the mat.'

Lewis whistled. 'Like something out of a fucking horror movie.'

Jen couldn't argue with that. 'I answered. What he said to me was nothing good. You've figured that out already.'

Lewis peered at her. 'That's it? That's all you're going to give us? Not what he said?'

Jen glowered at him. 'Didn't hear you giving much more. Just how a stranger offered you friendship and you lapped it up. And we're supposed to believe that?'

Jen felt a sting of regret as Lewis's face burned. She turned away from him. 'What about you, Bill?'

His sigh was loud. 'Duthie Park. I'd just parked up in the back car park.'

Lewis's tone was quizzical. 'And he just pounced and knocked you out? You never even saw him?'

Bill looked haunted. 'I didn't see him.'

Lewis grunted. 'Sounds like a pile of shite to me.'

Jen growled at Lewis. 'Knock it off.'

She jumped as the deep voice flooded the space: 'Think of these answers like an exam. Limited time.'

All three of their heads swivelled towards the camera, Jen seeing it as a living, breathing person as she spoke back to it. 'What do you mean, limited?' Her heart hammering as the voice continued.

'Seems you've nominated yourself as the team spokesperson. I'm sure you all want to get back to your lives. That isn't going to happen if you don't find those answers. If you don't do as I've asked.'

Lewis stood, knocking his chair back. 'Fuck you and your answers. What about you, huh? How about you answer some questions for us?' Lewis's fists clenched as he rocked back and forth, ready to strike. 'Like, what the fuck we're doing here? Save us all some time.' Lewis's legs clapped together as he rushed at the camera. 'Answer that, eh? What's the fucking point of all this? Is this how you get your kicks or something? Eh? Why don't you tell us?' Lewis's body was rigid beneath the camera, spittle flying, before he fell silent. Waiting. Staring. Challenging the voice to speak back.

'Temper, temper, Lewis – so brave when there's a stone wall between you and me. When you have a captive audience. I expect you already know this, but let me make sure that you do. The only person in charge here is me. The only one asking the questions: me. It's your job to find the answers.'

'Fuck you.' Lewis spat at the floor.

The voice tutted twice as if admonishing a child. Reminding Jen again of that phone call. Putting her right back in her hallway at home. Wishing more than anything that she was back there. That she hadn't done what he'd told her to do. That she'd instead gone running screaming from her door, knocking on any and every door until someone had let her in. She closed her eyes as the voice assaulted her ears.

'I expect you're all hungry. Needing a little fuel to think. To calm down a little, perhaps.'

Lewis was back snarling at the camera. 'Fuck calming down! Why don't you man up, instead? One to one. Come in here and try me now, instead of spiking my fucking drink in the pub. Instead of hiding behind that fucking camera.'

Jen stared at Lewis's back. 'You said he came up to you in the street. You never said anything about a pub.'

Lewis's frame softened; his back still turned to them as Jen continued. 'You asked what made me leave my home after that phone call. But what made you go to a pub with a complete stranger? What—' She stopped as laughter filled the room.

'The only ones hiding are each and every one of you. Behind all your lies.'

Jen glanced at Bill, then to the back of Lewis's head again as the voice went on.

'I want you to tell the truth. To tell your real stories. The ones you haven't told anyone else. Those are the answers I seek.'

Lewis spat again. 'I don't give a fuck what you seek.'

'*Lewis.*' Jen jumped at Bill's voice, surprised at the hardness to it. The volume. Enough to make Lewis stop and turn around in his anger. Bill sighed. 'Just sit down. You're not achieving anything.'

The speaker crackled again. 'Ah, the voice of reason. With age comes wisdom. That is, if you can remember that wisdom. Isn't that right, Bill?'

Bill looked at the floor.

'I said, isn't that right, Bill?'

Bill looked up, towards the camera. 'You're a son of a bitch. She's all alone.'

The voice ricocheted around the room. 'Not for the first time, Bill. Didn't seem to bother you then.'

Lewis turned on Bill. 'You never mentioned a "she". You said your son might be looking for you. Who's "she"?'

The words seemingly hitting like bullets as Bill's face changed and fell, his chin dropping to his chest. That same look on his face that Jen saw on herself every time she looked in the mirror.

'My wife.'

Jen closed her eyes, no idea what or who to trust, the voice bellowing out of the speaker cutting into her thoughts, pressing down against her in the small space.

'Why don't you start, Bill? Kick things off. Tell your truth.'

Jen looked over and saw panic in Bill's eyes. She had no idea what he'd done. Clueless as to why it would matter to their captor. What it was that he wanted from them. Knowing that, whether they liked it or not, he was going to show them.

Dreading when it would be her turn to speak.

Chapter 41

Then

I KNEW YOUR SECOND name by the end of our first date. Sorrie. Beth Sorrie. I couldn't imagine you ever having to be sorry for anything.

It was late October, the threat of winter in the breeze. We went for a walk along the beach, grabbing a coffee from one of the beachfront cafes before we set off. Of course, it had to be coffee.

It was meant to be a simple date. To be easy. But it wasn't. Sharing you was hard.

I didn't expect that. I couldn't have known. I'd never had anything to myself, not as a kid, not since Mum and Dad. I'd existed, skirted around the edges, and now you were bringing me to centre stage, and I wanted to bask in that spotlight with you. I just didn't want anyone else hogging the limelight, and I definitely didn't want an audience.

'You really are intense, Casey. In the two times I've met you, I feel like there's a whole other world going on in that head of yours.'

'You make me sound like some psycho.'

You laughed. 'Maybe you are. I hardly know you.'

'But you like what you know.'

'Modest too, Casey.' You smiled. That dimple. 'I'll admit I'm intrigued. I want to see what that world of yours is like. Mine can be pretty mundane.'

'I'd like to get the chance to change that.' I stopped, glaring as a guy brushed past you.

'Relax.' You nudged me with your elbow. 'See what I mean? You looked like you were ready to take him down.'

'I should've. Getting up close to my girl.'

Your eyes widened. '*Your* girl? Presumptuous too.'

You hooked your arm through mine, as into it as I was. As ready for it as I was.

What I wasn't ready for, and never would be, was seeing how other men looked at you as we passed by. I don't know why; I should've expected it. You were beautiful. I was aware of it the first time I saw you – running towards me across Union Street that rainy night. I knew they saw it too, but you seemed oblivious to their glances and stares; of being admired from afar, probably up close by the brasher ones amongst them. Years of being looked at had done that to you – you'd grown used to it.

But I hadn't got used to it – didn't ever want to – no matter how much I told myself that you were with me; that you had picked *me*.

I wanted you all to myself. I wanted you away from there. From them. Back at that table, out of the rain, just the two of us, the world around us off happening somewhere else, to everyone else out there in the dark.

I hid my discomfort that day. I hid it every day from then on. At least I thought I did. The last thing I wanted to do was scare you off, to send you running into the arms of one of those men who stared at you as we approached, and then looked back over their shoulder after we'd walked past. Some of them even hand-in-hand with their own woman, who happened to be looking the other way.

I was relieved to make it to a third date. By then you trusted me enough to tell me where you lived. I already knew but I didn't tell you that. Your life was there for all to see on Facebook.

On the fourth date, you took me home to meet your flatmate. The closest thing you had to family in Aberdeen. I took that as commitment. I took that as meaning something. You liked me. A lot. You wanted to show me off. You wanted others to like me too.

I hated your flatmate at first sight. The feeling was mutual. You told me that you shared with a fellow student, but I hadn't expected a male nurse. Cameron. *Cammy* – his preference. He was tall, dark, and . . . competition.

When we walked into your flat the first time, he was lolling on your sofa like he owned the place. A poky little two-bedroomed tenement rental overlooking the Kings Bar on King Street.

'So, you're the stalker.' He laughed, but in a way that was intended to make me think that you and he were in on some private joke.

I stared at him. 'Intense, I think she called it.'

You laughed at the same time as his face fell.

Shady neighbourhood. Shady flatmate.

This wasn't one of those guys watching you as we walked along the beach. He was living and breathing the same space as you. All those times . . . when I wasn't. He wasn't looking back over his shoulder with envy. He didn't have to. Cameron was the guy you went home to.

And now that guy was lying on burst cushions covered by a faded blanket, scooping cereal from a chipped bowl, watching telly. I had already silently refused to call him Cammy. He didn't even bother to drop his spoon when you introduced me, barely said a word in fact, but I watched his eyes follow you around the room, saw the way he glowered at me when you disappeared through to the kitchen, and I knew.

One night soon he'd come in drunk, jealous of what you and I had, when he'd always wanted you but was too chickenshit to make a move. He'd force himself on you, mistaking your kindness and care for your way of showing him that you wanted him.

But you couldn't see that, not yet, and you couldn't possibly know that it wasn't safe for you here.

The place stank of his scent. But I was there now, and I was going to make sure I invaded his territory. I'd make sure to piss all over the place.

Be sure to let him know I was there to steal his bitch.

Chapter 42

BILL LEANED FORWARD IN the chair as if bracing himself for impact. Aware of the tremor in his hands, wondering if they could see it. Old age, worsened by nerves.

He felt like he should stand, state his name and, instead of declaring he was an alcoholic, admit what a terrible husband he was, a shitty example of a human being.

But he didn't stand, doubting his shaking legs would hold him up. Instead, he leaned forward, staring down at the floor, avoiding eye contact. Not able to look anyone in the eye if he was about to give what he'd been asked to give – not even strangers.

'I'm not sure where to start, so I guess I'll just start. My wife, Patricia, has dementia. She has it bad.' Bill spun his wedding ring around with his other hand.

'We moved up to Aberdeen from Whitley Bay four years ago. My son, Simon, and his wife, Kelly, were already up here for work. Had been for a while. They'd come down and visit but we couldn't come up because of my health.' Bill stopped spinning his wedding ring and leaned back in the chair. 'But I got better. Around the same time that my daughter-in-law fell pregnant. A happy time after a long, rough one. New beginnings, if you like.' Bill sighed at the memory.

'I knew that, with the new baby coming, Patricia really wanted to be closer to them. We were both retirement age by then, so I figured we had nothing to lose. Simon liked the idea of us being closer too, what with us getting older, and, yeah, I guess we were built-in babysitters.' Bill smiled, the gesture disappearing just as quickly. 'So, we moved up.' Bill looked at Jen and then at Lewis. 'I'm sure you're bored listening to all this.'

Jen shook her head. 'Not at all.' *I'll take listening over speaking, any day*, Jen thought. She looked around the room, her gaze settling on the blinking red light.

Lewis said nothing, just scuffed the toe of his trainer against the stone floor.

'Anyway, we moved up and, for a while, it was great. We got a lovely semi-detached on Cairncry Road, not too far from our son. Got wrapped up in our new grandson. Other things. We'd always been active as a couple, with our own interests too. We started going to bingo. Patricia got involved in crafts at the nearby community centre. I got to know some of the boys at Murdo's Bar. I'm not a big drinker, but I enjoy a couple of pints.' He clasped his hands in his lap. 'Or at least I used to.'

He felt Jen staring at him, listening. Lewis not looking anywhere but at his trainer as he kicked at the ground. A guy who probably wouldn't be interested in anyone but himself.

'Anyway, it was only months before I started to notice things with Patricia. Little things. She seemed to forget stuff we'd not long talked about; didn't appear able to sit the same, to enjoy doing her sudoku. But it was the speaking that really got me. Forgetting the right word or stumbling over what she was trying to say. That just wasn't my Trish. She'd always been articulate – a teacher all her working life.' Bill stared at nothing, seeing Trish in his mind, his wife in her prime.

'Anyway, I hid a lot of it from our Simon and Kelly. Didn't want to worry them. Thought maybe it was all to do with the women's change, or whatever they call it. I knew she'd already come through all that, but still.

'Then I thought maybe it was just all the other changes at such a late stage of our lives. New city, new home, new friends. But then things started getting worse; in time, so bad I no longer felt I could leave her in the house alone. I told Simon and Kelly that I wasn't bothered about missing a pint, what with how expensive it was getting. I don't think Simon ever believed me, but he never questioned it.

'I'd still drop Trish at her crafts mornings but, by then, I'd wait outside instead of heading home for the hour. Eventually the woman who ran the class came up to me in the car, asked if Trish was OK. Something daft had happened. I knew then it wasn't just my imagination, that whatever was happening wasn't going away.'

'That must've been so difficult.' Jen sounded genuinely sorry.

Bill nodded. 'It's true what they say. By that stage you start to feel that person in front of you is already gone.

Dead. Except you're made to watch them die a little more each day.' Bill wiped at his eye. 'I know most would probably say this about their partner, but Trish was my life. Forty-five years married this month. She was – *is* – a good woman, who's given me a great life.'

Jen leaned forward. 'Most *wouldn't* say that, you know. I think how long you've been together, and that you still speak so fondly of her, is a rare thing to find these days.' Jen looked to the floor.

Bill thought he saw a sadness there. He glanced at Lewis, who was still giving nothing away except that he'd changed feet and was now hitting the floor with his other trainer.

'I still think fondly of her. But I also think about cheating on her.'

Now Lewis *was* looking. Staring. Jen too, her eyes wide.

Bill held her stare. 'Didn't expect that, huh?'

Bill rubbed a hand down each thigh, as if trying to push away the dirt within him. 'She's the woman who has given me this life, but I've been betraying her. Talking daily to someone else. Talking to someone in our home. With Trish there right beside me.'

Lewis sounded impressed. 'For an old codger, you're all right.'

Bill didn't look Lewis's way, not wanting to grace such a stupid comment with any recognition.

Jen spoke softly. 'Have you spoken to your son about how you feel?'

Bill glanced at Jen, reminded of the old Trish in a way. The same calm temperament, similar kindness in her tone. 'How do you even tell your son something like that?'

'I don't mean about this other woman. I mean how hopeless you feel about the situation. Surely that's what it is? Can you not ask for help? Maybe get a little respite? Even a couple of hours up at that bar you spoke about?'

Bill laughed – no humour in it, though. 'That need for respite, for company, is what led me here.'

'What do you mean?' Jen cocked her head.

Bill was back fiddling with his wedding ring. 'I've never wanted any help in looking after Trish. Not from anyone, including my son. She's looked after me all her life. Me and everyone else. It was my turn to do the same for her. I wasn't going to ask for respite from caring for someone that I'd shared my life with. Someone I loved and who loved me. What kind of man would that make me? There was no one else who could care for Trish like I could.'

Jen shifted her chair a little closer to Bill. 'I believe that, Bill, but what you're dealing with, day-to-day – that would take a toll on anyone. You owe it to yourself to take some time off now and again. You'd be better placed to look after Trish with a break.'

Bill shook his head. 'That's just it. I told myself that. Fooled myself into thinking I was only taking a break. Starting with the garden; making the back garden my escape. My sanctuary. Tending to it. Preening it. Telling myself that Trish could watch from the window in the colder weather, enjoy being in it on the warmer days.'

'It sounds great.'

'Yeah, except that Trish wasn't interested in being out

in the garden. Only wanting to do the same old thing. Over and over. She wouldn't be talked into anything else. All she wanted to do was stare at the television all day. Television with tea and biscuits. No idea of what she was watching or how long she'd been watching it for, but needing to do just that. We went from being a couple that had our shared interests – enjoying meals out, theatre, holidays, weekends away – to two people existing alongside one another. Barely talking. All those shared jokes, all that life together, forgotten.'

Bill stood and paced, going nowhere. 'I began to despise her – hate her, almost – for all her complaining and repeating and talking gibberish. I became angry, bitter. I'd lose my temper with her. I slowly began spending more and more time out in the garden, pretending she wasn't there. Forgetting about her inside. Blocking her out of my mind on purpose. Some man, huh?'

Jen reached an arm out towards him, brushing his wrist as he passed her to sit back down again. 'Bill, you seem a good man. What you're saying is hardly the end of the world. I think anyone would feel the way that you do.'

He swallowed. 'I had been so ill before we moved here. She nursed me back from the brink. And how do I repay her when she's ill? When it's my turn to look after her?

'Worse still, that garden was no longer enough. I wanted more. I went looking for more. Online. Convincing myself it was only for company but . . . I got writing to a woman online. Norma. I kept writing to Norma. All hours. Sometimes at the expense of seeing to Trish, to her needs. Never telling Norma about Trish. Not thinking enough of Trish any more when I said yes to Norma's invitation to meet.'

Bill jumped as Lewis sprang from his seat: 'For fuck's sake, Bill. It's hardly the crime of the century. So, you're sick of staying in, you think about cheating on your old lady. So what? I could kill someone for a fag right now. I think about squeezing my mother's throat every fucking day. You reckon that's the truth this guy wants?' He looked towards the camera. 'You think that's the worst that's going on in Aberdeen?'

Lewis was back at the camera, jabbing his finger up at it. 'Come on, you fucker, just spit it out. Why we're here. What the fuck it is you want from us. Get whatever this bollocks is over and done with.'

He jumped back as the voice burst out from beside the camera.

'Sit down. *Now*.'

All three of them froze. None of them saying a word. Lewis doing as he was told.

The speaker buzzed static. 'I expect Bill could do with a drink after that. Maybe a little something to eat too. That fuel I promised – I think our Lewis needs it more than anyone. A moment to calm down.'

Jen's arm was back on Bill's. Wanting him to know his story hadn't been forgotten about. Imagining everything he'd said had to be hurting. She spoke to the camera: 'What about our clothes? Our underwear?'

'No need for either. At least, not yet. Something to look forward to, let's say. Stay seated. The lights will go out. The door will open. If any of you move. It's all deals off.'

Chapter 43

Then

I SAT TUCKED BEHIND an industrial waste bin. Everything ached. My backside numb and my fingers frozen. I'd been there for an hour. Sitting, squatting, kneeling – changing to whatever position I could to keep the circulation going whilst I stayed hidden.

I'd told you I was going to see a movie, some new release I knew you wouldn't like. I'd even gone to the trouble of entering the cinema, buying the ticket, making sure to get the cinema attendant to make his small rip in it as he pointed me towards Screen Four. I stayed for the adverts then slipped out, the movie still playing as I sat behind that bin, the ripped ticket folded into a small square in my pocket.

I was dressed all in black, the hood of my top over my head and pulled tight around my face, the packed small blue rucksack flat against my back. I would stay there until he came. Until Cameron came. Afterwards, I would strip down to my underwear behind the bin and change into the clothes in the rucksack, putting the discarded ones in the bag before I fitted it with a red elasticated rain cover, leaving some three hours later, a different guy from the one who had entered the lane.

Student flats lined one side of the lane. I could have gone into any one of those doors – and come out of any one of them. No cameras to tell, no one to see me arrive in the dark. I'd been sure that no one would see me leave.

I'd prayed that everything would be on my side. That he'd follow the same pattern as he had the three Saturdays previously. When I'd watched, and then followed him.

For a big guy, he couldn't hold his drink. Mind you, I hadn't seen how much he'd sunk before I'd got there.

Drummonds was packed the week before. Wall-to-wall bodies seething in the stink of stale sweat and just as stale beer. The band were shit but Cameron and his buddies seemed to rate them – so into them that he didn't see me coming into the bar and he didn't see me leave behind him and his two pals when the band had finally decided that a third encore was probably enough for what they were being paid. Last orders had been shouted and the bouncers had herded the punters towards the door, out on to Belmont Street.

It had been four weeks since I'd first met him at your place. I hadn't warmed to him; none of my doubts about his intentions towards you had thawed. Four weeks since I'd started watching him, and he had only proved me right. He was a testosterone-pumped prick, and it was time someone burst his balloon.

I followed at a distance, getting nowhere fast as he

and his pals weaved from one side of the cobbled street to the other. I knew he would break off from them at the Back Wynd. The same as he had the previous two Saturdays. The two others pouring themselves into separate taxis, going in the opposite direction from each other and from him. Cameron opting to walk.

I stepped into the empty doorway of O'Neill's as he waved them off, then fell into step behind him as he walked along the Wynd and on to Schoolhill. The same route as last week, and the week before that.

I crossed over Schoolhill from the Back Wynd towards Boots the Chemist, down past Wordies Ale House, as Cameron went by the back of the graveyard, on the opposite pavement. The street was deserted, the shops and pub closed and in darkness. Him and me. No one else.

I didn't keep up pace – I knew where he was headed. I watched him cross the road up ahead, turning left, knowing he was headed for the Brae. He'd walk down the Brae, stumbling probably, and he'd risk crossing at the lights without waiting for the pedestrian crossing. From there he'd cut through on to King Street.

Both weeks before now, I'd followed him through there. Not another soul to be seen. Relieved when he did the same again.

Relieved again when he didn't disappoint this time either.

I heard him further up the lane from where I was hiding. Singing one of the shitty songs the band had probably just played, singing just as badly as they had. The baseball bat was where I'd left it earlier, beneath the bin, no fingerprints on it and none from my gloved hands afterwards, when I left it behind.

He didn't hear me retrieve it. He didn't hear me lift it high above my head.

He didn't hear the whoosh as it dropped hard through the night air.

Maybe he heard the crack as it hit his head.

But I couldn't be sure.

Chapter 44

Jen grasped the edges of her flimsy chair with both hands as the stone-walled space around her plunged into darkness, her eyes snapping shut even though she could see nothing. Bracing herself against whatever was about to happen. Waiting for God-only-knew-what.

Her heart lurched at the sound of metal scraping against stone. The door opening slowly, bringing with it a rush of cold air. Bringing *him*.

Jen forced herself to open her eyes, turning her head right, towards the door. Bright white torchlight beaming towards her, blinding her. Déjà vu. Seeing nothing behind that light, not even a silhouette, as she closed her eyes again just as quickly and tightly. Nothing but the bright-white imprint left behind her eyelids.

No footsteps to be heard. Wondering if he would venture far into the room. Her foot twitching, threatening to act out, willing her to move. To move and propel her towards the door. To challenge him before it was too late.

Jen planted her foot on the floor. Wondering if Lewis might make the move. Or if all his shouting and threats were nothing but bravado.

She jumped as something clattered to the ground.

Had Lewis come through after all? Had he struck in the silence, catching their kidnapper off-guard?

She dared to open her eyes again, hearing Bill's breath by her side, as ragged as hers.

Her question answered as no sound followed the clatter, nothing except the slam of the door as it shut, mere moments before light flooded the vault again. Her eyes squinting against the light as she looked over to the door. Seeing a tray on the ground. Three paper cups on it. Three croissants alongside them.

How thoughtful, she thought.

Jen looked at Bill, at Lewis. Neither of them had moved. Perhaps as scared to as she was, no idea whether they'd make it to the open door in the dark. Whether their captor might hold a weapon.

No way of knowing what was beyond that door, even if they did make it. What the repercussions might be if they tried to find out. That fear and their rumbling bellies, as well as the dawning realization that they may be here for some time, had made their need for water, for food, even greater.

The fact they were being fed and watered gave Jen a scrap of hope, comfort almost, that surely he wouldn't be feeding them if he had no intention of letting them go? Maybe that's why she hadn't moved. Still believing that the answers he sought would buy them their freedom. That maybe doing anything other than providing those answers, anything of risk, would rip that chance away. All three of them therefore making the decision to do as they were told. To try to give him what he wanted.

For now.

Lewis lunged for the tray, snatching up one of the croissants and ripping at it with his teeth. Mumbling something about it being stale, before lifting one of the paper cups of water and gulping at it. Not bothering to bring the tray over to her and Bill.

Every man for himself.

Jen rose and went to lift the tray, bringing it back to the chairs, offering it to Bill first. All as Lewis sucked his fingers, croissant already gone.

Jen took her time. Savouring every bite. Bill doing the same by her side as Lewis looked on like a salivating, begging dog. Neither she nor Bill caring that the pastries were as tough as old boots. Soon she was left with just an empty paper cup.

A cup which she now rubbed back and forth between her hands. Feeling a little more human after food and water. Wishing it had also helped her to feel a little more ready to tell her story. Knowing that nothing was ever going to make her feel that. Jen sighed.

'I'm not from Aberdeen either. You probably guessed: Edinburgh. My husband, Tom, and I moved up here four years ago. With our daughter, Daisy. She's six. She should have an eleven-year-old brother, Riley.' Jen hated the break in her voice, never able to contain her emotion when she spoke about him, always aware that it was better to avoid talking about it.

'We lost him to cot death. But there was a time, after

we lost him . . . Before the investigation, before the findings, where I blamed myself. I still did, even after.' She swallowed. 'Still do.'

Bill leaned towards her. 'I don't mean to interrupt but I'm so sorry to hear that. I can't imagine how hard the loss of a child must be.'

Jen said nothing, not trusting herself to speak further. Until she glanced at Lewis. He was still staring at the blinking red light, his legs sprawled open, the dirty, worn soles of his trainers pressed together on the floor. She wanted to punch him. Was surprised at how much she wanted to – seeing someone so blasé about the death of her son. 'Am I boring you?'

Lewis clicked his tongue, his eyes rolling up to the ceiling.

Bill looked from her to Lewis, his face darkening. 'Have some respect. Remember you've still to speak.'

'Whatever, man.' Lewis bounced his knee up and down, looking to the floor now.

Jen glowered. 'Maybe, Lewis, you'll be more interested to hear that I'm not the posh bird you think I am?'

He looked up.

Jen smiled, no happiness to it. 'A raving drunk, in fact. I don't drink in the type of bars you frequent; I just drink anywhere and everywhere else.'

Defiance in the way she said it, all of a sudden not caring what Lewis thought but, for some reason, the shock on Bill's face cutting deep.

She carried on, regardless. 'Bet neither of you were expecting that. So, similar to your words earlier, Bill: what kind of woman does that make me?'

Bill's face softened. 'Did it start after the loss of your son?'

Jen smiled – more of a curl to her lip, the disgust she felt for herself there, a sour taste in her mouth. 'In a way, I wish I could sit here and say that it did. That the grief drove me to drink. The truth? The truth is that I was drinking long before I fell pregnant with Riley. It was my normal. Tom and I were party people – we were in our twenties, nothing unusual about that.

'What was different was that unbeknown to Tom, I'd sink a bottle of wine before he came to pick me up from my flat. It would barely touch the sides, and I'd function as if I'd had just one or two drinks whilst getting ready. It got more and more over the years. Always in secret, never getting caught.' It was Jen's time to sigh now.

'I'd hide bottles all over the place. Even managed to keep up the charade when we moved in together. A bottle of red between us at night, starting whilst cooking tea. I'd be sneaking extra drinks in between the ones he knew I was having. Even on the nights when the drink would hit me hard, he'd just call me a lightweight. Thought it was funny.'

She shrugged. 'It only stopped being funny when I fell pregnant with Riley. When Tom didn't want me to drink during pregnancy, but I couldn't stop. Then he realized how much I was drinking, how much I'd probably been drinking all that time.

'I was going to be a mum; I loved that life growing inside me, but it seemed I loved the drink more. Then Riley arrived and things changed.' Jen rubbed at nothing on her palm.

'Something hit – that I was so lucky he was healthy and that this was real now; that I had to stop. To be his mum. I had to be better for Tom too.' Jen stopped rubbing at her skin, her shoulders slumping.

'Tom's a paramedic and he was doing so well at work. He wanted to take on night shifts, but he said he didn't want to leave me overnight with the wee one. I knew what he really meant. He didn't trust me to be left on my own. I vowed to change. Promised him I would. For a time, I did.'

Jen closed her eyes to the memories. 'It didn't last. Wasn't long before the lies started up again. The hidden bottles. I told myself I deserved a drink now and again. That it was hard; that it was because Riley was a baby who didn't sleep.'

Her eyes sprung open, her voice hardening when she spoke. 'What I should've been is a mother worthy of him. Happy. Protective. Not caring about how tired I was. Just because he was there. But the only thing I was aware of was my exhaustion. How he never slept. Ironic that I ended up wishing he'd never gone to sleep that night. That I hadn't sunk those two bottles of wine. That maybe I would've heard something. Sensed something.'

Jen shook her head. 'But I did drink them, and I didn't hear a thing. All I know is that whatever happened in that cot meant my baby boy went to sleep and he never woke up.'

She inhaled a sob. 'But you know what makes it worse? What the hardest thing has been to cope with?' She looked between Bill and Lewis. 'Not just the death of my son. But *Tom*. Tom, the ever-supportive husband who loves me. Loves me so much that he's never held me responsible for Riley's death. And why? Because of a flimsy piece of paper. The official report findings. Saying it wasn't my fault. That piece of paper so fragile yet strong enough for my husband to turn a blind eye to those bottles, to my problem.'

Jen gave a smile, though there was nothing happy in it. 'We even got pregnant again. And did I learn my lesson? No, I didn't. Now I blamed grief.' Her hands were gripped tightly together now, her voice softening. 'Until my body couldn't take it any more. Until I was told that if I didn't stop drinking, I was going to die. That the baby would die too. But that both of us still had a chance. If I stopped.'

She clenched her eyes shut, ashamed. 'So, I stopped. I went to the meetings I was told to go to. I did everything they wanted me to. To keep Tom. To keep Daisy.

'Once Daisy was born, I got even more help. Help that meant I could start afresh. After I was back on my feet, we moved. Not just house, but city too. Tom thought it was for the best. That we would do better starting again somewhere. So, we came to Aberdeen, and, for a while, he was right. We were busy with a new home, then with Daisy starting school and a new job for Tom. Everything was better. I was better.'

Her eyes opened slowly. 'But eventually there was nothing left to set up, nothing left to sort out. Tom's hours started creeping up and I ... I started feeling lost. Like my son wasn't near enough any more – not only his grave, but the memory of him. That I wasn't close enough to him. That I'd left him behind. That I'd let him down – again.

She sobbed, tears dripping down her face, soaking into her top. 'That's all I could see. Even with Daisy's beautiful face right there in front of me, needing to be loved.' Jen tipped her head back, staring at the stone ceiling, wiping at her tears.

'I fought it. For so, so long. Thought I'd won. But I was kidding myself. It started up again, about six months ago. Slowly at first. The odd sneaky drink whilst Tom was on a night shift. And now? Now it's more or less back to what it was.' She stared at the floor. 'I don't think Tom knows. I'm a dab hand at masking it – functioning alcoholic, it's fondly known as. No real smell to vodka. Besides, I don't think for a moment he believes I'd put us all back there. Not after everything.'

Jen took a deep breath. 'But I'm in danger of doing just that and I'm scared; have been feeling scared long before I ended up here, before *he* threatened to tell everyone. So scared that Tom would leave if he knew. That he would take Daisy with him. What my family would think. What all the school mums would say. So, I did what *he* told me to. But now, now I'm here, I'm terrified. Petrified that my being missing will bring it all out in the open, regardless.'

She gulped, rubbing at her mouth. 'But most of all, I'm scared that I'm never going to get out of here to make things right.'

Chapter 45

Then

SOME GIRL CALLED MANDY was there when I arrived at your flat. A friend of yours I'd never met. Another student on your course. Female, at least.

'So, you're him.'

Female but just as charming and prickly as Cameron. 'I guess so,' I replied. Because what was I supposed to say to that?

It was 2 p.m. and the police were there. Cameron having been found at 8.40 a.m. by a passer-by who used the lane to get to work. No luck for me that the passer-by had to work a Sunday.

They'd taken their time to find out where he lived – to find you, to let you know. They estimated he'd been lying there six to seven hours. Not a bad guess. Said it was a miracle he'd survived the hit to his head. It was a small miracle, when you phoned to tell me, that you weren't there to see my face. Cameron wasn't the only one left with a headache, after the realization that I hadn't hit him hard enough.

Of course, I did what was expected of me. I got to yours as fast as I could. I wondered if Cameron might've somehow seen something; if I might be in the police force's sights. But I knew there was no way he could have. That you wouldn't have called me if that had been the case.

I was surprised to see the girl there, irritation rippling that you might've thought to call her before me. She was on the sofa by your side, cradling you as you both cried. No room for me on the two-seater. I sat in the armchair whilst the two officers stood. I offered to make them coffee – they accepted. Mandy asked for wine.

I went to the kitchen and filled the kettle, my finger brushing against the folded cinema ticket in my jeans pocket – different bottoms from the night before, but the ticket transferred over. I turned to one of the officers, who was leaning against the kitchen-door frame. My fingers working overtime against the ticket as she asked me questions. Just a chat, but I was aware it might be much more than that: How long had I known you? Had I met Cameron? What was it like working as a barista? All things I answered carefully and lightly, waiting for the killer question, the one where I'd whip out that ticket and give her the answer. But it wasn't long before I realized she really was only hitting for small talk. I was of no interest to the officers other than as the provider of a steaming mug of coffee – confirmed when they didn't stop me from nipping out to the closest shop for Mandy's wine, me hating that I was being made to wait to find out what was happening, that she was comforting you when it should've been me.

I didn't even know if he was awake. Even worse, was

he lucid? Was there any chance things could lead back to me? I'd been careful, both following him there and afterwards. But still . . .

I brought back a box of white. I felt we might be in it for the long haul. I was fixing my face with a look of innocence, having checked and rechecked that the ticket was still in my pocket before I ventured up the tenement stairs. Genuinely surprised but filled with relief – elated – to find the police had left. Mandy was up and pulling the box from my arms before I'd even got over the threshold.

She didn't thank me, already glancing back over her shoulder at you as if I was some delivery guy not worthy of her time or a tip. 'I mean,' she called out, 'how long do you reckon it'll be before we know?'

Before we know what? I wondered.

She flounced to the kitchen, a total of five steps away from the living room, and I wanted to steal the free seat beside you on the sofa, but I guessed you'd think more of me if I went and helped her with the wine.

She was already pulling glasses from the cupboard. It turned out Mandy didn't see it being a pity party for three – pretty evident when she got out only two glasses before she started ripping at the box. I was good enough to pay for the stuff, but not to share.

I said nothing and followed her back through to you in the living room. I just wanted her to bloody spit out what kind of state Cameron was in.

'Are you not wanting some?' You asked, looking at me quizzically.

I could've kissed you in that moment, as Mandy

sighed and knocked past me to go and grab another glass. A 125ml glass to your 175ml, but I took the win.

Mandy tutted. 'It's so horrible. Who would want to hurt Cammy?'

She plonked herself down beside you on the two-seater, pointedly looking at me, forcing me to take the armchair by the window. *Bitch*. I wondered whether the look was to prove she was in charge or whether it said she suspected me.

You looked across at me, your gaze soft, making sure I was OK, silently apologizing for your friend's rude behaviour, I'm sure, before you spoke. 'It's scary shit. What if it's not Cammy, you know? What if he's not *our* Cammy when he comes round?'

I took an extra slug of wine in celebration. So, he wasn't yet conscious, and if he was to wake as a different Cammy, it would only be a good thing. The dickhead should've been thanking me.

Mandy shook her head. 'I don't even want to think about it. Like I say, who would want to hurt him?'

She was looking at me again. Maybe I was expected to put in my tuppence worth, now I'd been allowed a share of the wine.

'What are they saying at the hospital?'

Mandy looked at me as if I should just shut up and stay in my corner.

You folded your legs up underneath you and hugged the glass of wine with both hands. 'They haven't been able to tell us too much yet. His parents are travelling up now.'

I had no idea where he was from, but I already hoped

that, when he did wake up – *if* he woke up – they wouldn't want to let him stay in a place of such danger. That they'd bundle him off, back to wherever he'd come from.

'What have they been able to tell you?' I tried not to rush too much, but a little bit of give wouldn't go amiss.

'They've had to put him in an induced coma due to the swelling on the brain. They reckon there may be some brain damage.' Your voice cracked. I wanted to hold you, and I wanted to jump for joy.

No amount of care was going to nurse him back to full health. Brain damage. Never able to return to university. Crying shame.

You were crying. 'What if they knew him? What if it wasn't a case of wrong time, wrong place? They might've been after something we don't know about. They might know where he lives.' You took a too-big gulp of wine, grimacing as it went down.

Mandy placed her hand on your thigh and rubbed it. I wanted to rub her face off.

'I'm here, Beth. Nothing's going to happen. It was just some nutter. Wouldn't even have known who Cammy was.'

I took exception to being called a nutter, but I bought into it. 'There are a lot of strange folk out there – dangerous. Random acts carried out by people that probably don't even give it any thought.'

Mandy glowered at me. 'Helpful.' She shook her head, that hand of hers still lying on your lap. 'I can stay a few nights. I'd have you at mine, but there's no room.'

There was no way she was staying. I had my sights

set on pouring her out of here after the wine box was drained. Getting you all to myself.

You bit on your bottom lip. 'I don't think I want to stay here.'

I wanted to smash the air a high five. You didn't want to stay here; you couldn't go to Mandy's. She'd said it herself.

I needed to strike fast, before Mandy opened her gob again. I may not have finished the job as planned, but I could still use things to my advantage. It was time for me to be the one to scoop you up.

'You could come stay at mine for a few nights. I've plenty of space.'

Mandy's face contorted, out of view of yours. I had no idea why the girl had taken such an instant dislike to me, but the feeling was mutual.

You untangled your legs from beneath you and planted your feet on the floor, the almost-empty wine glass dangling in your hands between your legs. Grounding yourself, giving my proposal real thought. Mandy's hand left to drop to the sofa, lonely, just like she would be when you came to stay with me. She wasn't giving up yet, though.

'Don't be daft. You can't uproot because of it. I can stay. Until Cammy's back.'

You shook your head again. 'Until he wakes up, we don't know if he'll ever be coming back.' You wiped at your nose. 'This place *is* Cammy.'

Exactly why I wanted you out of it. 'Come stay at mine. Just until you know what's happening, or at least until you feel safe again.'

We could be safe together. The same way you'd made me feel after years of being exposed, of being looked at, prodded and gossiped about.

You looked at me, Mandy forgotten. 'I don't know. I mean . . . are you sure?'

You *did* know. So did I. It took all my resolve not to beat my chest. Tarzan: the rugged hero Beth wanted to be with. Me. Not Mandy.

You stood, not confirming anything, and went to refill your glass. I took the chance to stare Mandy down, to let her know that the confirmation would come.

Round One to me, which was enough for now.

Because I intended to make you feel so safe, you'd never want to leave.

Chapter 46

'This is bullshit.' Lewis balled one hand into a fist and punched it into the palm of the other. 'I'm not married and thinking of getting it on with someone else, and I don't have sprogs. I don't have anyone I feel responsible for, and I'm not addicted to drink or drugs. I live with my ma. *My ma*, for fuck's sake. And I've no fucking idea what I'm doing here. Why I'm listening to all this shit.' Lewis lifted his arms wide, palms to the ceiling.

The voice booming from the corner of the room, louder than ever, made them all turn. 'Try again, Lewis.'

Lewis stared at the blinking red light. 'Fuck you.'

Bill spoke. 'Lewis?'

His syrupy voice made Lewis want to gag.

'Lewis, just do as he says. We're not here to judge.' Bill stood, tucking his hands into his pockets. 'You said yourself that what I told you isn't the end of the world.' Bill shrugged. 'And you're right, it's not.' Bill turned to Jen. 'And, Jen, of course her story is heartbreaking, but she hasn't done anything to harm anyone intentionally. Not as far as I can see.'

Bill looked back at Lewis. 'But, regardless of that, he wants us to tell each other our secrets. Things we ourselves are ashamed of, no matter what anyone else thinks. So why don't we all just do that? Then try and work out why. Try our best to get out of here.'

Lewis tightened his lips to a thin, straight line, still glaring at the camera. The challenge in his eyes faltering as the invisible voice spoke again.

'Yes, Lewis. Tell your story. Or I show them. You know what I'm talking about.'

Lewis's stomach turned, having known why he was here all along. As soon as Jen mentioned bloody mistakes. Hoping he was wrong. Aware there was no way of him being wrong, not when he lived every day in the shadow of those mistakes. Unable to stop making them. Even after everything that had happened. Knowing full well why no one came near him. Hating himself right now for the hurt he felt that Mitchell hadn't been real. That he'd dared to believe he might have a friend. Someone who didn't know. Finally.

But Mitchell had known all along. He'd clearly seen the video splashed all over social media. Posted by people who didn't understand him. Those same ones who had made what he'd done into something dirty.

And to think he'd thought this guy understood him . . . What a fucking joke. Lewis shifted in his chair, turning away from the camera, his trainers squeaking against one another as the speaker boomed again.

'Tell them, Lewis.'

Lewis spat at the floor, wiping his chin as he looked anywhere but at Jen or Bill. 'Jesus Christ . . . I got caught talking to girls online. All right?' He glowered at the floor. The voice expected before he heard it.

'No, Lewis. The *whole* story.'

Lewis spat again, phlegm landing at Bill's feet, the old boy looking like he might go for him. He swallowed down what was left in his mouth. 'You want the whole story? There's fuck-all to tell. Nothing to say other than I'm attracted to girls. Girls younger than me.'

Lewis turned to Jen's stare and held it, seeing the slow curl to her lip, probably thinking about her daughter, whatever her name was. Bill's eyes narrowing, fists clenching and unclenching.

Lewis shrugged. 'Do I *want* to be? Attracted to them, I mean . . . The number of times I've been battered because of it, the way my ma speaks to me about it. My own brother attacked me; won't let me see my niece.'

Jen didn't disguise the uncertainty in her voice. Uncertainty laced with disgust. 'When you say younger, do you mean younger than you, or underage? . . . Kids?'

'Underage legally but not kids. I'm not one of those sick fuckers who go after toddlers and that. Anyway, I was just talking to them. Nothing else. Turns out I had some nosey fuckers tracking me online. Every girl I thought I was talking to was actually some bloke.'

Lewis tutted. 'Bastards turned up at my door. Online vigilantes they call them. Stuck cameras in my face. In my ma's face. But that wasn't enough for them – wrecking my life, bringing shame to my ma's door. Nah, they had to post it on their website. On YouTube. The footage and all the conversations they'd monitored. Sent the whole fucking lot to the police.'

Bill's voice had lost its sugar when he spoke now. 'What happened after the police?'

Lewis studied Bill's face. All that guff he'd said about no judgement. What a pile of shite. 'Nowt. Nada. Cos I didn't do anything. Never touched them. Talked to them. That was it.'

Lewis leaned back in his chair, its front legs lifting from the floor. 'Laugh of it is, there's supposed to be all this understanding these days. Takes all sorts, or so they say. But me? Something I can't help? Something I was born with? I'm just fucking scum.'

Lewis looked at Jen and Bill in turn, waiting for that same understanding they seemed so keen to give one another.

Getting nothing.

Chapter 47

Then

YOU NEVER DID GO home. Cammy, as I could now affectionately call him eighteen months later, had not been the same man when he came round from that coma.

He never made a return to uni or to your flat. Back living with his parents, who were basically his carers. You called him from time to time. He seemed genuinely happy for you, that you'd made it into the career that he hadn't. He never asked to talk to me on one of your calls. I got that. I'd pissed on his patch royally, and now you were mine.

I had been promoted to Store Manager at the coffee shop, or at least I had finally been officially recognized for a job I'd been doing since before we met. Not that it mattered. That was nothing but a cover. Casey Carter needed a job and Casey Carter had got a job.

I knew that as we had a home with no mortgage, and enough money in the bank to be able to sleep at night for a long time to come, we had nothing to worry about.

Not that *you* knew that. I didn't want you being with me for anything else but me.

Of course, you'd asked straight away, that first night you ever came to mine, how I could possibly afford a home like that with what I earned as a barista. I didn't take offence. I knew that questions would be asked.

I told you a lie that would become our truth. I told you how one of the carers at the home had taken a particular shine to me. An old woman nearing retirement when I hit my fifteenth birthday. More of a shine than I'd realized, in fact: when I turned eighteen I found out she was a spinster and would be leaving me 100 per cent of her will. That she'd chosen me. Not the home. Me.

I thought it the greatest story. It gave hope to the sad childhood I'd sold you. It showed I was the most loveable amongst all those other kids. That the woman had seen something in me that she'd failed to see in others. I wanted you to see I was special, that you were right to love me.

You never questioned that story. Why would you? You trusted me completely. We were happy. You were happy. You were loving your job at Aberdeen Royal Infirmary, and you were settling in well.

Everything was good. Except for Mandy. The woman who didn't know when to give up, the same one who had followed you there. The two of you ending up working on the same ward. Mandy had been victorious in Round Two. I had to give her that.

You spent endless hours together on that ward and I endured endless hours listening to you talk about her.

So, it was a bit ironic when she told you that she thought you spent too much time with me. Expected, but ironic.

You started to worry that she might be right. You were like that. You cared what people thought. You cared in general. It's why you wanted to be a nurse. It's one of the many things I loved about you.

I got that too. I could see why you might give those concerns time. We were young, it had been a whirlwind. You'd moved in temporarily after what happened to Cammy, and you'd never moved back out. I'd spent the last year and a half being your world. But Mandy couldn't know what we had.

Not that I ever said it out loud, or that I would. But, in my opinion, it was Mandy who didn't deserve your time. She wasn't worthy of your care in particular, yet you thought of her like a sister. I tried to understand that too – I did. Being far from home, you were forced to try to build a family. I could support that. But you had chosen one of the ugly sisters, not realizing that you were her Cinderella and that she didn't want you going to the ball.

Or at least, she didn't want you with me.

We rarely saw one another, Mandy and I. Both of us living vicariously through you. I knew her innermost workings, but I knew she didn't know mine. How could she, when you were only able to tell her what I was willing to reveal to you?

She and I tolerated one another on your fortnightly wine nights at my home. On my home turf, I made sure she took her turn of buying the wine and I made sure I drank my share. But we did not warm to one another. Let's just say we thawed enough to keep you from noticing.

You said she was nice, she was funny, she was hard-working, she drank too much wine at home on her own. She was alone, she was damaged, she was anxiety-ridden. Alone because – long before you ever met her – her boyfriend had cheated on her with her ex-best friend. Damaged because she'd never recovered from their betrayal. Anxious because she spent her time obsessing about them. Stalking them online, torturing herself with pictures of their happy little life together.

You told me all of this. All the little details and how Mandy had so much to offer as a friend, how any guy would be lucky to have her. I'd keep a straight face and nod understandingly.

You fretted over her problems like they were your own, enabling her by listening to her updates on her ex-boyfriend's and her ex-best friend's social media posts. I never dared to say that maybe there was a good reason that they were both exes. I had nothing but respect for the guy for running at full pelt from the bitch, making sure to take her best mate over the finishing line with him.

Mandy was our third wheel, but it was me who she went out of her way to make feel that way. That's why no one was more shocked than I was, that night she tried to kiss me in the kitchen.

Brushing past me to reach for the bottle opener as I refilled the crisp bowl. Taking my surprised turn towards her as some show of encouragement from me, pinning me against the worktop with her hips before planting those poisonous lips on mine.

Of course, I pushed her off, just as you were flushing the loo in our downstairs toilet. The loo that you and I had christened together the second night you moved in.

Mandy thought my rebuff was out of fear of being caught. How wrong could a person be? How wrong could I have been? All that time she'd been a bitch, and it turned out it was out of jealousy. You had something she wanted. And I had thought she wanted you.

I was torn whether to tell you. She was your best friend. It would break your heart that she was no friend at all. Instead, I made it my mission to find out exactly what Mandy was all about. There wasn't much work required before being surprised, yet not surprised, to find out the ex and ex-best pal who had spurned her were as real as my supposed foster-home inheritance.

After that little find, I made sure I was never there again for those wine nights. Taking on extra late shifts at the cafe, telling you that we were short-staffed. Two of those wine nights passed – a month – before it started. Little jokes at my expense. Barbed comments from the lovely Mandy about how I followed you like a little puppy. That I was a bit strange. That I was smothering, controlling.

I knew because I'd set up a camera just above the curtain pole in our front room. Already in training for a future job I didn't yet know that I'd have.

I suspected you wouldn't take her words seriously, but still, I worried that you didn't put her right, that you didn't fight my case hard enough.

I mean, how could I be some needy little puppy one minute and some controlling monster the next? I was as loyal as a puppy, for sure. Controlling? In no other way other than I liked to make sure you were happy, safe, that no one was taking advantage of you, that no one was ever going to hurt you.

And I knew that sooner or later, Mandy would.

Chapter 48

Jen wanted to smack Lewis's smarmy face. A hard slap for his constant shitty attitude but also at the thought of what someone like him might do to Daisy, given half the chance. The room had fallen silent after he'd finished talking, no one sure what to say to any of it.

Bill stopped walking, something he'd been doing since Lewis had gone silent. As he'd skirted the stone walls, his eyes flickering back and forth to the camera above, he reminded Jen of a caged animal. Perhaps he could be as unpredictable as one too.

Daisy. Was she safe? Did Tom have her? Could Jen trust that everything would be OK, if she followed this maniac's rules? If they found the answers he was supposedly looking for? A man who thought it normal to bring three strangers together, under duress, with the threat of exposing their innermost shame, bringing them *underground* to expose it.

She couldn't trust anything. Or any-*one*. But where did that leave her? The panic that she'd fought to keep down earlier was rising again. 'What if he has no intention of letting us out of here?' She hadn't wanted to say it out loud, but she couldn't keep the thought from escaping her mouth.

Bill reacted first. Calm, steady Bill. 'That can't happen. As we've already said, people will be looking for us.'

Jen shook her head. 'When? After Daisy has been left at school, crying and scared? Bill, it's probably been so long now. I can only assume Tom has her, that they're looking for me right now.'

Tears of frustration and fear collected at the corner of her eyes. 'Is Tom thinking the worst of me, what he's probably been fearing all along? That I've finally given in – surrendered to the drink, all the way? Somewhere on some bender, only caring about the next drink?'

Jen turned to Bill. 'What about Trish? How long before she tries to do something that puts her in danger? Before she cooks something, leaving that stove on? Or tries to get out of the house and succeeds? How long before Simon realizes she's all alone?'

She looked to Lewis. 'And you? Who sounds like his family hates him, that they'd be better off without you here. Are they even going to care that you're gone?' She saw what little light there was in Lewis's eyes fade, hating herself for the venom pouring from her mouth, as acidic as the vodka she poured down her throat every day. Desperate for that drink. Always that fucking drink.

Panic and self-hatred gathered in the centre of her gut, mixing with rage now. Rage that bubbled up into her throat, refusing to be held down.

She spun on her heels towards the camera. 'And you.

We've all told you our shit, like you asked. You haven't said a word since. Nothing!' Shouting, aware of Bill staring at her, of Lewis's stunned but fucking-impressed face. *Impressed*. Which only made her angrier. She didn't want or need the approval of someone like him, but she couldn't stop, her eyes back on that camera, on *him* – the guy behind the voice. 'What's your story? Huh? What the fuck is this all about?'

Her heart raced, her right eye twitching with adrenaline, lack of food, her body missing alcohol, fear, the shame that she was here because of her own weakness. That her daughter was potentially alone because she couldn't stop putting the drink to her lips, not even after Riley.

She ran and grabbed her chair, spinning around with it, the seat flying through the air with her. Lewis ducked.

Bill shouted: 'Jen!' He rushed to her, his hand cupping her elbow. She shrugged him off, racing towards the camera, wishing she could just reach up and smash its lens; putting the chair beneath it instead, stepping up on to it, not taking time to balance herself before reaching to the camera, wanting to pull it from the wall above the door, to drag him and his watching eyes, his patronizing voice, to the ground with her.

She grunted like a wild animal as her outstretched fingers grabbed above her head at the camera, falling short as she tried and tried again, up on her tiptoes, as Bill came to steady her, holding her legs, probably aware that to fight her efforts would be pointless.

'Come here, you bastard.' Stretching up, her body lengthening in the process, the plastic coverall lifting up higher and higher. Bill's hands moving upwards as she reached, trying to find her centre, fighting to balance her, the coverall bunching up above her waist, his cold fingers meeting the bare skin at her stomach.

Jen flinched as he touched it, recoiling from the camera like a snake after its strike. She pushed his hands away, off her skin, and jumped down from the chair. Her face burned as she crumbled to the ground, letting her tears flow. A half-hearted attempt to pull the coverall down over her stomach, knowing there was no point.

Bill and Lewis still staring at the plastic where her skin had been exposed.

Chapter 49

Then

Mandy walked into the coffee shop on a Thursday evening. I sensed her before I saw her – she brought a chill that lasted long after the door had closed behind her.

I was finishing up serving a regular, one of three customers who were in the shop. The day had dragged. I was counting down the time until I finished my shift; willing the minutes to pass even faster, now that she had appeared.

She smiled, a knowing smile, probably thinking I'd been avoiding her because I'd apparently wanted her when she tried it on with me that night. Her inflated ego struggling to accept that there might be any other outcome.

'Join me for a cuppa?' She looked me in the eye for that little bit too long.

I looked down to the counter. 'I'm kinda busy.'

She looked around at the three occupied tables. 'They all look like you've seen to them.'

And there was no mistaking that's what she wanted too. For me to see to her. For me to return that kiss from all those nights ago, willingly and with passion. To bend her over one of those tables and cheat on the love of my life. To betray her best friend. She was the worst kind of scum. I hated that she was there, and I detested what she was doing to Beth. What she was doing to our memories here. The place we met.

She ducked her head, trying to get eye contact. 'I've just been to see Cameron.'

I looked up because there was something in the way she said it. With him being down in Dundee, you didn't 'just' go and see him. Mandy and Beth had seen him two, maybe three, times since his accident. There was a hint of some threat, meant to strengthen my decision whether to sit with her or not.

I stopped scrubbing at the clean countertop. 'How is he?'

'Not the Cameron we knew, as you know.'

As I know. 'Such a shame.'

Mandy picked up a pack of shortbread from the display, flipped it over in her hand and put it back down. 'Amazing they've not found his attacker.'

I rearranged some steel jugs on the machine behind me that were already where they needed to be. 'Doubt they will now, after all this time.'

'It was always going to be kind of difficult when he was dressed all in black and with a hood tight around his face.'

I turned. She looked into my face, searching for something. I came out from behind the counter and led her towards a table, making sure it wasn't the one where Beth and I had sat.

She smiled, the gesture sending a chill down my spine. 'Not so busy after all.'

I hated her as I sat opposite her.

'He really opened up this time I visited. With Beth not there. I guess he never wanted to scare her, or maybe he wanted to protect her.'

'Protect her from what?' I looked down at the wooden table between us.

'He doesn't remember much about that night, but he was sure there was no one behind him. Reckons someone had been hiding out there, waiting on him. Like, whoever-it-was knew he'd be coming; that he'd take that shortcut home, at that time.'

'Scary shit.'

'Yeah.' She took her time ripping open the sugar sachet.

I felt her stare, hot on the top of my head.

'It was tragic for him, but lucky that Beth had somewhere to go so she felt safe – you know, when it was clear Cameron wouldn't be coming back.'

'I guess.'

She wanted more from me; I could feel it.

'He doesn't remember much about that night, but he remembers you. And I remember his chats to me about you, before that.'

'Chats? The guy barely knew me.' I stared at the spoon as she over-stirred her coffee.

'He knew enough. We both knew enough.'

My heart thudded. Did they know my real name? That I was The Butcher's Boy? Did they know I'd not been entirely honest with Beth?

'Knew what?' It took me all my time not to close my eyes against whatever was coming.

'That you're too into Beth.'

I breathed out. 'I'm *too* into Beth? What the fuck does that even mean?'

Mandy shrugged, going for the silent-assassin approach. 'I don't mean as in love; I mean as in an unhealthy way. You're jealous. Controlling. Scary, sometimes.'

I frowned. 'This, from *Cameron*?' He definitely didn't get to be called *Cammy* today.

'Yeah.'

'A guy who was clearly obsessed with Beth, but didn't have the balls to come out and say it?'

Mandy smirked. 'You think he said what he did about you out of jealousy?'

I tutted. 'He was an arsehole from the first time I met him.'

She laughed this time. 'Funny, he said the exact same about you.'

'Then what's your argument?'

She stared at me. 'My argument is that there's a difference.'

'How?'

She lifted the cup to her mouth, sipped, taking her time to place it back down in its saucer. 'Let's just say, I've never heard Beth say Cameron's too full-on, but she's said it plenty about you. That, and the fact I don't like you.'

That, I wasn't expecting.

She sat back, thinking she was the one in control now. 'There's something about you that doesn't sit right with me. I can't put my finger on it, but I don't think you're good for Beth. I don't think you're right for her.'

I grunted. 'I don't think that's for you to decide, and it's a bit rich given you tried to make a move on me.'

She flicked at her hair. 'Not because I like your arse. *Please*.'

I wanted to pull her head to the table by that same hair, but she wasn't done.

'I wanted to test you. I needed to see if you'd bite.'

I shook my head. 'And I didn't. I pushed you away. I've avoided you ever since. I'd say, I passed.'

She shrugged again. 'Maybe it was the wrong test. You're obsessed with her. I've watched the way you are with her, the way you've slowly steered her towards you and taken her away from everyone else. From every-*thing* else.'

'Bullshit.'

'I don't think so. I think it was you that night. I think you attacked and injured Cameron. I think you're a dangerous son of a bitch.'

My turn to smile. 'So dangerous that you've come here alone, to confront me with all this bullshit?'

She leaned forward. 'You don't scare me, Casey. I've got your number. Beth can't see it, but I can. I want you to leave her alone.'

'Why not go to the police with all this, if you really believe it was me?'

Mandy looked around the cafe. 'Because I have no proof. Besides, I wouldn't take out the bottom of her world like that. It won't change what Cameron has become. But I'm willing to bet you have an all-black ensemble stuffed at the back of your wardrobe somewhere.'

I stood, done with the crap spewing from her mouth. 'I can't believe you're coming to me with this shit. You need to leave.'

She leaned back, crossed her legs. 'No, it's you who should leave. Leave Beth the hell alone. Tell her it's over, let me be the one to pick up the pieces.'

Her face had the decency to register shock as I pulled her up by her arm, not caring about the customers who turned to look. 'I'll never leave Beth – you'd better accept that. I think there's more to your feelings for Beth than you're making out. I think that's the real problem.' She tried to tug her arm free of my grasp, to stop me from removing her.

I continued to march her to the door, my voice a hiss in her ear. 'You're a sick fuck with a fake ex and a fake ex-best pal, all engineered to gain Beth's trust and sympathy – all this depths-of-despair shit you peddle to her.'

Her face paled, her mouth not denying her lies as she gathered herself and turned as we reached the door. 'One day you're going to trip up and I'm going to be there to catch Beth when you fall.'

I pushed her out the door and shut it hard behind her, already knowing as I watched her leave that the only person that needed to take a fall now . . . was her.

Chapter 50

Jen was back in her chair, tears dried. Docile. Complacent. Doing what was wanted. What was needed. Calmed and about to give the camera, to give *him*, what he'd been waiting for.

She swallowed. 'We've all said how he approached us. Lewis, you in the street with a promise of friendship. Bill, unaware he was even there. Me, the phone. What we haven't said is exactly how he got us here.'

Jen could feel Bill staring at her, as he had been since he'd asked about the scar on her stomach. The one that she'd exposed when she'd reached up towards the camera. Nothing but a C-section scar, she'd said – all she was going to say – avoiding Bill's gaze as she spoke again, doing her best to stay on point. 'Maybe that's what he wants. The story in full before he gives us the ending.' She took a deep breath. 'I'll go first.

'I told you about Riley, about how I blamed myself for his death. I told you about the phone.' She looked to the camera. 'What I didn't tell you is that I'd been drinking all that morning. When the phone was posted. Drinking since I'd woken up. Hiding it in my coffee, in the same old insulated travel mug. Thinking no one would ever know. My tolerance is to be commended.'

Jen felt as bitter as she sounded. She scratched at her forearm, wanting to dig in hard enough to draw blood. 'Tom was on an early shift, already long gone to work. Daisy and I were running late. I was going to walk . . . It started raining. Heavy rain. Daisy went to put on her wellies, begged to take the car – it's only a five-minute drive.'

Jen crossed her arms, hugging herself. 'So, I took the keys. I drove, sipping coffee laced with vodka as my daughter sat in the car beside me. So in need of that bloody drink that I didn't notice the little boy crossing the road up ahead, outside the school, as I drank. I swerved at the last minute, missing him by inches and hitting the kerb. I shot my arm out in front of Daisy, the cup banging against her chest, droplets splashing on to her jacket. Congratulating myself on that gut reaction as I withdrew my hand and put the cup back in the holder.' Jen rubbed at her eyes. 'Totally denying the truth in my head that I could've killed that little boy. That I could've killed Daisy. That every time I put that cup to my lips, I was endangering her. Risking my marriage, my own life, everything I had.'

Jen sobbed. 'The school mums saw that accident. Came running to see we were OK. To comfort us.' Her face tightened. 'Only making me feel worse. *He* saw that accident too. Saw the boy. And my daughter. He took videos of the whole thing.' Jen closed her eyes, remembering the footage. 'He must've planted a camera inside my car. Must've been at the school itself, waiting and watching us. Probably been waiting a good while, knowing something was bound to happen eventually. Something I knew deep down myself but wouldn't admit.' She sighed. 'The videos he sent . . . of my face up close inside the car, from a distance outside the car. Filming the whole thing as it happened. He sent me those videos on that phone he posted.'

Bill frowned. 'But it could've been nothing but an innocent accident. He wasn't to know you'd been drinking. He couldn't prove that.'

Jen shook her head. 'No doubt about that when he sent me the photo – of me with a forty-ouncer of vodka in my kitchen, pouring it into the coffee-machine jug. The picture time-stamped. Me wearing the same clothes as later in the videos, also time-stamped. He'd been in my garden, metres from me and Daisy, taking photos through my kitchen window.'

Lewis and Bill stared at her.

'Filming us going about our day. Taking pictures of my life when I thought no one was watching.'

She wiped at the tears falling again. 'Of course, I didn't know that. Not when I went home after the accident and told myself that was *it* – that what I was doing had to stop. That the drinking had to stop. I went and got all the bottles I'd hidden throughout the house, took them out to the garage, and hid them again. But I didn't empty them. I didn't get rid of them. Told myself I'd go make soup to calm down – good old bloody soup. That I'd take the bottles to recycling later. And then that phone came through my door. Into my home. On to my mat. Ringing.'

Chapter 51

Then

I NEEDED TO WAIT, but not too long. Not long enough to risk her poisoning you against me – at least, not any more than she'd already tried to. But long enough for her to be the maker of her own demise. I knew it wouldn't take long. She didn't disappoint.

In the weeks after our encounter at the cafe, Mandy upped her game to command your attention. Not threatened by the fact I'd told her I knew what she was up to, most likely believing that she supposedly had enough on me to keep me silent.

News of her ex-boyfriend's hugely romantic proposal to her ex-best friend really ramped up her need for your support. You willingly gave that support and I allowed it, because I knew it wouldn't be for much longer.

I watched her when she was alone, when she was in company. Always perfectly happy until she was in *your* company, when she'd have you believe her world was crumbling around her. Scary how well she could turn it on and off. I never told you that, though. I never said a word. It would pay to let her play out the drama, to garner your sympathy.

The night I showed up at her maisonette, I left my mobile phone lying on the sofa of our home. Knowing that, on your shift break, you might want to see where I was. It was comforting for us to see where the other was; sometimes that was enough to feel connected. So, you would check, you might even phone, but you'd know I was most likely soaking in the bath, as I often did at that time – and that there was no way I would've gone anywhere without that phone. Never. It would be like leaving you.

I knew I'd be back in time for your return home from work, time to run the bath, apparently forgetting to drain it – something that drove you mad but you'd still laugh – and more than enough time to wet a towel and dump it by the washing machine. No one to say I had ever been out, and all once I'd paid Mandy a little visit.

When Mandy failed to invite me in on that visit, I burst through her door and she finally looked scared. Realizing at last who she was dealing with. Especially when I took her by the throat and shoved her backwards, kicking her front door closed behind me, moving at speed down her small, narrow hallway, her tiny bare feet treading air, trying to find ground.

She fought hard as I spun her to the ground, pinning her there with the weight of my knee against her back as I bound her arms and legs. Not too tight, not enough to leave any marks. Just enough to keep her there, where I wanted her. Until I was ready.

She lay there trussed up, belly down, looking like she was skydiving. I knew she'd be in the air soon enough.

She'd ripped the place out when she bought it. Wanted the best of everything – down to the bloody wooden beams she'd added to the ceiling: the 'cottage feel', she called it – in the middle of a cramped residential street in the Bridge of Don suburb of the city. Still, as I looped the rope around the central beam on her living-room ceiling, I was thankful for that home décor choice.

The noose was a thing of beauty. She squealed like a pig when she saw it, wriggling like one for the slaughter as I dragged her up on to the oak side table that seemed picked especially for the moment, so perfect was its height for the task ahead. The noose dropped around her neck just as perfectly, tightening as easily as if I was some pro. Only then did I untie her arms and ankles. Once it was too late. Once she had nowhere to go.

The more she struggled, the tighter that noose got. Still, she thrashed, knocking the table the way she would've planned to if she'd been the one to engineer her end. Knocking it, but not quite hard enough. It was the same story with me and my hit to Cameron's head – not hard enough. But that wouldn't happen this time.

I looked up into her eyes as I kicked the table on to its side, clear of her dangling legs. I watched those legs kick until they stopped; her wide, terrified eyes until they bulged, trying hard to escape their sockets. Still trying even after the light had left them.

Then I dropped to the floor, watching her white body sway like a pendulum. Until her time finally came to an end.

And I saw Mum again, hanging there on that hook.

Chapter 52

Bill was twisting his wedding ring again. 'But you wanted to stop it, Jen. You wanted the drinking to stop.'

His fingers stopped fiddling. 'That stuff I told you about ... The whole online thing. Talking to that woman. It all started after a particularly bad day. A day when things had been awful with Trish.' Bill looked at them both. 'You don't need all the details. Let's just say I wasn't in a good place. I just wanted it all to go away. I was needing something. A distraction. Trish was in bed – finally. I was downstairs at my computer.'

He looked at Jen. 'I spend a lot of evenings there, watching old programmes, listening to music. The Beatles, mostly. Loved them, back in the day. But that night, sitting there, it was like someone was trying to give me the answer.'

Bill sighed. 'I didn't mean to. It sounds pathetic, but I didn't really think about what I was doing when I clicked the link.'

Lewis looked up. 'Link?'

Bill closed his eyes. 'To a dating site. Senior Singles.'

Lewis laughed. Bill's eyes shot open, giving him a withering glare. 'Glad you find it funny.'

Lewis shook his head, still smiling, but he shut up.

Bill looked back at Jen, needing the support she was giving him in her features as she listened. 'I only wanted someone to talk to. Like I said, distraction. Friendship. Anyway, I got chatting – to Norma. We chatted for a week. A lot. Before she asked to meet up.' Bill dragged a hand through his hair. 'I knew it was a crazy thing to do. Not only what I was doing behind Trish's back, but what I was doing to our marriage and what I'd be doing to my son. Not just if he found out I was meeting another woman, but if he discovered I'd left Trish alone.'

Bill looked to the floor, his eyes filling as he got up from his seat, moving away from Jen as she lifted an arm from where she sat, trying to reach his hand.

He shook his head. 'Please . . . I don't deserve the comfort. Anyway, I agreed to meet. Norma suggested Duthie Park. That we meet at her car. She told me what to look out for and I said I'd see her there.'

Bill took a deep breath, trying to gather the strength to carry on, and Jen spoke. 'Bill, it was friendship. That's all it was – company. Anyone would understand that, maybe even your son.'

Bill looked at her, the tears gathering in his eyes threatening to run down his withered cheeks. 'That's just it. I don't think even I can be sure that it wasn't going to be anything more than friendship. I didn't tell the woman about Trish. Why didn't I?' Bill stared at Jen through his tears. Taking a moment before carrying on.

'When I arrived at the car park, I didn't see the car at first. Not until after I'd parked up myself and got out. It was tucked away in the corner, at the back of the park cafe. I went over but couldn't see her in the driver's seat, or by the car. So, I went right up to the car, just to be sure. He came out of nowhere. Next thing I knew, I was waking up here.'

Bill let himself sob, not caring about Lewis and his insensitivity, only realizing now how stupid he'd been.

'I can only presume that Norma never existed. That he somehow knew I was on that site. Because what's the alternative? That he followed me there? How would he have known I was going to meet her? What she looked like? What car she was driving? But, worse still, if he did, has he done something to her too?'

Bill slumped in his chair. 'This sounds terrible, but I have no real feelings for the woman – I hadn't even met her, if she is even real. But to think I might somehow be responsible for her coming to any harm.'

Bill wiped at his face. 'The worst thing is that telling you all this makes me want nothing more than to see my wife. To see Trish right now. To make sure she's OK. To hold her, tell her I'm sorry.' Bill was sobbing again, not caring, letting the tears flow freely. 'To tell her that I love her. More than anything. No matter what's happening to her – to us. That being here has made me realize more than ever that all I want is *her*. To look after her. Her and our life together.'

Chapter 53

Then

You were broken after the loss of Mandy, but I was there, the glue to help put you back together. To make you whole again.

You were so wrapped up in your grief that you were unaware of my sleepless nights. Of my tossing and turning, convinced I'd somehow left something to chance, that everything I'd done to stage Mandy's death as a suicide, the lengths I'd gone to in order to leave no trace, would somehow not be enough. That they would come for me, and I'd lose you after all. Hoping you'd tell them you could vouch for me. The bath, the phone tracker. But I needn't have worried. The doorbell never rang and, after the official cause of death by suicide was recorded, I dared to breathe again.

I was breathing for both of us, as hers was a death that hit you hard, but it only made you more grateful for me. For what we had. You raged that Mandy was robbed of that connection. You began to build your own hate campaign against her ex-partner and her former friend. I didn't have the heart to tell you the truth.

You spent your own sleepless nights immediately after her death wanting to go to the police, to tell them this wasn't as simple as suicide. That Mandy taking her life was tantamount to murder, and that her ex-boyfriend and ex-friend were wholly responsible.

But in the cold light of day, you knew. You knew that they could never be held responsible for something she'd done to herself, no matter the reason she'd done it.

You jacked yourself up for the funeral, so sure that they would attempt to show their faces. Your hyped-up conviction for your cause had no place to go when it seemed they didn't even have the decency to try. So, you waited. Waited until you were able to approach her parents at the wake. Parents you'd never met but who you felt deserved to know the truth. You wanted to make it easier on them, to give them a reason for the senseless loss of their only child. I watched you pull them aside. I let it happen. Better that it came from them than from me.

It's fair to say that your world spun on its axis when they told you they had no knowledge of either person ever existing. That Mandy had never had a sweetheart, that her best friend had left their friendship when she moved to Australia with her parents.

That news, that awful truth and all it meant, only tilted you further towards me. As always, I was there to catch you. Your one constant, your pillar of strength, as everything else you knew crumbled around you. You could trust no one. Not the randoms – whoever or wherever they were out there, the ones who had attacked Cammy so ruthlessly down that back alley; not even Mandy, the person who you thought closest to you, before you met me. Your best friend, your confidante – the one who had your back. A girl who told a lie so big it burned a hole right through your world, leaving you wondering whether you ever really knew her, questioning exactly why she had taken her life. Ultimately, pondering whether all those years of friendship had been fake.

You were left wondering if anything she'd ever said about me was true. Clinging to me now because I was the only truth you knew.

I did what I felt was the only way to show you how much I was there for you – to be sure you knew that I loved you, that I would never leave you like all those others. I proposed. And you accepted without hesitation.

In the weeks after, I would lie awake at night fretting that maybe I'd taken it too far – made my proposal too soon; that one day you might feel too hemmed in by me. That you might grow strong again. That I might lose you.

I was knee-deep in thinking of ways to make sure that would never happen when the solution presented itself to us, with no input from me. Well, that wasn't entirely true, because it was precisely because of my input that it had happened.

We were going to have a baby, and I couldn't have been happier.

Chapter 54

Lewis glowered at the camera. 'This is like something out of that old Jeremy-fucking-Kyle show. You two with your sob stories and regrets. Which I guess makes me the baddy, the guy that storms the stage. The one who isn't sorry, who doesn't care what the fuckers in the audience think.'

Lewis stood. 'I don't give a shit whether I tell you why I'm here or not. Why? Because I have fuck-all to lose. I don't have some wife to save, or a kid. I don't even have a fucking life. Not one anyone would want anyway.'

Pacing now. 'And this isn't some sob story – it's just fact. I ended up here because he wanted to be my mate.' Lewis kicked at the ground 'There. There you go. I was that fucking needy for someone, anyone, to like me.' He turned to the camera. 'Happy now?'

Nothing, until Bill spoke. 'How did he get you here?'

Lewis spat. 'I told you. He came up to me in the street. I'd been watching a girl at the school just down from me. During the day. A primary school. Taking photos of her on my phone when I thought no one was watching. I had to be careful, after everything that happened. My ma would've gone apeshit if she knew I was still at it.' Lewis smoothed at the coverall.

'Anyway. Couldn't do much in broad daylight, but the other night, I was late home from the local. Lights still on in the school. Cleaners in as usual – thought that was all it would be. Except she was there too. Some after-school club. Couldn't believe my luck when I saw her coming out – all knee-high socks and gym gear, unbelievable – at least, until she disappeared into a car.' Lewis swallowed. 'Her ma picking her up, probably. I went back every night, looking for her. Then a week later, there she was. Thought my luck was maybe in. I just wanted to talk. Be up close. Get a cheap thrill, I guess . . .' Lewis paused. 'No, I ain't going to lie – I've no reason to. Nothing to be scared of now, saying maybe I would've wanted more.' He shrugged.

'Then *he* showed up. Blew my chance. But him and me got chatting. Next day he was outside my flat, inviting me to tag along to the pub. I went. Saddo? Probably. But one pint in and I was out of it. Woke up here.'

Lewis spat again – he'd finished – as Bill and Jen stared in disgust at the spittle on the stone floor between them. Jen looking like she wanted to be the one spitting. At him.

Bill cleared his throat. 'So, after all that had happened – those people at your door, the stuff all over social media, the fact no one wanted anything to do with you . . . You still didn't stop?'

Lewis tutted. 'It's not like I get to fucking choose. I

know where the truth of who I am gets me. Last time, when it all came out, it got me shouted at in the street whenever I went out. It stopped people from talking to my ma at the local shop, but not from talking behind their scabby hands as they passed by.

'It got me battered countless times too. Graffiti all over the front of our flat, across our front door. Windows broken by bricks – on the fucking top floor. No one wanted to be seen near me, no one wanted to talk to me. And I still couldn't stop. Not even to have any kind of life. And then Mitchell showed up.' Lewis shifted in his chair. 'Call me a needy fucker. I can deal with that.'

Silence stretched. Jen eventually stood up, breaking it.

'So, we've said it all. All there is to say.'

She stared at the camera, at the door. 'And still, he doesn't speak. Still, he waits. Everything we've said, everything all three of us have said, it's bad. Bad, but far from the worst. Not by any means the worst that goes on in the world every day. So, there must be more. There must be something else he wants.'

Jen's gaze dropped to Lewis, still pinned to his chair.

Watching just as his mouth began to open.

As the lights went out and the door flew open.

Chapter 55

Then

I WAS GOING TO be a dad. A chance for me to give someone something that I never had myself: a happy childhood. Security. Love. Protection. I vowed as soon as I saw those two blue lines on that stick that our child would want for nothing. That they would never come to any harm.

You weren't so sure about the prospect of parenthood. Lukewarm at the news of what was already going on inside your body. I understood that. You'd worked hard to qualify as a nurse. You were just getting started in your career.

But it wasn't just that. You were scared. You told me so one night, lying in bed. When I knew you were still awake, when I sensed you were staring at the ceiling, kept awake by your thoughts.

So many bad things had happened, you didn't dare to think that this baby could be your new beginning. Our new beginning – happy again. That you deserved to be happy. There'd been so much loss, but also the awareness that, in all that grief and loss, our whirlwind had intensified, whipping itself up into a tornado.

However, I knew there was always calm after a storm. I knew it would come. You would be ready when the time came. Born to be a mum. That caring nature of yours made for the job. They say there's a reason your pregnancy lasts nine months. It prepares you, carries you through all those crazy hormonal ups and downs, taking you from not ready, to counting down the days until you meet the life growing inside you. The life we made.

And that's what we'd done. We'd made a life together; we were going to continue making a life together. All three of us. Forever bound together.

Making certain that we were, I whisked you off to the registry office and we sealed the deal with a kiss, two rings and two witnesses. Small. Intimate. Bound. You, me and our unborn child.

We would make our union, our little world, work. I didn't need to be making coffee for a living. We had all the money we needed. I'd be the full-time dad to let you work shifts. To let you have it all. We'd bring up our kid together.

The first eight months of growing our child, you carried on working. Taking care of others, coming home to me caring for you. I had you all to myself. No more wine nights. No more Mandy. Even the calls to Cameron dwindled, the dynamic bent out of shape without Mandy, with Cameron's likely jealousy of our marriage – our growing child. The show of our commitment and love dictating his distance.

We were happy. We would continue to be happy.

There was nothing and no one to stop us now.

Chapter 56

Something clattered into the chairs in the dark. Heavy. Knocking over their empty chairs, after they'd shot up from their seats at the noise of the door opening and the sudden darkness.

The lights blazed back on, all three of them staring at the body that now lay at their feet. They jumped back as it uncurled, dragging itself up to a sitting position. Male.

Lewis growled. 'Who the fuck are you?'

Jen gasped. 'Are you OK?'

She reached down to the half-naked man, only his bottom-half clothed. Bill was close behind her. Each taking an arm either side, helping the man to his feet. Jen motioned to Lewis to pick up one of the fallen chairs to let the man sit, not missing the begrudging look on his face at her request.

The man wheezed as they lowered him into the chair. 'I'm OK. Honestly. I'm OK.'

All of them waiting. Wanting to know who the hell he was. What the hell was going on.

Jen watched as he straightened in the chair, his body pressing back against the backrest as he tried to catch his breath. Exposing his bare chest.

Jen froze as he spoke.

'Sorry, the shove to my back winded me. I'm OK. Apart from being down here, of course.'

'How long have you been here?' asked Bill.

The man looked at them all, perhaps wondering if he'd recognize any of them from somewhere. 'I've been down here a while. Don't know how long. In another room, much the same as this.'

Jen stood staring at him, trying to make sense of what she was looking at as her stomach lurched. *Were there others?* She forced herself to move. To talk. 'We were all put in here, one after the other. Were you in with other people?'

The man shook his head.

Jen spoke again, not taking her eyes from his chest, her mind working overtime. 'What's your name?'

'Danny. My name's Danny.' His breath steadier now.

'I'm Jen. This is Bill, and that there is Lewis.' Jen knelt on the ground in front of him, letting Bill fetch the fourth seat, still leaning against the wall. The spare suddenly making sense.

Bill sat and turned his attention to Danny. 'Do you know why you're here?'

Danny's eyes flitted from Bill's to the door. 'Can you tell me why *you* guys are?'

Jen was still staring at Danny's chest, waiting for his response. Wondering, as she stared, exactly why they *were* here. If they'd been wrong all along.

It could be nothing.

It could be everything.

She turned towards Bill as he spoke again, his finger pointing at Danny's bare chest as he asked him, 'How did you get that scar?'

Chapter 57

Then

I WAS LADEN WITH packs of nappies – three different sizes, because who knew what we'd need – and carrying the beige changing box with the picture of the fluffy brown teddy bear on the front that you wanted.

I told you to rest, to make the most of the four weeks' maternity leave you had before our lives would change beyond recognition. I would take care of anything needing done. I was the hunter returning to the cave, bringing my woman what she needed. What our child-to-be needed. The provider. Hunter and gatherer, bringing home the essentials for survival. Your due date close.

But you weren't waiting to throw open the front door for me, like normal. For the last three weeks, whenever I'd gone out, you'd been hovering by the window, looking out for me arriving home. Knowing I was near with that tracker. Telling me it was out of boredom, that you weren't used to sitting about all day. I laughed; told you there was no need to lie about being excited to see me.

I looked towards the front-room window, then along

to the right of it, to the kitchen window on the other side of the door. Maybe you were in the toilet. You peed so much now that I thought about getting a Portaloo strapped to your back, to balance out the weight of the ever-growing bump at your front. Our baby. I was loving that bump as much as I already loved our child. He or she would have the best childhood, the best life. They would always have two parents, and I would not only be the hunter, gatherer and provider; I would be the protector. No harm would ever come to my pack.

I dumped the shopping bags on the step, and unlocked and opened the door, expecting to hear the TV blaring in the front room. You needed the background noise, but I heard nothing but silence. My heart pounded, scenarios racing through my mind – none of them good.

Shouting your name; panic rising when you didn't reply. I found you in the front room, lying on your side on the sofa, your feet curled up beneath you, foetal. Mirroring the scans of our baby-to-be that plastered our fridge.

You looked like you'd been washed up and beached there, but I knew not to make that joke. Not when you were crying. I looked at the telly to make sure it was off. You were a ball of hormones, capable of crying at puppy adverts, but there were no puppies on the screen. Nothing on the screen but black, as dark as the smudged mascara beneath your eyes.

Only then did I notice you holding a sheet of paper to your stomach, stretching across it, wallpapering your bump.

'Is the baby OK?'

You looked up at me, said nothing. Gulping for air, crying.

Please don't let it be the baby.

Your face was ashen, red eyes making you look like you were in the grips of some illness. As scary as one of those zombies – the undead. I moved towards you – you snarled. I thought you might bare your teeth and lunge at me.

I jumped back. 'Beth?'

'Don't come near me.' Your voice like gravel, words hitting like stones. A voice I'd never heard before. A stranger, looking at me. Seeing me for the first time too. Of all the scenarios that had flown through my head, this wasn't one of them.

I was desperate, needing to fix whatever had broken you, struggling to think what that piece of paper in your hands could be. Hearing the ring of a far-off alarm bell, getting louder, shriller, as possibility niggled beneath.

The alarm screaming in my ear as you spat those four short words from your mouth.

'Welcome home, Wesley Harris.'

Chapter 58

'My scar? I got it through heart surgery.'

Jen stared at the long, pink vertical scar running down the man's chest. Danny, he'd called himself. She was willing herself to speak. Telling herself the surgery might've been a bypass. Might've been anything. She nodded, remembering Danny's question.

She gave him the short version of all their stories, as Bill and Lewis sat in silence, both looking at the scar on the man's chest as she spoke with him. Jen's mind whirring as she talked.

Danny sat still a moment before reacting to what Jen had said. 'So, you all think you're here because of things you've done?'

Jen licked at dry lips, her eyes travelling the raised welt on his bare chest. Questioning in her mind why he had been thrown in without his top. Thinking that it had to mean something; that what she was thinking, what she thought she knew, had to mean something. Feeling sick as she asked, 'What was the surgery?'

Danny searched her face, talking softly as he answered. 'Heart transplant.'

Jen didn't miss the look on Bill's and Lewis's faces as they looked from Danny's scar to her. Down towards her stomach beneath the plastic coverall. Most likely thinking back to when she'd jumped up at the camera in her rage. When they'd stared at her exposed flesh.

Jen closed her eyes against their stares. Taking a moment to breathe before she stood.

Chapter 59

Then

A SOLICITOR'S LETTER. DAD's brother; my uncle. An uncle that I hadn't seen since before my mother's murder. One of the only remaining family members who could've stepped up, who could've saved me from the care system and sheltered me from the media storm. But didn't.

He'd croaked it in his crumbling cottage on the outskirts of Aberdeen, leaving the house and three acres of land. To me.

Guilt before the grim reaper came knocking? Maybe. More likely a final 'fuck you' to my father, who he had never got on with in childhood and never visited in prison as an adult. The only other person that was left for him to leave anything to: a man rotting in prison. Which left me.

My uncle had failed to do what was right by me in life, and now he was still screwing me over in death.

'I wanted to tell you.' It sounded feeble. Nowhere near enough, standing there in front of you, our unborn child growing between us. 'It's still me, Beth. The same person you know – just a different name.'

Fear mixed with anger in your eyes. 'I don't know you. I don't know jackshit about you. Jesus, Casey. My married name isn't even your name.'

I wondered how much you'd already found out. If it was just the name. I dropped to my knees, reached for your hands, but you pushed me away. I backed off to let you stand.

'It's not just the name. You lied to me. Jesus, Casey ... *Wesley* ... whoever the hell you are. Your mother was murdered.'

I hated the way that name sounded on your lips. My name. Someone I once was, bringing me back to all those things you now knew. The wonders of Google. Everything ready and waiting to be uncovered in seconds if you knew where to look. I was losing any ground to be the one to tell you anything that was left to say, to salvage something from the shock. Fearful that the day I had always dreaded had finally arrived. I was going to lose you. Worse still, I was going to lose our child.

'Beth, please.' You paced whilst I knelt on the floor, pathetic. Begging. 'Beth, I was ashamed. Tired of being talked about, pointed at, pitied. I wanted my own life. I didn't want anything to do with my father, with what he'd done.' I stood up, shuffled towards you. 'I didn't want *you* pitying me.'

Now all I wanted *was* for you to pity me, to think I was pathetic, needy, in need of you. Whatever it took for you to forgive me, to make you stay.

You walked back to the sofa and perched on the edge, still there but ready for flight. 'It's not just this. It feels like something I've been waiting for.'

I frowned, wanting to touch your hands, scared that you might pull them away from me. 'What do you mean?'

'All of this, ever since we met, I've never felt like I've really known you, tha—'

'Beth, what are you talking about? We were meant for each other. You know me better than anyone else ever has.' I held on to your hands, tried to stop them slipping from mine as you pulled them away, just as I'd feared.

You shook your head. 'That's just it. I don't think anyone else has ever known you either. I don't think you've ever been close to anyone. What I've always meant about the intense thing – it's scary sometimes. *You're* scary.'

I stepped back from you, on to my knees, not knowing what to say, what it was that you needed me to say. Not expecting to hear what you said next. The complete change of subject throwing me.

'I thought it was about your will. The letter. It's the only reason I opened it.'

I jumped on the statement anyway, whilst my mind continued to process that you could ever fear me. 'I know that, sweetheart, and I've changed it. That's how much I love you, how much I want to be there for you – for you and our baby. Joint names on this place, everything to be left to both of you, should anything happen to me.' I moved towards you, still on my knees, stopping myself again from reaching for you. 'And now we have this cottage – and my uncle's land – we could sell it; we could do it up, we—'

'Is any of your childhood true?' Not even able to look at me.

'The care home is true. This place . . .' I looked around the room. 'This place didn't come to me from someone at the care home. It came from them – my parents. A trust fund in the bank too.'

You looked horrified. 'This isn't where they lived, is it? This isn't . . . ?'

I shook my head. 'No. Christ, no. I didn't keep the house or the butcher's. That shop became like the House of Horrors. After all the media finally left the doorstep, the local kids would dare each other to go up to the boarded-up doors and windows, to look through the letterbox. The brave ones would break in, then dare one another to stay a whole night. I never set foot in the place after the day it happened. It was decided for me that I wouldn't want it, or the house. They were right. Neither place would sell; no one wanted to live where The Butcher's Boy and his family had lived or worked. They knocked them both down, eventually.'

Your turn to look around now. 'And this?'

'Came out of the family business and the land the house sat on. It wasn't a business I wanted to continue, as you can imagine.'

'And what about since then? Have there been any more lies?'

'What do you mean?'

You looked into my eyes, like you needed to see the answer there for yourself. 'When I say I sometimes feel I don't know you, that you can be scary, I get now that maybe it's because of what happened to you. But I need to ask you, I need you to tell me the truth . . .'

Your eyes glistened, the pulse beating in your neck.

You, the one scaring *me* right now. 'What? Ask me. Just say it, Beth.'

'Did you have anything to do with Cameron or Mandy?'

I looked deep into your eyes, almost believing that, with our child growing inside you, and the fact that all we had was each other, you'd forgive me for the truth. That you'd forgive me for anything. Almost.

My answer played on my lips, but I hadn't voiced it before you added, 'Did you have anything to do with . . . your mother?'

The moment gone. The answer swallowed and regurgitated into something palatable. Because everyone has secrets. Everyone. For good reason. A tale they want the world to know – that allows them acceptance. Things that they hide; things *I* would continue to hide – all for you. For you to accept me. And yet, you would still never know the real strength of my love.

You stared into my eyes. 'I need to know everything. *Please.*'

I would give you what I could, more than I'd ever given anyone. But I wouldn't give you the truth. I couldn't.

'Beth, sweetheart.'

'Casey? You must tell me *all* of it.'

Casey. You called me Casey.

'I had nothing to do with my mother's death.'

You breathed a sigh of relief.

Suddenly, there was hope.

Chapter 60

JEN LIFTED THE PLASTIC coverall, not caring that she stood in nothing but a nappy beneath. The room was silent. All eyes on her. She looked down, holding the coverall up with one hand, using the other to trace the red scar with her forefinger. The scar looking like a large three-pointed star, akin to the Mercedes-Benz company logo.

She looked at each of them in turn. 'Bill, Lewis, when you saw this, you were probably wondering what caused it. You'll remember what I said about being told if I didn't stop drinking, I'd die. I nearly did. I would have, if it hadn't been for this. After Daisy was born.'

Jen stood there under the glare of their stares, Danny's too, before she dropped her coverall back down. 'An ugly-looking scar, I admit, but with the beauty of a gift beneath it. A gift that saved my life. A liver transplant.'

Bill whispered. 'A second chance at life.'

Jen nodded. 'One that I grasped with both hands at the time, one that I now piss over every day, every time I put that drink to my lips.'

She looked at Danny. At Lewis. Both wide-eyed. Surprised as she looked at Bill, to see the expression on his face. Her eyes never leaving his as he stood. His face chalk-white, legs visibly shaking.

Jen thinking he was about to offer her comfort.

Dread filling her instead when he started to lift his own coverall.

Chapter 61

Then

That's what we called her, our daughter. Hope.

Because that was the overriding emotion I felt when she came tumbling into my world.

Hope.

Hope that I could be normal; that I could be happy. Hope that you would trust me now and be mine for life, our daughter forever binding us together.

What I hadn't expected was the love. Pure. Fierce. Obsessive.

I hadn't thought it possible to love anyone as much as I loved you, yet I loved our child with a passion I'd never felt before.

Yes, you were mine, and Hope was an extension of everything you were, but she: she was *truly* mine. Flesh and blood. Made by me. The intensity of what I felt for her, for everything I wanted to give her – the life I never had – was overwhelming.

I know it overwhelmed you too. So much that you struggled to bond. Another thing I hadn't expected. The baby blues were cruel to you, but I was there to scoop you both up in my arms, to hold you tightly, to rock you both. Nothing could ever break our circle.

I became the provider, the protector, the nurturer, the feeder. Letting you sleep. Allowing you to heal.

My favourite moments were rocking on that chair in our front room, Hope in my arms. Watching night turn to day against the bare magnolia wall, and back to night again. Watching my child feed from the bottle, growing, developing, becoming her own person. Those big blue eyes staring up into mine as if I were her whole world.

I'd whisper again and again, *'You are mine and I am yours.'*

Everything good in the world, everything perfect in that small room, in our little bubble. But nothing is ever perfect. If anyone should have known that, it should've been me. Until Hope, you and I never argued. After Hope, all we seemed to do was bicker.

I feared you hadn't really recovered from that day you found out my true identity. Perhaps telling me what you thought I wanted to hear because of our child. Because you could see no other way out, had nowhere else to go. No one else to go to. But I was too scared to ask, too frightened to hear your answer.

I told myself it was the baby blues. You just weren't yourself. I tried to understand, but my empathy just made you angrier. You blamed me – for you missing out on the bond with our daughter, accusing me of not letting you be a mum. Of being fixated with our child at the expense of our relationship.

Enraging me. I had read about jealousy, but it was

always the father, not the mother. But I hid that rage. You loved me so much you wanted me all for yourself. I understood that. It's all I'd ever wanted from you. Until Hope.

Everything would be OK. You were a born carer, a nurse. You would learn to love our child. You would find enough love for both of us, as I had. That cloud of misery would lift. We would be happy again.

Days, weeks and months passed. Eventually you returned to work. Money allowed us the luxury of staying at home, but you said you needed to remember who you were. I supported that, becoming a full-time, stay-at-home dad. A modern man. A father of the times.

A year passed, and another. You learning how to love us both. Things becoming normal again. A new normal, but normal nevertheless.

A family. Parents to an almost-three-year-old. We even got a dog – a puppy, Bruno. I was *that* guy.

Hope grew, she and I never losing that special bond, never forgetting those words I used to whisper to her in that rocking chair.

Changing over time as she found her voice, giggling and throwing her chubby little arms around my neck, her button nose squashed against mine.

'You're all mine, Daddy.'

I'd laugh, kiss her back. 'I'm all yours, baby, and you are mine.'

There would never come a time when we wouldn't be each other's.

Or so I thought.

Chapter 62

JEN WATCHED BILL'S GNARLED fingers fumble, lifting the coverall higher and higher, the scar beneath revealing itself inch by inch.

He looked up at her, his stomach exposed. 'Kidney transplant. The reason my health was in bad shape. When I told you Trish had to look after me for a long time.'

Lewis staring open-mouthed as Jen listened. Danny sighing and closing his eyes against this latest development.

'This is what made me well enough to move up here. To be beside Simon and our grandson. A second chance, like you. After all Trish did for me in the years on that waiting list . . . How lucky I was. And yet all I've been doing is moaning about the injustice of her illness.'

Jen couldn't help but stare. 'Why? I mean, why did you need the transplant?'

Bill dropped the coverall. 'Why? I asked myself the same question when I first got the news. Over and over.

The funny thing was, I didn't have a clue. Felt totally fine. I'd left my job and was gearing up to start a new one, excited. Went for a routine medical and the test came back showing blood and protein in my urine.' Bill shrugged. 'As simple as that. Next I knew I had a chronic kidney disease diagnosis. Spent years on dialysis, up to five hours a day, before I was put forward for the transplant list. More years of waiting before I finally got the kidney.'

Jen sat stock-still, stunned as Danny opened his eyes again and turned to her. Staring at her as he spoke: 'How long?'

It took her a moment to process what he was asking. 'Since the transplant?'

He nodded, his mouth slack.

Jen counted back in her head. 'Six years.'

Silence. And then . . .

Bill whispered, 'Same.'

They looked at each other before turning to Lewis. Lewis crossed his arms. 'This is fucking bullshit.'

No one spoke. No one moved.

Waiting, before the words spat from Lewis's mouth: 'I had a lung transplant, OK? I had a fucking lung transplant.'

Jen didn't need to ask how long it had been.

Chapter 63

Then

IF I HADN'T LOST my grip on the dog's lead, my daughter would still be alive.

There. There – you have it.

My life in one sentence, reading like some shitty prompt your English teacher, most likely a failed writer, might peddle to spark a story.

That's my jolly little tale. The beginning and the end.

The middle? That's the part I lived after. The part I live now. A day-to-day existence of sorts. No story. Static. Like the life I was leading before them.

But all you really need to know – the real takeaway from this particular story – is that I am the villain. It was all my fault.

I have often wondered what might have happened if we'd stayed at home to finish the drawing Hope had started. Like all those 'what ifs' on the day my mother was murdered.

In Hope's case, it all came back to a brightly coloured crayon version of me and Beth. You, the woman who had saved me – our stick fingers touching in front of a squint-cornered rectangular house, the fat, circled start to our dog's head suspended mid-air between our thin stick legs. Before Hope had stretched her own little chubby legs down from the breakfast bar stool, leaving Bruno's crayon body still to be drawn beneath that circle, but only once we'd taken his real body out for a pee.

Hope burst from the back seat of the car into Westburn Park, as excited as Bruno. The collie puppy straining at the leash in his attempt to keep up with Hope's white Velcro-fastened trainers as she ran ahead of us, totally ignoring the kids' playpark and the skatepark; running onwards, over the grass, heading straight towards the two ponds and the flowing waters of Gilcomston Burn beyond, running through the south side of the park.

The narrow burn snaking beneath a little metal footbridge and a drystone one further down, both of which Hope loved to stand on, throwing pebbles into the water, giggling as she watched them splash when they hit the surface.

Red, orange and yellow leaves fell in the breeze, crunching beneath her tiny feet – the little rainbows stitched into the outer edge of her white shoes blurring with her speed. Me, feeling overwhelmed, as I often was, that something – someone – so innocent was mine, that she loved me as much as I loved her. That I had a family. That I even had a bloody dog.

Westburn Park had become our place when you were working a day shift, more so since Bruno had been fully vaccinated and was able to explore beyond the front garden.

Hope's trainers thumped on to the stone bridge, surprisingly loud for feet so small, quickly followed by the tap-tap of Bruno's clawed paws. The dog's nose was down, tail wagging manically, already sniffing for those who had gone before him as Hope ran down the other side and on to the sloped bank of the stream, throwing in a stick she'd picked up along the way. Her white trainers already muddy. You were going to have a fit.

'Careful, those leaves at the edge are slip—'

The words were wrenched away into the wind as Bruno pulled me away from the bridge, on to the grassy field alongside. My arm was being yanked straight out in front of me, painful and forcing me to jog a little, surprised as always at the puppy's strength. My fingers loosened on the lead as I steadied myself, grappling to keep a hold, but failing as Bruno took full advantage of my wobble, breaking free and pelting off across the field towards the never-ending stream of traffic on Westburn Road, the leash dragging along behind him.

'Bruno! Heel!'

I ran, all too aware that the lights were never at red for long, with traffic always coming from one direction or another.

'Bruno!'

The woman jogging along the path on the outskirts of the field saw me frantically waving to her, her attention captured even though she was wearing earphones. She ran, of course, first stamping on Bruno's lead, stopping the pup in his tracks, before crouching down to snatch up the lead into her hand.

'Stupid dog.' I laughed as I reached the woman and

took the lead, thanking her too many times, suddenly aware I'd left Hope at the water. I glanced back, but could no longer see her. Shouting to her, hoping to be heard over the breeze, thinking she'd perhaps crouched down on the stone bridge to pick up more pebbles. I shouted again. 'I've got him, Hope! One second!'

I started to run back; the woman forgotten. 'Hope?' Something creeping up the nape of my neck as I shouted her name, the same thing working up from my stomach, wrapping itself around my heart. Maybe she hadn't heard me. Maybe I couldn't hear her.

I picked up speed, the dog bounding in front of me as we neared the pond. My feet stopping dead, heart lurching in a way that felt the same as my feet. Unaware I'd let go of the dog until I saw him splashing in beside her.

Hope floating.

Swimming. *Yes, that's what she was doing.*

It took a moment for my brain to catch up with my eyes. Her arms outstretched either side of her, legs splayed. Only the heels of her trainers above water, the little stitched rainbows submerged. None of her limbs moving.

Not swimming. Knowing deep down she hadn't learned to swim yet.

I ran across the nearby wooden platform spanning the pond, jumping into the water, wading, screaming her name again and again.

Flipping her on to her back, face up, terrified by what I saw. Pulling her from the water, laying her on her back on the stone bank of the burn, pinching her nose and tilting her chin up, blowing into her mouth, forgetting what the count was; whether I should be pumping at her chest too. The dog darting back and forth beside us as I did both, moving between mouth and chest, desperate for her to breathe.

No idea how long I tried. Ignoring my tiring arms and chest as I screamed towards the jogging woman for help – she already running over, calling for an ambulance from her phone before she'd even reached us.

Aberdeen Royal Infirmary was literally across the road, blocked from my view only by houses. A&E maybe a ten-minute run if I hadn't been carrying Hope. If I hadn't been trying to keep her alive.

So, I waited for the ambulance, breathing. Breathing for her as I heard the wail of the siren. Knowing only that Hope was alive when we burst through the doors of A&E, but that by night-time it was just the machines that were keeping her that way.

Chapter 64

Then

Bleep... Bleep... Bleep... Bleep...
The machine constant.
Beat... Beat... Beat... Beat
Electrical breaths but a reminder that, still, she breathed.
'But it's the machines that are breathing for her.'
Me not giving a fuck because it didn't change the fact that she was still here. That there must be some promise in that. That the specialists were wrong when they told us nothing else could be done.

You sat by my side, both of us upright and uncomfortable in wooden-armed chairs not built to encourage a long stay. It didn't matter. Different chairs, another room, none of it would've changed anything.

Our daughter, our Hope, was about to be left to die in front of us. Us, her parents, sitting together, caught in some sick home movie, about to watch it unfold.

Together, but not together.
Not truly together for a long time.
Not talking, not touching.

No chair yet invented that would bring comfort to any of this.

She had a pulse – a pulse! I felt it. Faint but moving beneath my fingers. Telling me she was still there. That she was alive. Silently shouting, *'Don't you dare give up on me, Daddy!'*

She'd been breathing. With my breath. I saw it – her chest rising and falling as I breathed air into her lungs. The ambulance speeding, blue and white lights flashing, through the narrow, stone-pillared entrance of Westburn Park, its wheels ripping up the wet grass as the siren screeched – as they crossed the field to get to us.

I was breathing for her, *with* her, both of us joined together, skin on skin, touching one another through that thin veil between life and death.

You are mine.
I am yours.
You're all mine, Daddy.
I'm all yours, baby.

Saying it in my head, over and over again. All the way up until they tubed her, then seemingly flew her across the grass into the back of the ambulance. Me following, wondering who or what was powering my limbs, hellbent on keeping her within my line of vision.

Clambering in behind them, refusing to be told *no* as they reluctantly bundled Bruno into the front of the ambulance, as I grasped her hand and told her again and again that everything would be OK. I had her.

You are mine and I am yours.

I wouldn't let anything bad happen to her. No one was going to be giving up on her.

Those moments slowing as the ambulance pushed at speed through traffic lights, feeling like hours rather than minutes, the A&E literally two streets away. Our arrival at Emergency: them physically breaking my hand free of hers to get her out of the ambulance, me left behind as they ran with the stretcher, rattling across the pavement, in through the double doors. Me screaming inside my head when they told me to stay behind, to wait in reception, not sure if I was also screaming outside as I watched those doors slam shut behind them, swallowing my daughter, my Hope, whole.

I have no idea how long I sat there in that waiting room. How long it took the world around me to sneak back into my senses. It was long after the receptionist told me I couldn't keep the dog there. A good while after she told me she could take him home for me, if I had no one else to come and get him. That Bruno would be fine overnight with her dogs until I knew what was happening. That we could exchange numbers and keep in touch. Her kindness almost breaking me before I realized what she'd said. *If I had no one else*. But I had you, Beth. In the very same hospital, working your shift, no idea we were there.

No father, no husband, should ever have to make that call; should ever have to say those words. Should ever have to hear their wife's silence, then her howling like a wounded animal.

No husband should have to see their wife run into the Emergency room. To be unable to recognize the woman he loves because of the pain etched on her face, the agony weighing down her body. Neither you nor I having any idea, as I rushed to catch you before you collapsed, that it would be the last time I would hold you.

Both of us eventually sitting on hard, plastic chairs, hunched forward, hugging cups of coffee long gone cold, willing the black hands on the white plastic-framed clock above the reception desk to move, for those double doors to open, to bring us news of our daughter. At the same time, wanting to stop time, to turn it back – when those doors finally opened for us and we were shuffled into a quiet side room by a stern-looking male doctor in a creased white coat. Praying for his face to soften, waiting for him to smile, to tell me it's all been a terrible mistake. That my daughter was fine.

But she was far from fine. About as far away from fine as she could get yet, somehow, still be with me. Starved of oxygen long enough to cause brainstem death, he said.

Shaking my head. My head still shaking, faster, as I argued that she was breathing. I had been breathing for her. She couldn't have gone any time without oxygen.

That niggling voice whispering in my ear about how long she might've been face down in that stream before I got to her. And all because I'd put Bruno first. Knowing even then that if anything happened to Hope . . . If she . . . I would never be able to look at that dog again.

Then being told by the doctor that there may be a glimmer of hope. That tests would be carried out over the coming days, that they might find some brain activity.

Those days spent hoping and praying, you and I so far apart, when we should've been clinging to one another.

The crushing devastation of us being back in that room again. This time being asked about the possibility of switching off the machines now keeping her alive. Being asked if we were willing to agree to the murder of our daughter.

I had expected you to be as adamant as me in our answer to that. In no circumstances would it happen. The shock I felt when you nodded silently, tears trickling down your face. Not even a glance towards me. Not even a question as to whether I would agree.

'It's for the best,' you sobbed once we were left alone. 'There's nothing more they can do,' you croaked. 'She's already gone.'

You wouldn't even look at me. I left then. The door of that quiet room thudding shut, echoing in the corridor as I strode down it. I should've stayed. With you. But I hadn't trusted myself with the rage bubbling beneath. The grief. The despair. The hopelessness of not being able to stop what was happening; of not being able to make it all OK. Breaking my promise that I wouldn't let anything bad happen to her. The realization I was giving up on her.

But nothing could've prepared me for what you did next. The decision you'd already made, expecting me to agree to it. Letting me think you were listening to all my arguments, my pleading and begging, letting me think you might change your mind.

Eventually ground down by my grief, being forced to support your arguments, instead, thinking it may ease my guilt. That it was the only way we might find our way back to one another.

If I did it. If I agreed to this one thing. The one thing that went against everything in my being – but what I wouldn't give to help you, my wife, in your own grief?

At least that's how it seemed in those moments, so wrapped up in what I could see that it rendered me blind to anything else. To you and your own guilt. To just how much that decision of yours might come to affect you.

There was no way of telling then, as we sat together in that room, that within days your small red car would be found at the cliffs of Cove Bay. The driver's door still standing open, your mobile phone and all your belongings left inside the car – everything except the small colour photograph that you used to keep tucked behind the sun visor. The picture of the three of us, smiles beaming for the camera, captured in happier times. Together.

My pain, the unbearable agony in the aftermath of losing you, would be softened at least by the thought that you had clutched that photograph in your hand, that it had somehow comforted you at the end. That we had somehow been there beside you when you jumped to the freezing depths of the North Sea below.

But, as I said, as we found ourselves sitting there, waiting to watch our daughter die, I couldn't have known any of that.

There were six other people in the room with us. I was surprised, even in the numbness, to find it's not like they do it in those dramas on the TV. They don't just turn off the ventilator that's breathing for whoever is lying in that bed.

Our daughter. Hope.

It isn't one socket and one switch flicked before that white line flattens and drones, continually telling the world that person is gone. Instead, they withdrew all the tubes and cannulas that had entered her body. Drawing out the process, our pain, as we watched.

As I watched our daughter's body slowly shut down. Each of us holding her hand either side of those starched white hospital sheets enveloping her tiny body. She, already dressed as an angel.

Watching her body slowly go to sleep.

Waiting for her heavily medicated heart to stop on its own.

Her heart. One of several organs you said they could take from our daughter's body. That you wanted to give away.

You.

Me, the howling animal when they told me she was gone.

No idea I was about to lose you too.

Chapter 65

Jen stared at Lewis, the vault silent. None of them wanting to say what they were all thinking, to pose the questions that might give them answers they didn't want to hear.

Jen eventually asking what seemed to be the only safe question, the same one Bill and she had already answered. 'What happened, Lewis?'

Lewis's eyes flashed as he looked at her. 'You really want to know?'

She nodded.

Lewis squirmed in his seat, glaring at the ground as he spoke. 'What happened was that I was brought up by my sick fuck of a father. Only thing he gave me, my ma and my younger brother was a beating. Daily.'

The silence stretched.

Lewis wiped at his nose, his eyes not looking up from the spot he stared at on the floor. 'I've never told anyone this shit. Only my ma and my brother know.' He looked up for the briefest of moments, not making eye contact with any of them, only looking at the walls of the vault, and the camera.

Jen felt a shift within her, a slight softening towards Lewis. Seeing the pain there. Something had hurt him badly. His own father. Where he should've felt safe, where he should've *been* safe. She thought of Daisy in that car when it mounted the kerb, about the danger she had put her own daughter in; the risk she took every day she drank, in all areas of her life. She looked at Lewis, imagining Daisy sitting there with her own tales to tell as an adult. Jen's insides hardened with shame as she repeated her question to Lewis.

'What happened?' She couldn't ever pretend to feel sympathy towards Lewis's desires, but she could understand that there may be a reason, a mix of nature and nurture.

Lewis shifted in his seat again, the discomfort of the memories clear in his head. 'My da kept pigeons. In a shed out the back of our garden. He'd take me in there. Every day. Pretending it was for us to spend time together, but it was nothing but an excuse to tell me everything I was doing wrong – all the ways I wasn't living up to the person he'd hoped his son to be.'

Lewis swallowed, the sound loud in the stillness.

'He beat me every one of those days. Pushing my face down on to those splintered wooden planks. Planks covered in bird shit, feathers . . .' Lewis's nose curled like he was smelling it all now. 'Held my head down in it as he beat me. Breathing in the shit, trying not to open my mouth to breathe because I could taste it on my tongue. The ends of the feathers would pierce my skin, make my face bleed . . .'

Jen's eyes blurred. 'What about your mother, didn't sh—'

Lewis spat back at her. 'My ma knew. No way she couldn't have. She was too scared, probably glad he was beating on me instead of her, that he was away from her baby boy, my brother.'

Lewis pinched at his nose as if trying to get rid of the stench, before letting his hands fall to his lap.

'There was no window in that shed. We spent hours in the thing. When I got ill, really ill – long term – I told ma. I told her it was being holed up in there so much. Da said I was a wuss, that I was making excuses not to help with the birds. It was a schoolteacher who eventually stepped in. The school who got me seen.'

Jen sat, surprising herself as she reached out to Lewis, stopping when he shrank away from her hand. 'What was it, Lewis? What was making you ill?'

'Pulmonary fibrosis. Fanciest words I'd ever heard. Caused by the stuff in the bird shit and feathers.' Lewis smiled, no warmth there. 'Bird fanciers' lung, they call it. Anyway, long story short, I eventually ended up with a transplant.'

Jen stood. *Find the answers.* Thinking of her own drinking. Of Lewis's smoking. That with Bill perhaps it just came down to not appreciating what he'd been given. That none of them had been grateful enough for what they'd been given. Those answers . . . The links between them . . . The question left being how strong those links were, and what it meant for all of them.

She wiped at her forehead, pacing. 'So *that's* what this is? We all had transplants at the same time. And he knew. How the hell did he know?' That fingernail was scratching again, at the fact that none of them had had the same organ transplanted.

Bill mumbled. 'I don't know. But *he* does and he was somehow able to find us.' He shook his head. 'I don't understand how. It's all wrapped up in red tape. Confidential. The donor's family doesn't know and neither do we. Made that way for a good reason.'

Jen turned, walking back the way she'd come. 'Yeah, well he's managed to cut through all that. Somehow he knows we were all given a second chance.' Jen's stomach turned. 'He's mad, angry, thinking we didn't take it. That we haven't lived the way we should've, the way we could've with that chance.' Bile rose in her throat. 'Especially me. Me and my liver, yet I'm still drinking.' That self-hatred was now greater than ever.

Lewis grunted. 'So, what's my fucking story? That I smoke? I got the transplant when I was no more than a kid, and because my dad was a violent, sick fuck. So, tell me, what the fuck have I done to piss him off?'

Jen looked to the pulsing red light. 'What we need to be asking is how he knows we all had our operations around the same time.'

Jen kept pacing, her head hurting from thinking. 'Maybe it's someone who was somehow involved with our care? Before the transplant or after? That would make sense. More sense, surely, than someone being able to access confidential records.'

Lewis laughed. 'Yeah, sure, someone involved in our care. He really seems the caring type.'

Jen spun towards him, surprised at how quick the

loathing for him came back. 'Well, what have *you* got, then?'

But it was Danny who answered, silencing them all. 'I don't know how he did it, but I know why we're all here.'

He sat propped up against the wall as they all turned to stare. 'I know who he is.' Danny closed his eyes and pointed to his chest. 'Because I know whose heart this is.'

Jen's voice cracked as she spoke, realizing what Danny was saying. 'None of us had the same organ transplanted.' Her voice a whisper. 'We all have different organs. All of them from the same donor. Someone he knew.'

Danny stared up at Jen. 'Bingo.'

He turned to Lewis. 'You asked what the fuck this has to do with you?' The smile bitter on Danny's lips. 'That lung transplant you had? You're living and breathing when his daughter no longer is – with the lungs she used to breathe with.'

Chapter 66

OUR DANNY THINKS HE knows me. He has no idea who I am or what I'm capable of.

He's been down here longer than any of them. There was never any question that he wouldn't be. My daughter's heart beats within him. Precious. Special. Hers.

I've read all I can about that age-old debate. The one as to whether anything remains of the person. Within the donated organ, I mean. A residue of sorts, within the tissues. The recipient feeling the emotions of the person who went before, their personality changing under the influence of that ghost.

Of course, I tried to get as close to the truth as I can. Seeking the answer to the biggest question I asked myself when Beth made the decision she did. The biggest fear. That my daughter, Hope, would remain, that she would endure and have to suffer being dispersed into pieces. I never believed all that rubbish about her legacy living on but, rather, that the soul of her would remain trapped within those organs – inside the bodies of strangers.

But the answer eluded me and all I was left with was hope. Hope that if she was still within her organs, the recipients would value her gift, they would look after her. It's the reason I tracked them down, why I'm doing what I am now. I needed to know. And now I know that they didn't. That they haven't.

Hope was love. She was loved. She deserves to remain loved.

I know that Danny loves. I've seen it, up close. Watching him kiss his love on the front doorstep of their home. Libby, he calls her. Her small feet balancing across the threshold, him standing one step down, craning his head and body up towards her. In full view of all the houses surrounding theirs. My need to watch Danny, like watching that family video at home over and over again. Jealous of his love. Of their love. Libby looking desperate as their lips parted, hands grasping either side of his face as if she didn't want to ever let him go. Both oblivious to anything, and anyone, around them; to me, sitting in the car across the road, just past their driveway.

The car visible, but not me. The engine idling, my eyes watching in the rearview mirror that I'd been fussing with as if I wasn't interested in what they were doing. Angling it so I could see exactly what they were doing.

Watching and thinking of all I had lost. The people responsible for that loss. Danny. Lewis. Jen. Bill.

All people painstakingly found because of what they took from me, rage making me want to spring from the car and charge up that path towards them.

Instead, I tooted the horn. Danny turned and waved his arm at the car before stepping back off the bottom step, then reached the same arm towards Libby's outstretched one, their fingers joining. Their toddler daughter, Charlotte, appeared at her mother's legs and giggled as Danny went back up a step, pulled her up into his arms and showered her face with kisses.

Dragging out their family moment, making me wait, my blood boiling and bubbling, before I blasted the horn again.

Eventually he passed Charlotte to Libby, kissed them both again and turned, before walking down the path. I started up the engine, knowing that there would be no opportunity right here, that Libby would stand there until the car was no longer in sight, Charlotte staying balanced on her hip.

I straightened at the wheel as he opened the boot and hoisted his carry case into it, probably already deciding not to give me a tip, as he banged the boot lid back down. In the rearview mirror, I saw him glance down. I knew that he would see the number plate I'd fitted the night before, after phoning just three taxi firms before finding his booking and cancelling it.

Amazing how easy it is when you have a name, address and a destination. Moments after that call, I was fitting the plate I'd stolen from the saloon belonging to the taxi driver who lives four streets over from me.

Danny opened the passenger door, still waving back at his family as he ducked inside and closed the door.

'Going to the station?' I didn't look his way as I pulled away from the kerb.

'Yeah.' He clicked his seatbelt, glancing back over his shoulder as we left the street.

My fingers tightened on the steering wheel, my hand itching to reach out and ram itself back against his windpipe. For him to pay for having that love. That life. But I kept my head centre, with steely focus on the road ahead. On the task ahead.

'Busy, driver?'

I forced myself not to groan at the inane drivel. 'Not bad. Away on business?' Knowing he was going nowhere.

'Yeah, 'fraid so.'

I don't know if I imagined it, but I felt him staring at me. Maybe expecting more small talk from a man he probably assumed made a living off speaking shit and getting tipped for it.

The next street would be a right turn only, left being a leafy dead end. I didn't yet need to indicate, but I did hit the button on my armrest that locked all the doors.

Danny turned, staring at me. 'The area's not *that* rough.' His laugh was forced, the smile dropping when I said nothing in response.

His gaze danced from me to the car radio, to where the taxi meter should be. He looked up to the space above the rearview mirror too – another common place it might be – and frowned.

He slowly slid a finger to the door button on his armrest, pressing it lightly, as if I might not notice. No sound of the click of locks, which I assumed he was hoping for. Like me, he stared straight ahead. Now not so keen for chat.

The junction was approaching; no need to indicate as there was no car behind us. And not wanting to indicate, to risk giving the game away too early. I turned left without a word.

The lines on Danny's forehead deepened as he peered out of the passenger window. Then out through the windscreen. Then at me. 'What are you doing?'

I said nothing as I jerked the steering wheel, the car veering towards the kerb, mounting it, coming to stop beneath the sprawling trees marking the end of the road.

Danny wasted no time reaching for the door handle, perhaps hoping it would magically unlock. He pulled – once, twice, three times – staring at the door, willing it to open before he turned to look, open-mouthed, at me, his gaze darting back and forth between me and the street beyond.

I stared at him, wondering, again, if he was fancying his chances of going for the lock button on my armrest. Ready for him. But he sat still. Unsure. Maybe wondering if this was some kind of joke, the uncertainty clear in his voice as he tried to recover ground.

'I asked, what are you doing?'

I smiled, his eyes widening as I did so. 'I'm doing what needs to be done.'

His eyes crinkled, confusion clear. I could almost see his mind ticking. *Is this guy for real? Will he stop if I laugh, if I appreciate whatever this wind-up is? Or should I lunge for him, to hell with misplaced violence?*

But he did none of that. My hand was already reaching down into the door pocket for the wet rag, my left arm coming up just as quickly as his survival instinct kicked in, blocking his attempts to shove at me, ready for him as he came at me, ready before he even moved. My body twisted towards him, my right hand shoving the saturated material against his lips and nose. One of his hands still pulling again and again at his door handle, the other hand trying, but failing, to remove mine from his mouth.

There was a flicker of recognition in his widening eyes, right before they rolled into his head as he slumped sideways against the passenger door.

Danny going nowhere but where I wanted him.

Chapter 67

THEY'D PUT THE PUZZLE together, but no voice boomed out of the speaker.

'He has no intention of letting us out of here, has he?' Jen looked over from Bill, straight up at the camera, nothing to lose by saying it out loud. Either she was stating what their faceless watcher already knew, or she could live in hope of being corrected by him.

The ensuing silence confirmed the worst.

But something didn't add up, something that had been scratching at her in the background. The medication. Or rather, the lack of it. She had been told she would most likely be on immunosuppressants for the rest of her life. Daily tablets that would prevent her body rejecting the transplanted organ. She'd never missed a tablet, had no idea what would happen if she did, but she'd heard stories of rejection within days.

She looked at Bill, Lewis and Danny in turn. None of them looking particularly bad, apart from the obvious effects of what they were going through. 'He may have no intention of letting us out of here, but he must have a reason to be keeping us all alive. And I don't just mean whatever his end goal is. I mean with our medication. He must somehow be administering our medication.'

Bill looked up at her, no surprise on his face, as if he'd already been thinking the same thing. 'It's figuring out how he got it in the first place.'

Danny sighed. 'Easy enough with me. I had it in the suitcase I was carrying when he got to me.'

Jen saw herself in her mind's eye, back in her home, as she ran into Daisy's room in her search for coins; as she sped into another room too. 'It was the only thing I took with me without him knowing. In the pocket of my coat. But I guess he knew all along – was banking on it. Even then, given the cameras and how close he got to me and my life, I expect he'd been in my home.'

Bill nodded. 'I think the same. It would have been easy if he'd been watching for any length of time.' Bill dropped his head, blushing at what he was about to say. 'I keep a key in the mailbox outside my house.'

Lewis tutted. 'I'm not that stupid but I did take mine with me when I left the house. Had no idea if I'd be home that night.'

Jen thought of all those broken memories when she woke up here. 'So it wasn't just water that he was forcing down our throats.'

No one spoke. All of them lost in their own thoughts.

Eventually, she sat down, between Bill and Lewis, and shuffled her chair sideways, the metal legs scraping and screeching on the floor as she brought herself as close to Bill as she could go, forearms touching. She looked at the camera, Lewis watching her as she then turned to Bill and twisted to place her other cheek against his.

'The thing to take from all this is that he's keeping us alive. But why? Why not just kill us all? One by one, as he found us. Why here, together?'

Bill sat silent, shaking his head. Jen didn't want to say what she was about to, but had no choice. 'I think this guy sees us as walking body parts. Parts of his daughter. So, what we have to figure out is what this is: does he want to make us somehow pay for not taking care of them, the way we should've?'

Bill kept his head facing forward, talking in a whisper. 'I don't think we can assume anything. What we do know is that he's gone to a lot of trouble to get us all here, and to keep us well whilst we are here. Now we know why. Put yourself in his shoes. If it was Daisy, if your grief had somehow altered your mental state, what would you be doing with us?'

Jen thought about all the true-crime documentaries she'd watched on TV, about the book that had stayed with her long after she'd read it, *The Silence of the Lambs*. How people were driven to crazy things, things that made no sense to anyone except them. The trophies they would keep, stolen from the bodies of their victims – jewellery, clothing. *Skin. Body parts.*

'Jesus, do you think he wants them back?' It sounded crazy as Jen said it, but not so mad that she couldn't believe it.

Bill didn't move. 'I don't know what to think, but we need to be ready. Ready for when he comes for us. Prepared to fight.'

Jen pulled back from Bill's ear, seeing the steel set of his jaw. The determination clear in his features. Hearing it in his voice.

He whispered to Jen what they would have to do, that if they did exactly as he said, then they might somehow survive this nightmare, that they might just see daylight and their families again.

All things that, after he was done talking, she repeated to Lewis – every word, all of them whispered, hidden from the camera, from *his* eyes. Then bringing the same to Danny.

Jen praying that what they'd said was quiet enough to avoid being heard by anyone else's ears.

Chapter 68

I UNLOCK THE DOOR to their room, repocketing the keys as I enter. Knowing they've put the last pieces of the puzzle together; that now we have the full picture, there will be no more need for medication.

This time they don't listen to my instructions to stay back. Instead, they come at me like rabid dogs protecting the rest of their pack. A four-strong row of them, all bared teeth and wild eyes. The whites of those eyes turning to flags of surrender when they see what's in my hand.

They back up, proverbial tails between their legs, as I raise the cattle prod and run it across their torsos like a stick across bar chimes. Each of them swaying, wavering and falling back against the force, their tuneless growls switching to pathetic whines as they back away, shuffling and stumbling, until cold brick stops them from retreating any further.

I study the runt of the litter, the fight in his eyes dimming – the brave man who had almost punched me, a stranger, in the street, nowhere to be seen. He cowers and shivers, squatting against the wall like he's about to shit himself, like the mutt he is.

The others crouch beside him, licking their wounds. Big old puppy eyes looking up from bowed heads at me – their master, unmoved.

Lewis's head is down, avoiding eye contact. Hoping he won't be picked. Where's the fight? Where's the man who strutted down the street, keyring swinging?

I nudge at the plastic material over his stomach with the prod. He yelps as the others uncoil and jump to his defence, howling and retreating again as I strike them each in turn.

Misguided loyalty, I think you'd agree.

I lift my other hand, all eight eyes flickering from my face to the prod and then to the new addition. Real terror there now. No charge in this rod. Only a steel noose at its end, the silicon coating removed from it, kindness not a consideration here.

They stand, ready, thinking they can somehow avoid what's about to happen. I extend the catch pole, slowly, the stiff noose contacting the wall above Lewis's head, and lower it. He ducks and dives like some shitty amateur boxer, the others either side of them pulling at the noose, back and forth above his swaying head, believing they might save him – or perhaps they're fighting to be first.

A swift hit of the prod and they're back on the floor where they belong, the noose slipping easily over Lewis's head. I tighten it around his neck as he bucks, pulling to catch my hound. A hound for the pound. A dog to be put down.

I yank the noose towards me. Lewis topples, then regains his balance before standing – pulling against me, the fight returning briefly before he's stunned by the prod, suddenly pliant. He shuffles forward as I step backwards, the prod and the noose fully extended in my hands.

Snot runs from his nose, down over his lips.

Snivelling wuss.

The other three scream obscenities. False in their conviction to stick together as one, as a pack, when they don't even attempt to move away from where they're leaning against the wall. Their whispered promises of loyalty and unity, before I entered the vault, already forgotten – now it's every man for himself.

A return to the lying scumbags that they are.

Chapter 69

I push Lewis forward into the room. He stumbles at a metre's distance, our bodies separated by the cattle prod. His body rigid in its fight to stop his feet moving, to stop them from heading towards the inevitable.

His breath catches. The runt looks around the room – though I'm behind him, I can tell from what little movement he has in his neck. His new surroundings are causing him to breathe too fast for his chest. He's wheezing. Heaving.

The metal gurney gleams beneath the temporary strip light. The sheen of the gurney competing with the shining glare of the rows of tools lying on the square table on locked wheels beside it. The only other obvious feature: four double steel hooks in the corner, hanging down from a steel beam that's been drilled into the ceiling. A macabre coat rack.

'What . . . the . . . fuck . . . is . . . this?' A gulp between each word, perhaps attempting to swallow the reality before him. But, even now, even when faced with his fate, he still tries for bravado in the harshness of his words, the quiver of his voice telling me otherwise.

'This is justice, Lewis.'

He tries to turn his head towards me in the noose, but I hold him fast. I want him to see his end. To really contemplate it.

'What . . . are you . . . going . . . on . . . about?'

'I think you know, Lewis. Enough for you to end up here. To follow my rules.'

'The . . . girl? At . . . the school?'

His breathing slows. Trying to calm himself. Thinking he somehow has a chance to fight his case. 'I didn't touch her. I didn't . . .'

'Only because I got there first. You *would* have.' I force him towards the table, his hip bones banging against it. 'You'd been planning it for a good while, even after all the warnings – the threats and the exposure.'

He flexes his wrists, pulling against the leather cuff restraints, which I put on him straight after I pulled him from the other vault, having applied the prod to briefly stun him into submission.

Lewis grits his teeth, spitting, as he hisses at me: 'I couldn't help it. I couldn't fucking stop it.'

I shove at his neck, bending his scrawny upper body over the gurney, his grubby feet lifting off the floor. I drop the cattle prod but keep hold of the catch pole that Lewis's neck is on the end of.

'What the fuck?!' Strangled words, his face turning puce as he fights against the force.

His feet are elevated enough that I can use my free hand to flip his lower limbs up further, his body spread out almost flat, suspended, looking like it's in flight, but going nowhere.

I grab the remaining cuff restraints hanging from my belt and go for his ankles. He kicks out but stops when his head and shoulders start to tip towards the concrete floor on the other edge of the gurney. I pull hard on the catch pole, his head and neck jerking backwards, as he chokes out a groan; his brief moment of compliance makes it almost too easy to scoop his ankles in before hooking them together.

I grab both of his feet and pull them to my left, spinning him on the smooth, cold metal gurney like the glass bottle in the centre of a truth-or-dare circle. But there's no dare here. There is only the truth. A truth we both already know.

I loosen the neck noose a fraction and flip him over, before tightening it again. He's flat on his back, his tied hands behind him, forcing his pelvis to jut upwards. Splayed. Where I want him.

'Please! I'll stop. I promise I'll stop.'

I pull the neck noose as tight as I can, panicking him, giving me time to lift the heavy buckled rubber strap dangling from the table in front of me. To lean over and lift the opposite strap up, fastening them tight at his centre before securing his shackled feet to the gurney. I move to his chest, do the same there.

'I didn't know. I couldn't have known.'

I say nothing.

'It's because of the transplant, isn't it?'

I move the gurney up to the table and take out the gun that's been tucked away in the pocket of my cargo trousers.

His eyes follow me, the blue irises almost disappearing upwards in his vain attempt to see over the top of his head. Squirming. Thrashing. To no avail.

I move down into his line of vision, needing him to see what's happening, rewarded with wide eyes as they follow the gun in my hand. Darting from my hand to my face, those same terror-stricken eyes pleading, imploring.

'What the fuck is that?'

He can be forgiven for asking; it's not your standard gun. I take my time loading it. Giving him time to think of all his terrible decisions, the mistakes that led him to this moment.

He chews his lips. 'Do you think this is what she would want?'

Nice try, arsehole.

I unlock the wheels on the small square table with my foot, gently pushing it out of my way, some of the tools rolling around and clanking against one another with the motion.

The move brings me level with his bobbing head. Blue and purple veins popping at his neck and temples as he tries to keep his head up, neck extended to breaking point as he stares down the table at his imprisoned limbs.

I finally look at him. *Really* look at him. Standing over him, staring down into his watery blue eyes.

I knew it would be impossible, even if a part of my daughter did remain in the tissues, that I would see any recognition there in those eyes, but I pause anyway, long enough to allow for it. But I see nothing. I'm grateful for that, at least. For what it means, after everything he's done.

'I'd love to rip those eyes from your skull. But they're not what I need.'

He understands exactly what it is that I need and want from him. What I want from them all.

He goes to say something, but stays silent.

Still. Shock, perhaps.

I take it as acceptance of his fate. Revelling in justice being served as I press the stun gun against the side of his head. And fire.

Chapter 70

'What was that?' Jen was wide-eyed.

Bill swallowed, sick to his stomach. He looked at her, glancing over at Danny, the look on Danny's face telling Bill that he was thinking the same, neither of them wanting to be the one to tell Jen.

He had recognized the cattle prod, knowing what it was used for from having watched so many documentaries about animal cruelty, back when Trish played with being a vegetarian after first learning about it herself.

Bill was acutely aware of what that prod could do to an animal; of what it could do to a human. He also knew only too well what would happen next. Not wanting to let that thought in, not willing to admit it even to himself, not until he had heard the muffled shot.

'Bill? Bill?' Jen's voice was high, terror as clear in her eyes as it was in her voice.

Bill looked at Danny, his eyes pleading, searching Danny's for answers they could give her.

What could they tell her? A young woman who had

already lost so much, someone who wanted a chance to make things right, a mother who only wanted to know she would see her child again.

Danny stood. 'We're going to get out of here, Jen.' He pulled her to him as she sobbed into his shoulder.

Danny stared at Bill over her head, both knowing they were anything but OK, that unless they could think of something, fast, they were going to the same place Lewis had gone.

Bill's eyes filled. He did nothing to try to stop the tears forming as he thought of Trish sitting in that armchair at home. He would do anything to be there refilling that plate of biscuits.

His home, where he had felt the walls closing in for a good while now, a place where he sometimes thought both Trish and he would be better off dead.

He was now brutally aware of the stone walls around him, of death knocking louder than ever before. His home, his wife – both, suddenly, a lifeline.

His need stronger than ever to slam the door in death's face.

Chapter 71

I WONDER IF THEY heard the shot. If the thick granite walls were soundproofed to death or not. If they were wondering, when that door opened again, which one of them would be next to the slaughter.

Knowing from the beginning, from the very first moment I started searching for them, the day I started watching them, that this was how it would all end. Needing to have them all come together. For them to be made to think about how they'd lived their lives. The mistakes they'd made. The lies they'd told.

Before what my daughter had given them and after. What they had abused. Never worthy of that gift. Soiling her memory.

I needed to hear them tell the truth. To admit it to themselves. To finally realize, in their captivity, how lucky they had been in receiving that gift, how fortunate they were to have been given that second chance. To realize what they'd done. What they'd wasted – that chance and their freedom to live.

All of them coming together in that realization.

Then, and only then, could I take back what was never theirs to have.

My daughter.

Take back what should have always stayed hers. Things that should never have been taken from her. Handed out to others, as if we weren't in danger of losing the essence of her.

Not any more. All of those parts coming back to the man who made them. The man who had loved all of them. Within her.

Forever loving all of her.

Knowing all along that there would be no freedom granted for these people. Not for any of them. That there would be nothing after. For them, or for me.

Feeling a sadness that I won't ever see the streets above again. The streets I watched for so long. Beside Robbie – the only person who still meant anything in my life. Regret that I won't see him again either. That all of this will play out, yet I can't let him see it. Unable to give him his moment – that moment he's dreamt of. The moment he gets to be the hero.

I wonder what he'll think of me. After. When all is done.

After the days, weeks, months or even years before someone stumbles upon these vaults, when they bring up the bodies from beneath. When they bring me up too.

Will I still be his rock star? Once the kid known as The Butcher's Boy?

I imagine the press will go wild. I hope then, at least,

Robbie will have his moment. That he will tell his story. The one telling the world what it was like to befriend a killer. To live and work alongside him.

A star in his own right. His story becoming the prized possession in his collection of true-crime magazines and books. In time.

All of that is still to come. With me no longer here to watch it play out.

But, for now, I still watch; I watch as they play out their final moments in front of me.

As I play out mine. Enjoying their fear. Seeing it. Hearing it in every move they make, every word they utter. The last movements and sounds they'll ever make.

Danny has his arm around Jen, comforting her as she weeps. I hear her ask them what I'm doing with Lewis. Right now.

They pacify her with their theories. I look over at Lewis hanging there on the hook, his lungs gone and, although I don't hear any of them say it out loud, surely that must be the resounding theory. The one they're all thinking in those heads of theirs.

But I guess no one wants to think about their end, not when theirs is going to mean taking the one thing from them that had promised them a second chance at life.

I watch them playing with the idea of how I will enter the room next time. Already suspecting that, if I lead with the cattle prod, there will be none of the fight of last time. I may even hold out the catch pole alongside it; tap the top of each of their heads in turn. Eeeny, Meeny, Miney, Mo. Already knowing who's next, but where's the fun in that?

It's Bill next. I'm surprised to feel a sense of sadness about that. I've grown to like him in some strange little way.

I expect I'll be able to drop the hoop fast over Bill's head, before I tighten it around his neck. That it will be Jen who will jump to her feet, pulling at the handle, begging me not to take him. To take her instead. Commendable. Stupid. Because they'll all get their turn.

Regardless, she'll fight hard. Danny too, I'll bet. Gallant of him. But the cattle prod will fight harder.

Bill will stand and whisper to them that he's OK, accepting his fate with dignity. The last word he will utter, right there on that table, will be *Trish*.

Jen is talking on the screen. I turn it up, wanting to hear what she says, to hear what they all say in their last moments as a three, before I go and fetch Bill.

'How did you know it was his daughter, Danny? That our organs belonged to her? Mine was anonymous. I thought everyone's donor was?'

Bill now. 'Same here. Trish and I, we wrote a letter, to the donor's family. We wanted them to know how grateful we were for what they had done for us. We did that but we were told not to put in any information that would identify us. We never heard back.'

My fingers grip the laptop. I never got word of any letter.

I turn up the volume further, invested in Danny's reply. 'My story's a little more complicated.'

He looks between the two of them, probably wondering if what he is about to say is something he should share. Surely not thinking of lying – not now, when they're all here together, in the situation that they're in?

'You've heard of Share Your Wishes?'

I breathe out, relieved that he's decided to tell his truth.

Jen nods. 'Yeah, that website where people can post their wishes to be donors, share their stories of the gift a family member has given or the gift that they themselves have received?'

I'm sitting on the edge of my seat, here for this story. The tale of all tales. Because I already know the ending. That Danny shared his story, and someone else shared theirs.

That what they eventually shared together is a particularly nasty story. One of horror, because absolute horror is what I felt when I found out. When I found out tha—

'Casey?'

Chapter 72

I JUMP AT THE voice behind me, sending the laptop crashing to the floor as I spin in my chair, my mind taking its time to catch up before I see Robbie standing there. His eyes move from me to the laptop – the device upright and open on the ground – to the metal gurney and the thick steel hooks hanging against the wall. To Lewis swinging on one of them in the underground draught.

His voice no more than a croak when he speaks. 'Casey, what is this?'

I smile, because what else is there to do when you're faced with the unexpected? When you're left staring Batman in the face? My mind working overtime as my mouth turns upwards.

How did he get in here?

I glance at the monitor, no change to the view from the camera over the outside door above us. No intruder notifications or any noise coming from the laptop's screen or speakers, to tell me the door has been tampered with. I smile wider now, teeth bared. The Joker face to face with his adversary, already thinking of ways to outsmart him.

'This?' I spread my arms wide and look around, swivelling from side to side on my chair. 'This is me taking back what's mine. Welcome to your very own true crime in action, Robbie. Finally.'

Robbie's face is a strange colour. Whiter than white. Ghostly against the black of his T-shirt. Reminding me of the pints of Guinness he loves so much. It suits him, much better than the flushed look of clogged arteries he usually sports.

I smile again, acting, welcoming, nothing to see here. 'How did you find me, Robbie?'

He drags his gaze away from the table, from the hooks, from Lewis. Turns his head to the dark, deep tunnel behind him, the place from where he crept up on me, perhaps now gauging if he should run, sprint out of here, not caring how loudly his feet carry him. Up, up, and away. Out of here. Anywhere but here.

'I ... I got a Missing Person report in for Danny Anderson. To the desk. I ...'

I can't get my head around how that would've led Robbie here.

So, what was it? Had Robbie tracked Danny back through CCTV recordings? Possible confirmed places Danny might've been? Unlikely, given my knowledge of where every camera is, the fact I had manipulated them in advance to face a certain way and had taken care to stay out of view. There had to be something else.

'The truth, Robbie.'

He's looking at me as if he's never seen me before.

His podgy, dough-coloured hand, fat dimpling at its knuckles, rubbing at the tired logo on his chest, perhaps willing some of that Batman magic to materialize right out of that shirt, like the Bat-Signal light shining into the night skies.

'I was worried. You seemed a little off. Distracted. Not fully in the chair, when you always have been, if you know what I mean.' His eyes dart to Lewis's body, the gaze scurrying away again as it bounces off the gaping holes where Lewis's lungs once were.

I laugh, more of a chortle. 'Me having a couple of off days at work led you down here?'

The sound is met by terror in Robbie's eyes. 'Your . . . Your . . .' The plump hands by his sides furling and unfurling.

'Come now, Robbie. Spit it out.'

He blinks rapidly. 'I could tell you were lying.'

Ah, Robbie and his fucking true-crime programmes. Like I said before, he's always fancied himself as quite the detective. The reason he's in the job, I reckon. Waiting for his moment, the day he'll swoop in and capture the crime real-time on camera. The crime, the criminal, the accolade of being a real-life superhero.

'So, you did what, Robbie?'

He steps back, unsure whether to keep talking. Perhaps battling with whether he should trust that there's still a friendship here between us, one that he can use as a bargaining chip. That he's somehow safe. Immune to whatever's happening to those people he's seen on the laptop screen on the floor. To whatever's going to be happening in this room next. Surely knowing what's happened already, what with Lewis hanging there. Aware now of exactly where Danny Anderson will end up.

'Robbie?'

Stepping back again. 'When I asked if you were OK and you told me you were, I didn't buy it. I followed you after work a couple of times. Out of friendship. I thought you were maybe in some kind of trouble.'

'And?' Scanning my memory, retracing my steps.

'I followed you by car one night. I watched you in that street, watching that couple in their home. The couple with the kid. You sat there for hours, Casey.'

I nod, processing. 'And what did you think, Robbie?'

He shrugs, the movement exaggerated, slow, trying to buy time. 'I didn't know what to think. And then that Missing Person report came in and I recognized the guy – Danny. The one I'd seen you watching.'

Jesus, how could I have been so sloppy? So unaware of being watched when all I do myself is watch?

'But, Robbie, how did you know? To come here, I mean?' What I really want to ask is how he escaped my camera outside the door to the tunnels – how the hell he got past the alarmed door – but I'm loathe to say it out loud, to admit that I've somehow failed in having everything covered. But I *did* have everything covered. Had I somehow been distracted?

Jesus, had I really been outsmarted by Robbie? I stare at him as he takes another sliding step.

'I didn't. I followed you from your home to here. Earlier today. I saw you approach the tunnels, held back until I was sure you were a good way in, and then I caught up. But when I came out the other side, you'd disappeared.'

'And?'

'And I went back into the tunnels, tried to figure out where you might've gone. I knew you weren't far ahead of me, so you couldn't have been out of my sight by the time we both came out.'

I watch Robbie's face, his features animated even in his fear. Sounding like one of those TV detectives revelling in laying it all out for the baddie in the grand finale, right before the arrest. But Robbie, regardless of what he thought, was no Columbo like our Jen, and he wouldn't be taking me anywhere. Still, I'd give him his moment in the spotlight.

'What did you do then?'

Robbie looks towards the monitor showing the view of outside the external door, his eyes not wandering to the other screen – the one showing Jen, Bill and Danny together in the centre of the vault, upright on their hard-backed chairs. His stare remains fixed as he turns from the exterior view back to me, as if he knows that only something bad can come of looking at that other one. 'I went back into the tunnel, saw that external door.' He cocks his head towards the monitor. 'Saw the camera above it straight away.'

I wouldn't have expected anything less of Robbie's observation skills, both of us trained to see what others don't – no matter how much I'd gone out of my way to make sure everything was hidden.

'I actually raised my hand to knock but it just seemed crazy that you would be behind that door.' Robbie's eyes flicker towards the other monitor and dart back to my face just as quickly. Maybe thinking all kinds of crazy now.

'I left the tunnel, went above ground, on to Union Street, trying to figure out from the front where that door would access at the back, beneath the street. I realized it was the empty shop, the one Caffe Nero had vacated.' Robbie looked up at the arched brick ceiling above his head, perhaps picturing what was once above us. 'It's been lying empty a good while, that "For Let" sign flapping in the wind, and I remembered what you said that time we spoke about the crap coffee at Greggs.'

'What was that, Robbie?'

'About the coffee ... about how you always complained about the quality of the coffee, and you could teach them a thing or two from your barista days – from your days at Caffe Nero. I figured that had to mean something. That there was a reason you were here.'

Robbie looks to the floor, as if trying to silence himself, the normality of talking as if we're side by side on the operating room, just two pals chewing the fat, suddenly feeling out of place here.

'Well remembered. You really *would* give Columbo a run for his money.'

Robbie's face reddens at the same time as his chest swells, fawning in the warmth of the compliment. That true-crime obsession as strong down here as it is above ground. My words buoying him to launch into his next explanation.

'I figured the letting company had maybe put up the camera for security but, given how much you and I saw daily outside the main glass doors of the place, I wasn't sure they'd have gone to the trouble down here. So, I phoned them.'

If I hadn't already been sitting in silence, I would've been stunned into it now. I look over Robbie's shoulder, along the tunnel he'd appeared from, half expecting to see the staff of the letting company coming towards me, lanyards swaying around their necks or, worse still, the boys in blue. But there's no one. No one but me and Robbie.

Robbie turns to follow my gaze, then turns back. 'It's just me.' His face falls as he says it, realizing his mistake, making himself vulnerable. 'I didn't want to think you were actually down here, but, if you were, I figured there'd be a good reason for it. I didn't want to drop you in any shit, so I made up a bullshit story.'

Robbie continues to surprise me.

'I told them I worked for the city's CCTV, that we thought we'd seen someone trying to tamper with the cafe doors on Union Street. That there may be someone inside – squatting, if you like. That I was going to notify the coppers but wondered if the letting company might have keys to allow them access.'

'And they bought that?'

'Yeah, guy got really antsy about it, started laying off about damage to another building that he oversees. Told me he would happily come and gave them what-for himself if he wasn't working away. So, I did the right thing, told him not to worry and that if he told the local office I was coming for the keys, I'd deal with it all and keep him updated. I got my hands on the keys an hour ago.'

I close my eyes and picture the glass doors above, and the one you pulled open in that downpour all those years ago, then brought in the sea-change to my life. Doors I didn't even consider. An empty retail unit not accessed in months. The same cafe where I worked all those years, regularly using the staircase down to the storeroom, the one that also accessed the tunnels and vaults. I look up at Robbie and I can almost picture him wearing Columbo's crumpled beige overcoat, a cigar hanging out the side of his mouth, below his glass eye.

I clap, slowly, applauding his ingenuity. The swollen chest is gone, uncertainty clouding his face, those podgy fingers of his working overtime against one another. I stand. He jumps back another three steps at least. I raise my hand. 'Please – you're my wing-man. I'm merely stretching my legs.'

I walk towards the metal cabinet in the corner, the one housing all the tools I might need, the one I've been stowing the cattle prod down the back of whilst it recharged, next to the catch pole I've been keeping there for dragging the guilty, one by one, towards their fate – for unexpected moments like these.

'I need a good stretch.' I squat, straighten, then lean over the container, my eyes still locked with Robbie's. Seeing the shift in his eyes at the last moment, the flicker to the left of me.

To the left, where the cattle prod I was about to reach for comes slicing through the air, connecting with my skin, taking me out.

The room fades to black.

Chapter 73

'Hello?'

All three heads whipped towards the voice coming from the camera, confusion clouding their features at the sound of someone new. Robbie watched the woman jump from her seat, then hesitate, not daring to move any further. Maybe she wasn't willing to believe there could be any hope.

Her hand fluttered at her neck. 'Hello?' She turned, looking at the two men, her eyes willing them to join her, to speak out too.

The men stood up either side of her, the three of them peering up at the camera.

The elderly man spoke. 'Who's that?'

'Robbie, my name's Robbie. I'll explain it all later. First, I'm going to try and get you out of there.'

The younger man exhaled loudly, shoulders sagging, his eyes closing for the briefest of moments as relief flooded him. The other two faces slackening, stress and fear draining from their features as they all joined hands, then arms, seemingly needing each other to stay upright.

'Where is he?' The woman's voice still cracked with fear.

Robbie looked at the camera feed in the other vault, where Casey was shackled to his chair, his eyes fluttering, body twitching in its attempt to wake up.

'You don't have to worry about him right now. He's not going anywhere, but we need to get you out.'

Robbie felt stupid even thinking about asking the next question, doubting any of them had seen anything outside the stone walls they were imprisoned in, but he couldn't think of any other way.

'Long shot here, but do you know where the keys to the door might be?' He'd searched everywhere, including on Casey, to no avail.

The woman nodded, her head movement exaggerated, her whole body animated in its eagerness for all of this to end, for her to be free. 'His pocket.' She sped towards the camera, desperation powering her limbs, her stare burning into the camera. 'When he came for Lewis, he put them in his pocket.'

Robbie said nothing as his chin slumped to his chest – his mind trying not to think about Lewis hanging behind him, about the body he'd now covered up – in the knowledge that the keys weren't in Casey's pocket any more.

His eyes darted to the other camera feed.

Casey was awake.

He was the only person who could unlock the door.

Chapter 74

I COME ROUND IN the floodlit vault where I'd first held Danny. Before I allowed him to join the others. I'm upright in my chair, my lower legs splayed and tied on to it, upper arms already sore from how tightly they've been pulled back and fastened behind me. I feel pain at my wrists when I try to flex my fingers.

Was it Robbie who pulled me up into the chair, tying me to it, before wheeling me in here? Robbie, or whoever had knocked me out with that prod.

I have no idea how long I've been out. Long enough for my eyes to squint against the glaring light above. I turn my head to look left, right. No one else in here with me, just the blinking red light in the corner, on the camera there. Ironic. The watcher now the watched.

I'm surmising that Robbie is at the other end of the camera, watching from my laptop. The one I dropped, what seems like moments before, when Robbie walked into my vault. The same laptop also showing the camera feed into them.

I expect Robbie has already spoken with them. I hate to think what they might've said, but they'll still be in there, awaiting their fate, as only I know where the keys are.

Even when I think I'm alone, underground, no chance of being seen, I plan for someone watching; the job above ground ingrained. I've safeguarded the keys. Making sure nothing will get in my way. That what had started will be finished.

And this? (I flex my fingers again, feeling that pain, the sharpness there.) This is nothing but a minor blip.

Robbie, as if he can read my mind, filters into the room via the speaker. My wing-man, always knowing instinctively when there's a problem. 'I'm sorry, Casey. I don't want to hurt you.' Loyal, even now. 'But you need to tell me where the keys are.'

I look straight up at the camera. Strange to be on the opposite end of one from Robbie. For me to be on the other side of that lens. 'I'm not giving you anything, Batman.'

Silence, stretching between us as I move my wrists behind the chair, out of view – that sharpness again, remembering the broken innards of this chair, slowly rubbing the rope at my wrists against them. Never taking my eyes off the camera, my arm movement slow, hoping it's not picked up. And then . . .

'What about me, Casey? Will you tell me?'

That voice. *Your* voice. My face softens at the same time as my heart hardens, shattering into a hundred pieces all over again, doubtful that the cracks have ever fully healed from six years ago.

Beth.

The Robin to Robbie's Batman.

How?

Knowing how. At least, I was aware that you were still alive. I've known for some time now that you never jumped from that cliff. All those years I'd thought you were gone, dead, were a lie. The shock of that truth not softened with the passing of time, but instead driven home again and again, its current just as strong as that cattle prod, knowing everything that had come to pass after you faked your death.

I look to the floor, stilling my arms behind the chair. Suddenly snivelling like a child, not caring about that blinking red light. I'd prepared for the unexpected, but nothing could've prepared me for this.

The cafe where we met lying empty above, the vault beneath, here, on the corner of Union Street, the tunnels interlocking with more vaults beneath Market Street. So many memories, a whole other life led between the walls above. The moment we met; the night I fell in love with you.

I don't want you to see that I still love you, that I never stopped loving you. Not after what I now know.

I hear your breath over the speaker, the sound I'd listened to in our bed all those nights, all those years, we lay together. 'Casey? You need to let them go. Please. If not for me, then for Hope. This isn't right. You must know that. It doesn't give you back anything. It's just going to take everything further and further away from you.'

I look up to the camera, picturing those watery blue

eyes of yours, wanting you to see mine now. I feel the conviction in what I have to say. In what I must do.

'How could you do it, Beth? How could you have left me to believe that you were dead? Wasn't it cruel enough that I'd lost my child? That you'd gone on to take even more of her away from me? You had me believe that you regretted that decision, that you'd ended your life because of the guilt of what you did to her. And then I have to see you swanning around town on CCTV. You took everything from me. I have nothing left for anyone to take away from me.'

'That's not true. We can make this right. There's still time to make this right.'

I hear the crack in your voice and, even now, I would forgive you anything. Even now, when I know that the emotion I hear in your words is for someone else. Not me.

Still, I want to make the lie last as long as I can. 'That's all you have to say? I saw you, Beth. I thought I'd seen you so many times, but it was never you. And then that day, that day, there you were. Wasn't she, Robbie? Right there on that screen in front of me.'

'Yes.' He says nothing else.

Robbie now knows that you never really were a ghost. That I had once believed you to be dead, an apparition of my past that would forever haunt me, but that that had also changed.

Now he knows who the real ghost is. Someone he never knew existed. My daughter. Hope.

Hope, who somehow still exists in the bodies of others. In those who don't deserve to have her. No one deserving her because no one can look after her the way that I could.

'You took her from me.'

Your breath catches on the monitor. 'She was already gone, Casey. I wanted her to live on. To know that she was still out there, somewhere. That she was helping others to live.'

I shake my head. 'No, you let them cut her into pieces, like some piece of meat. An animal. Spare parts.'

'Casey, it wasn't like that. Everyone deserves a chance. The people through in that vault deserve a chance.'

I laugh, the sound loud and harsh as it reverberates off the stone walls. 'Is that what you thought *you* deserved? A chance to live free of me? Was life with me really that bad? Am *I* really that bad?'

Her voice is small. 'Why didn't you come for me? When you saw me that day on the CCTV screen? When you knew I was still alive?'

'Why? Because I wanted to know what had happened afterwards. To Hope. I wanted you to know. To come to you with that information – with all this.' I look around the vault. 'To show you what you did. To tell you that the decision you made for our daughter was wrong. So wrong. And then I wanted to take what I could from you after that. Everything. Because that's what you did to me.'

Silence.

I stare at the camera. 'You think you're worthy of a chance like you believe they're worthy of a chance? Of the chance that they've already been given? Cheating, drinking. Those young girls . . . Her heart going to—' I can't bring myself to say it.

Your voice shakes. 'They're still people, Casey. As human as any of us. As capable of mistakes and regret, as prone to hardship as the next person. And I know you've made *your* mistakes. We both have. Bad ones.'

I can't help but laugh, the sound cruel. 'Do you regret what you did to our daughter? What you did to me?'

The speaker crackles, your voice soft when you speak again. 'I have regrets every single day.'

I shake my head. 'That's not answering my question. How could you have me believe all these years that you were dead?'

You sob, taking your time to answer, the silence stretching, me doubting whether you're going to say anything at all, before you finally do.

'I was terrified, Casey. I had been for a long time. I still am. I live with that fear every day. Of seeing you. Of you knowing I'm alive. Of you finding me. Of what you might do. Of losing everything all over again.' She's crying freely now. 'But in my worst fears, I never saw this. You've just admitted you were planning to come to me. So, I was right to be terrified. You're not well, Casey. None of this is your fault. You've been ill for a long time. Since long before we met.'

I'm crying with her, licking at the tears trailing down my face, feeling like I'm drowning in them.

'How did you find them, Casey? How was it even possible?'

I figure I have nothing to lose now. 'You probably don't even remember. The Donor Family Care Service. Hope's details, our details, were passed on. After. They only contacted us once before you . . .' I can't bring myself to say it. 'Two weeks after they got our information. A gold heart pin and a certificate thanking us for the donation.'

'I remember.'

'After a month, we got a letter about Hope's donations. General, no detailed information. A year later, an anniversary card, as if I should somehow be celebrating what had happened. What you made happen.'

'Casey—'

'Don't. You asked, so I'm telling you.' I flex my fingers, forcing myself to carry on. 'I found comfort there, though. Even though it was only phone calls or emails, it felt like I was keeping Hope alive somehow. But I always wondered . . . I . . .'

'What did you do?'

'I said I wanted to write to the recipients. All of them. I did that but what I wanted to say, what I needed to say . . . well, the team read it, removed all information that made me identifiable. They told me the recipients would be made aware I had written to them, that what I'd sent would be forwarded to them, and they could choose to read it at their discretion. But not one of them ever tried to make contact in return.' I push the thought of what Bill said from my mind. 'And there were no links between us for me to know who they were.'

'So, how?'

'I left it for a few years. Until that day I saw you. On that CCTV screen. I couldn't ignore it any more. So, I travelled down South to the Care Service. I said I wanted to thank the lady at their offices who'd been in touch with me during that time. In person.'

'And she met with you?'

'Yes. But I already knew her. I'd been watching her for a while before I went to the offices. She had a son – a seriously ill son. A boy who needed help quicker than the NHS could give it. When I offered her the money to go private, as much as she would need and more – even allowing that she would lose her job if it ever came out – well, I guess in the grand scheme of things, it seemed a small price to pay.'

'She gave the details of the recipients.'

'Every one of them. It was so easy to find them online – in newspaper articles, Facebook, you name it; all you needed were the names. When I found out they were all in Aberdeen – one born here; the other three ending up here after, and all for valid reasons – it seemed a million-to-one chance. But to then find out that all of Hope's organs had gone to adults . . . well, that sent me down an even deeper, darker hole. To think that our child hadn't helped other children . . . struggling to see why these adults had the right . . . surprised to even learn that a child's organs could be donated to an adult. It all seemed so unlikely – a rarity, even. Think of the unbelievable odds of that alone . . . but for them all to be in Aberdeen too? It made it a billion-to-one chance, and it was all the sign I needed. The confirmation that what I was about to do was meant to be done.'

'Jesus, Casey. Does she know?'

'Who? The woman at the service? I think it's fair to say she would've understood I would do something with the information – just not what, I guess. But if she reads or watches the news, if she remembers those names – and I expect those names and what she did keeps her awake at night – then she'll know for sure soon.'

The silence stretches for the longest time, before Beth speaks again.

'I went to see your father.'

My head snaps up. Another thing I wasn't expecting.

'In prison. After everything that had happened, after we were no longer together, I needed to know if I was right all those years. If I did ever know you.'

I'm shaking my head, not wanting to hear about him. Not wanting to hear what he said. Not when I chose to bury my father the same day as I had my mother. Realizing that he had known you were alive, and he'd chosen to protect you. That he hadn't tried to reach out. To tell me.

'He loved you as much as Hope did. And she *loved* you, Casey. So much. She could only see the good in you, the healthy you.'

You're gulping back your tears, struggling to breathe as you talk. You sound like my father. That day in the butcher's shop. Not wanting to believe I was anything but good inside. Even after the way he found me. The way he found my mother. Still believing in me, so powerfully, that he was willing to take the fall for me. To give me a chance at life.

And I took that chance. Grabbing it. Taking the chance on you. You and Hope.

But I couldn't stay good, not with you, not even with Hope.

I couldn't look after you, or her. The same way Hope went on to give others a chance at life and yet even they haven't looked after her. And my father knew that I'd failed. That he'd failed. That you wanted to be free of me.

'Casey, please – just tell us where the keys are.'

Pleading. Giving me the ability to make your wish come true, to make you happy again. I could almost be lulled into this bullshit, if I didn't know.

But I do know.

I rub my wrists against the sharpness, against the pain. Daring to move as much and as fast as I can.

I know that it won't be me that you go on to be happy with, *if* I let that happen. I know who it will be instead. Who it has been.

That's why I must finish this thing. Why I must play my part.

Chapter 75

I LOOK UP INTO the camera. A good while after sitting silent, refusing to talk, whilst you and Robbie talked at me, as if back in that therapist's office again.

I stare at the lens, hoping that my eyes are burning into yours. 'You're right. I see it now. They're only people. Human, like me. I've made so many mistakes, like them. My biggest one being leaving Hope, letting her fall into that pond.' I close my eyes, not having to act out this part.

You speak. 'It was an accident, Casey. I know it was. After all the things you've done, I still know that what happened to Hope was an accident. I know that, at least. How much you loved her. How much she loved you.'

I smile through the tears. *'You are mine. I am yours.'*

'Yes, Casey.' Another sob. 'And she was. You were. No matter what happened after, that part will always be true.'

I nod. Now I *am* acting. Following the script. Not able to believe anything you say to be true. Not after telling the cruellest lie you could ever have told me. I see through you, Beth.

But you, you can't see the truth because you're incapable of reading what's between the lines. The fact that I have nothing if I don't have Hope. Nothing, if I don't at least try to right the wrongs.

There is no redemption for me. Or for them.

But I can't let you know that. I can't let you see, so I lie like them. 'I'll show you where the keys are, Beth, if you let me out. Let me be the one to free them. Let my father, you, and Hope, see that there is still good in me.'

'I wish I could believe you, Casey, I do. But . . .'

I'm forgetting about the small problem of Lewis hanging in the other room. The glaring proof of what I'm capable of. The reason you and Robbie have me tied up in here, rather than on that table. I expect that you're both so focused on watching me on that laptop screen that you're not looking anywhere near what's behind you, not looking at him hanging there on that hook.

You and Robbie have no intention of letting me go, of making things right. If I were to give you those keys, if I were to let them go free, to allow both of you to go free too . . . I would be left here to face my fate.

I expect those blue sirens would be en route as soon as you'd all gulped your first breath of fresh air. Up there. Above. If they're not on their way already.

'I assume you've called the police?'

Robbie speaks. 'No. No, Casey. I didn't want to believe what I might find down here. I wanted to prove myself wrong. I wanted to see it for myself. And Beth . . .'

'Casey, I've spent so long running, hiding, I wanted to

finally face that fear. To face you. To talk. To have that chance. Something I doubted would happen having the police here with us. We still trusted that you wouldn't hurt us, at least.'

I look to the ground, feeling some give from the rope tying my hands behind me. 'Then let Batman come and get me.'

I say this because I know the true-crime horrors Robbie has seen. I know that, even after seeing Lewis, he still sees me. His wing-man. His friend. The guy who works daily to protect people. To keep the city safe. By his side. Beth just said exactly that.

'Robbie, you can trust me. Keep my hands tied up, my feet too, if you want. Wheel me out of here if it must be that way. I'll direct you to the key. Just let me be with you to go get that key. Let me be part of letting them go.'

Chapter 76

The audio speaker clicks off. You and Robbie are considering my plea. Discussing the shit I've just peddled, most likely unable to see any other way, if I won't tell you where the keys are.

The rope loosens at my back, unfurling, my fingers grasping to catch it before it falls to the floor. Before you and Robbie see it on the camera. I cling to it, hoping none of the rope's length is visible beneath the chair.

It seems not, and that you might just believe that I want to do good, that I'm telling the truth, when Robbie opens the door, but not without the cattle prod in his hand. Stretched out in front of him, his face contorting between fear and trust.

I don't look at him, too ashamed – or at least making him think so. 'Wheel me through.' I gather the rope and curl it around my wrists as much as I can, to hide it from view.

He walks towards me, around the back of me, I hold my breath.

The speaker clicks back on, and you're there with us. 'I'm watching, Casey.'

Not close enough, clearly. I wonder what you think it is you can do anyway, sitting there watching from another room. Aware that you don't hold the power that I have, when I do the same above ground.

I sit, placid, as Robbie begins to push the back of the chair with one hand, having to position the prod down against the back of the chair so he can use both hands to get any traction.

He shifts me towards the doorway, leaving some space for him to come around the front, that prod grasped down by his side, and open the door, then comes back to wheel me out into the tunnel, towards my control room, entering the space. Where, on the hook, Lewis has been covered up by a blanket. Where you sit. *You.* My Beth. No longer my Beth.

I stare at you, almost reaching out my hand to touch your face but stopping at the last moment. Remembering. Desperate to touch you. One last time.

I swallow and sit still. 'The keys are over there.' I nudge my head to the right, towards the floor. 'Under the vent in the floor.'

You stay seated, watching me look past you. You, visibly shaking as Robbie walks in front of me, approaches the grate and crouches to the floor, his back facing me. His fingers poke through the hole of the heavy metal grate before he lifts it and places it on the ground to the side of him.

I'm up, pulling my hands free, you making a noise in your throat that sounds inhuman, me already apologizing in my head to my wing-man, to Robbie, as I spring forward, grab the grate and lift it high above my head – all this before Robbie has even turned to look, before he can gain any balance – whacking it down over his head, sending him sprawling across the floor.

Chapter 77

You stare at Robbie's body lying prone at my feet. 'Jesus, Casey.'

I'm staring at you, struggling to believe you're so close. That you're real. Wishing we could go back – back in time. To how things were. Before all this. Before we lost Hope.

You're so near to me that I could stretch out my arm and touch you. My fingers flex by my side, longing to reach, to hold you, and all whilst you refuse to even look at me, not lifting your gaze from Robbie when you speak again.

'What have you done?'

I want you to look at me, *need* you to look at me. I long to look into those eyes that have watched me in a whole other lifetime, the same ones that somehow managed to see me more than anyone else ever did.

'Casey, we have to help him.'

I force myself to look away from you, towards Robbie, seeing his foot twitch. 'He'll be OK.'

You finally look up at me, seemingly shocked that I'd care. That hurts.

'Please . . . Casey, please. Just tell me where the keys are. Let them go.' You step towards me. 'Let us all go.'

Even now, what you don't realize is that I can't. No way I can let Hope slip away from me again. It's impossible for me to let you leave me again, not now that you're here. I can't watch you go and live. I don't want to see you happy – to think that you could be, that you have been – without me, without Hope.

You're weeping, trying to steady your breath as you wipe at your eyes. I see you on the first night we met, that raindrop running down your chest, except that now the droplets running there are tears.

'Please, Casey.'

You look down at Robbie, seeing him move at the same time as I do, at the exact moment I lunge for the cattle prod, ready to put him down again.

You come at me, howling. Pushing me. Away from the prod, away from Robbie.

Sideways. Then backwards . . . back . . . back . . .

Your strength surprises me as I fight to find my footing under the force of your rage, your fear, whatever it is that's fuelling you. Trying to find the ground beneath me, not wanting to hurt you, never wanting to hurt you. Not even now.

My eyes are wide, mouth opening as I feel the sharp puncture between my shoulder blades, and your eyes become just as wide – your hands still pushing me back . . . back . . .

Pain searing ... then ebbing as you drop your arms and step backwards.

Me left there. Hanging beside Lewis. Flashbacks of Mum.

You fall to the floor in front of me, as if you're worshiping me, but I know that you're not. Not any more.

You're crying, groaning, rocking back and forth as Robbie crawls, blood streaming down his face, to you, slumping by your side. Both of you looking up at me, hanging there, as tears run down your faces.

Robbie, shaking his head, over and over. *'I'm sorry, Casey...'*

Sorry. Forever my wing-man, no matter what.

But I'm not sorry because he finally gets his moment.

A strange calm descends as I stare down at both of you.

As I look at you.

Deep into those watery blue eyes of yours, where I'm sure I still see a glimmer of what once was, as the light slowly fades from mine.

Then I see her. Hope.

Standing there, right in front of me. In front of you and Robbie. Whole again.

Whispering to me, *'You are mine.'*

I smile, tears mixing with the blood on my lips, dropping to the red blossoming at my chest. *'I am yours.'*

She smiles right back. *'You're all mine, Daddy.'*

As the blood seeps from me, I know that, before long, Robbie and you will get the keys from that vent. I know now that what I started will not be finished.

I am strangely, unexpectedly, at peace with that. Accepting of my fate, even knowing that you will go and save the father of your child. That you will go on to be happy, and that you will let the others live on too.

Not me. Not Hope.

But Danny. And Charlotte.

Your new husband. Your new daughter.

A new family.

Your new name: Libby.

Libby. The woman on that step with Danny that day I posed as his taxi. The same woman who Robbie watched me watching when he followed me in the car to your street.

Libby, the person he contacted when that Missing Person report came in for Danny. Phoning you directly. Telling you what he'd seen – you already knowing who I was, my name escaping your lips before Robbie even said it. Robbie bringing you here, after he'd already followed me himself. You, knowing why. Why it would be here.

Would any of this have happened if I hadn't seen you on the CCTV screen that day? Maybe not. Because it was seeing you, pushing a buggy, that set it all in motion. Being faced with you. The fact you were alive. That you had created another life. That you were living another life. With someone else. Cruelly reminding me of our daughter's lost life, of everything I had lost – knowing my life had effectively ended at the same time as hers.

It was unfathomable to me that you had found a way to move on. In that moment I was forced to think about everyone else who had been able to move forward after the death of our daughter, of all the people she had helped to live on afterwards, because of her. I needed to find out that her gift, the gift of life, was not given in vain. To find them all.

Lungs, liver, kidneys.

Lewis, Jen, Bill.

Never expecting what and who came next.

The heart of our daughter. Beating and alive inside Danny's chest.

The man who found you through your shared stories on that Wishes site. The man you couldn't help but fall in love with. No matter how you both tried to stay apart. No matter what others thought or said.

You wanting, *needing*, in your own way, to have Hope back beside you.

Just as I did.

And she is back. Our daughter. Somehow, she is here with me now.

With *me*. That dimple creasing her cheek, that sugary smell of hers all around me.

Hope curls her small fingers through mine.

I close my eyes as my hand squeezes that soft, warm flesh of hers.

And I whisper, *'I'm all yours, baby.'*

Epilogue

BETH CLUNG TO DANNY's hand as they walked across the gravel car park towards the chapel. She looked up ahead to the crowd congregating outside the church. A sea of black and white. She knew that sea would have been more of a puddle, had this funeral been under any other circumstances.

The funeral of Lewis Taylor. A man whose demise would never have been expected to draw the masses – until the unexpected happened.

It was two weeks since they'd all been released from beneath the streets of Aberdeen. All of them breaking free of those vaults, out into the light. Their lives changed for ever, their appreciation for those lives – for whatever their futures may now hold – in sharp focus.

Only Lewis had fallen, no chance of ever seeing that light again.

Beth moved towards the crowd, keenly aware of the last time she was at this chapel. For her daughter;

holding Casey's hand, their show of unity that day as fragile as Hope's life had been.

Casey was the only villain in this story now. Today, and in the countless stories that had flooded the news for the past fortnight. The man she had once married, the father of her first child.

Beth had barely slept in the days after the others' release, feeling guilty that she hadn't done more all those years ago. That she hadn't stopped Casey before it had ended the way it had this time. Fearing the repercussions of all of that. That more than anything, the memory of her daughter would somehow be sullied because of what her husband, Hope's own father, had done.

But that hadn't happened. Instead, she had been embraced, and had turned down interview after interview request to tell her story, to give some insight into the mind of a madman. There was no need. Nothing would be gained. Nothing could be changed.

What they had all suffered – she, Danny, Jen, Bill, Lewis, Robbie, and their loved ones – was enough. Everything else would remain her secret to keep, until her own day came at this chapel. She owed that much to their lost daughter.

Beth looked up and saw the funeral car and hearse crawl to a stop, watching as Lewis's mother, brother, his wife and their daughter stepped out to the flashes of cameras – reporters devoid of any respect for their grief.

Some of the press speculated about whether Lewis's brother would show, whether he would want to publicly grieve his sibling. But Beth had suspected he would come. And Lewis's mum had her own regrets as to what she might have been able to change all those years ago.

Beth stared at the mahogany coffin through the gleaming glass of the hearse. Knowing that the pieces of her daughter removed in those vaults by Casey had been returned to Lewis's body. Finding it hard to take in that a part of her daughter was inside a coffin. Again.

She wiped a tear from her eye, felt Danny's grip tighten round her hand. There as always. There yesterday, when a red-haired woman had skulked towards her on the street, Beth fearing that not everyone had embraced her. When the woman had reached out a pale, slim hand, placed it on Beth's forearm and spoken to her.

'I'm so sorry to approach you like this, at such a difficult time, but I had to. My name is Andrea Moss.' She'd looked from Beth to Danny, hesitating. 'It was me. I'm the woman that gave your husband the details of all those people.'

Beth had felt the tremor of the woman's hand, had seen the redness in her haunted, sunken eyes. Not knowing what to say as the woman's eyes searched hers as she spoke again.

'I will never forgive myself for what I did. I . . .' Her voice hitched. 'Those poor people. You. Your daughter. I've told my superiors everything. The authorities too. I'll make sure I pay for what I've done.'

And then she had dropped her hand from Beth's arm.

Beth had stood. Staring at the woman. Expecting to feel something. Rage; disappointment, perhaps. But instead, what she had felt was compassion. Beth herself, after all, had been at the hands of Casey, as had everyone else in that vault – before, during and after their ordeal – and probably in some way for the rest of their lives. She knew the reach he had. The hold. The man had caused enough damage and hurt for it to be everlasting.

Beth also knew what it was to have a fierce love for your child. To fear the loss of them. And for her, to have that fear realized.

Beth had let go of Danny's hand and reached for the woman's. 'Forgive yourself, Andrea. I do. I know my daughter, and all the others, will too. You have nothing to pay for. Casey was the only one who needed to do that, and he's paid the ultimate price.' Beth had then patted the woman's hand. 'I'll make sure to talk to your superiors personally. I hope your son is getting the help that he needs.'

The woman's mouth had opened and closed before she backed away, a whispered thank-you as Beth and Danny had moved on.

Now, at that memory, Beth squeezed Danny's hand. 'I love you.'

He turned to her, smiled. 'And I love you, Libb—Beth.'

Beth smiled. Danny had always known her real name, had always understood her need to hide from it. Now she didn't have to hide any more. She was free. She knew it would take some time for Danny to adjust to the change, but it felt good just to hear her name on his lips.

She saw Jen up ahead, standing with her husband, Tom, by her side. Bill too – his son, Simon, brushing something from Bill's suit-jacket shoulder.

'Wait up, folks!'

Beth turned. Robbie. Of course, Robbie.

As much a part of all this as they were. A man who had known a different Casey. A good Casey. A Casey who Beth had also known for a while, all those years ago. Both privately clinging to that memory of him, to that part of Casey they knew and loved, whilst still accepting the reality. The truth.

Beth looked between them all. Together in that truth now. Meeting up and talking several times on the phone since that day. Needing to. Something Beth hoped they would continue to do.

Her heart warmed to see Jen and Tom arm in arm. Hopeful for the future, all their secrets laid bare. Jen hadn't touched a drink since the crash with Daisy. It was by no means easy, but she was determined to do it for her family. And for Hope.

Bill had shared his own secrets too. His son had done nothing but embrace him. With Simon and Kelly's support, Bill was now making time for himself, striving to be the man he wanted to be, the one he knew he could be for Trish. His wish, now, was for them to live as full a life as they possibly could, together – their way of thanks for the gift that Hope had given them.

Beth linked arms with Jen as, all together, they walked through the throng, entering the chapel before taking their places.

One by one. Side by side. A part of Hope within them all, her memory and legacy alive. Forever strong. *All theirs.*

Acknowledgements

I love to watch the world go by. Sitting in those rare, quiet snippets of time to myself – perhaps a latte in hand – watching others go about their day. Imagining what their story is and what's brought them to that moment. What makes them tick. One day, sitting in a cafe, I thought, *what if someone were watching* me? A stranger putting together my imaginary story. But, even more than that, what if I wasn't a stranger to them?

It made me think about how much we are watched every day without us ever realizing. Whether it be an electronic trail we leave online, or those cameras perched around our home towns that we never stop to notice or think about – most of us having no idea they're even there.

And, from there, Casey Carter was born. Fictional, but someone to be given his own story. A tale where he would be watching others whilst I watched him – except that he'd already know their stories.

But it was the *why* that eluded me, and, for offering to bounce ideas about, I have to thank the ever supportive

Marion Todd. A top-class crime fiction author and an all-round lovely lady.

For giving me the eventual answer to the *why*, I thank the Mutch sisters: Nicola (who I dedicated this book to), Donna and Lisa. All three of those girls are ones I grew up with and who I still cherish having in my life now. Thanks for setting the story in motion.

Huge thanks to my wonderful editor, Finn Cotton. My first full project working with him and it's been such a fantastic experience to have his kindness, understanding, expertise and input. Thanks for putting up with all my daft ramblings.

Thanks to all the Transworld team who have worked on *I'll Be Watching You*: Holly Reed, Barbara Thompson, Alex Newby, Sarah Coward, Emma Fairey, Richard Shailer and Deirdre O'Connell.

As always, thanks to my fabulous agent, Oli Munson, for being the person willing to take a chance on me and my writing in the first place. Forever grateful, as you know.

Thanks also to everyone else on the A. M. Heath team who supports me.

Before writing this book, I was keen to find out more about the placement and workings of CCTV in Aberdeen, and, for that, three fabulous ladies from the city operation came to my rescue. Heartfelt thanks to Caroline Gray, Ann Proctor and Pauline Fraser for agreeing to meet for a coffee and for letting me pick their brains about how, when and where they watch all those people living out their stories on the streets of Aberdeen. It was an eye-opener and a blast.

For helping me to find out all I could about organ donors and transplants, I want to thank Gemma Smith at Aberdeen Royal Infirmary for answering all my rookie questions and helping me to figure out how I could apply fact to a good sprinkle of fiction. For anyone interested in finding out more about organ donation in Scotland, please take a look at www.organdonationscotland.org.

My usual thanks go out to all my friends and family who are always there for me – whether it be in day-to-day life or supporting me in this writing journey. I know how lucky I am to have you all for your unwavering willingness, for listening to my yakking and for replying to all those marathon texts and voice notes I love so much (blame the writer in me, ha-ha).

And, of course, I can't go without mentioning my two small people who aren't so small these days: Holly and Ellis. Thanks for being you and for putting up with me being me – especially when I'm hunched over the desk, approaching deadline, and promising I'll make it up to you both. Every day is an adventure (and a rollercoaster!) with you both. Love you more.

Thanks also to our two pooches, Harley and Milo, for resting your heads on the keys of my laptop as I try to work (!), hinting to go on those walks that get me out into the fresh air to think when my brain feels like mush.

I also must thank the girls who understood I work better in cafes and allowed me to overstay my welcome at times. So, for keeping me in coffee, and a seat, thanks to baristas extraordinaire Gemma, Sharon and Sophie at Costa, and to Wendy and Pamela at Starbucks.

And last but in no means least – because, after all, it's the reason I do this – massive thanks to you, the reader, for picking up and hopefully enjoying the stories that I write.

**Don't miss the first book in the gripping
DI Eve Hunter series**

A brutal murder.
A young woman's body is discovered with horrifying injuries, a recent newspaper cutting pinned to her clothing.

A detective with everything to prove.
This is her only chance to redeem herself.

A serial killer with nothing to lose.
He's waited years, and his reign of terror has only just begun ...

AVAILABLE TO BUY IN PAPERBACK AND EBOOK

**Don't miss the second book in this
award-winning series**

A young man, the son of an influential businessman, is discovered dead in his central Aberdeen apartment.

Hours later, a teenaged girl with no identification is found hanged in a suspected suicide.

As DI Eve Hunter and her team investigate the two cases, they find themselves in a tug-of-war between privilege and poverty; between the elite and those on the fringes of society.

Then an unexpected breakthrough leads them to the shocking conclusion: that those in power have been at the top for too long – and now, someone is going to desperate lengths to bring them down …

Can they stop someone who is dead set on revenge, no matter the cost?

AVAILABLE TO BUY IN PAPERBACK AND EBOOK

**Don't miss the third book in this
award-winning series**

In the dead of night someone starts a fire in a home for underprivileged children in Aberdeen. The flames spread quickly, and one person doesn't make it out alive.

But the victim wasn't found in their bedroom; they were discovered locked inside a secret basement underground. And DI Eve Hunter's team are about to find themselves in even darker territory.

Soon Eve unearths a horrific discovery at the heart of the property – one that turns the whole investigation on its head. Everyone in this home has something to hide, but who has a secret worth killing for?

'Taut and gripping, with a pace that never slows' ANDREA MARA

'Pacy, intelligent and so, so satisfying' MARION TODD

'Unmissable and addictive, Masson delivers beautifully crafted punches and red-hot twists' HELEN FIELDS

LONGLISTED FOR THE 2022 McILVANNEY PRIZE FOR SCOTTISH CRIME BOOK OF THE YEAR

AVAILABLE TO BUY IN PAPERBACK AND EBOOK

On a station platform, with nothing to read,
and a four-hour train journey stretching ahead of him...

That's where the story began for Penguin founder Allen Lane.
With only 'shabby reprints of shoddy novels' on offer,
he resolved to make better books for readers everywhere.

By the time his train pulled into London, the idea was formed.
He would bring the best writing, in stylish and affordable
formats, to everyone. His books would be sold in bookstores,
stationers and tobacconists, for no more than the price
of a ten-pack of cigarettes.

And on every book would be a Penguin, a bird with a certain
'dignified flippancy', and a friendly invitation to anyone who
wished to spend their time reading.

In 1935, the first ten Penguin paperbacks were published.
Just a year later, three million Penguins had made their
way onto our shelves.

Reading was changed forever.

—

A lot has changed since 1935, including Penguin, but in the
most important ways we're still the same. We still believe that
books and reading are for everyone. And we still believe that
whether you're seeking an afternoon's escape, a vigorous debate
or a soothing bedtime story, all possibilities open with a book.

Whoever you are, whatever you're looking for,
you can find it with Penguin.